C000077597

Andrew Ireland was born in Birmingham in 1964, and moved to Cheshire a year before the new millennium. Recently retired, he spent over forty years working in food retail, with the past twenty-five years living with his wife, Tricia, and their two children, James and Bethany.

His hobbies include playing chess on a daily basis and training for his annual effort at the Blenheim Triathlon.

His love for Victorian literature began in his mid-twenties, and *Unwelcome Legacies* is influenced by both that and Tricia's holiday fiction, which he reads on the beach in the South of France.

His favourite author is probably Anne Bronte, his favourite beer is definitely Timothy Taylor's Golden Best.

To my wife, Tricia, our two fantastic children, James and Bethany, and our three precious little bichons, Snowy, Archie, and Milou.

Andrew Ireland

UNWELCOME LEGACIES

AUSTIN MACAULEY PUBLISHERS™

LONDON * CAMBRIDGE * NEW YORK * SHARJAH

Copyright © Andrew Ireland 2022

The right of Andrew Ireland to be identified as author of this work has been asserted by the author in accordance with section 77 and 78 of the Copyright, Designs and Patents Act 1988.

All rights reserved. No part of this publication may be reproduced, stored in a retrieval system, or transmitted in any form or by any means, electronic, mechanical, photocopying, recording, or otherwise, without the prior permission of the publishers.

Any person who commits any unauthorised act in relation to this publication may be liable to criminal prosecution and civil claims for damages.

This is a work of fiction. Names, characters, businesses, places, events, locales, and incidents are either the products of the author's imagination or used in a fictitious manner. Any resemblance to actual persons, living or dead, or actual events is purely coincidental.

A CIP catalogue record for this title is available from the British Library.

ISBN 9781398435711 (Paperback)
ISBN 9781398435728 (ePub e-book)

www.austinmacauley.com

First Published 2022
Austin Macauley Publishers Ltd®
1 Canada Square
Canary Wharf
London
E14 5AA

Thank you to all of the team at Austin Macauley Publishers Ltd. for bringing *Unwelcome Legacies* to life and helping me fulfil my dream of becoming a published author.

Prologue

With air-time on the hour, every hour, seven days a week, the jingle that preceded the traffic update was as recognisable as it was repetitive. Gloomily, the news was not promising, a serious accident, and a subsequent road closure that was likely to extend well into the early hours of the morning.

Two police cars had already arrived at the scene, the officers making an initial assessment of the damage, laying down bright yellow warning cones, redirecting traffic, this was a nasty crash, a head on collision, and there would almost certainly be some fatalities. In the back ground the wailing of an ambulance siren could be heard in the distance, getting louder and louder, its blue flashing light illuminating the darkness, it was going to be a long night, and it was just starting to rain.

Traffic had already started backing up, thirty, forty yards, a queue of cars quickly building up, the raindrops irradiated by the ever-increasing line of stationary headlights. Drivers, too inquisitive to be distracted by the foulness of the weather, leaned out of their windows, their necks craned for want of a better view, a young man, in his impatient twenties wearing a thin blue anorak, had stepped outside of his rundown Vauxhall Astra and was pacing up and down, his hands stuffed deep into his trouser pockets, his back hunched against the elements, frustration and tension building up in equal quantities.

The orange cab of the fifty-four-foot articulated lorry was fully intact, barely a scratch, the forty-eight tons of steel behind it having soaked up all of the impact, the driver, a rotund man in his mid-fifties sat frozen in his seat, unable to move, his hands stuck fast to the steering wheel as if by glue. Six inches in front of the lorry's radiator was the wreck of a silver Ford Focus, its boot wide open, the passenger door completely detached from the body of the car and lying on the grass verge, leaning against a spiked rampion, seemingly propped up by the plant's creamy white barbs.

The front of the car had completely disappeared, concertinaed by the force of the impact against the front bumper of the lorry, the bonnet and the front seats crumpled up and pushed back into the rear-seating area, the roof a twisted and tangled mass of metal, the airbags deployed, but totally ineffectual.

One of the officers, a fresh-faced constable in his early twenties, a torrent of rain water cascading over the surface of his bright yellow fluorescent jacket, his hands made red by the cold, bent down and peered over the top of the buckled driver's door. Through the broken glass of the shattered window his exhausted eyes rested on the two bodies, their heads clean through the smashed windscreen, their faces, hands, and clothing all covered in blood.

Almost immediately he turned away from the carnage, his body shaking uncontrollably, for whilst he had no recollection of the man in the passenger seat, he was very familiar with the driver, for they had lived in the same cul-de-sac for the past twenty-two years. His cheeks soaked in both tears and rain water, he turned to his colleagues.

"It's Reg, Reg Johnson. Christ, they didn't stand a chance, and what the hell were they doing on the wrong side of the carriageway?"

Chapter 1
Monday

The chrome wire meshed letter cage vibrated unobtrusively against the front door as the brown manila envelope announced its arrival, plunging through the letter box.

Still only fifty-eight, and some three years into his retirement after a lifetime of working for the County Council, Reg had already slipped into the contentment of someone with nothing to do and all day to do it in. His Monday routine of a cup of coffee at midday with the newspaper and a catch up of the weekend's sport was a luxury he simply could not have afforded when he was still at work, shackled to his desk in the office, or out on the road somewhere miles away from home.

Allowing himself a brief smile, he lifted himself out of the tired brown leather arm chair and ambled slowly into the hallway, chuckling to himself that you could set your watch by the postman, he raised his wrist up slowly towards his face and gazed at his own timepiece, it was exactly one o'clock.

Sinking back into the soft cushion of his favourite chair, a clamour at the front door suddenly brought his peace and solitude to an abrupt halt, Anna and David were home from a morning at the shopping centre, and judging by the racket they were making, had obviously had a good time of it.

Keeping the promise made to his mother whilst the family were regaling themselves of their regular Sunday treat of a latte and a pastry at the Café Narino, David had been up first, and, at a quarter to nine was standing in the short driveway holding the passenger door of his red sports car open, his mother eagerly clambering inside and onto the black leather seat. Three hours later and the two of them were back at home, staggering into the living room, laughing and joking, their faces red through effort, their arms laden with shopping bags.

Reg's eyes rested on his wife, examining her, marvelling at her beauty as he had done on so many occasions before.

At fifty-six, she was just two years younger than he was, her carefully sculptured eye brows looking down on her sweeping eye lashes, her shoulder length brown hair framing her perfectly formed cheek bones, not a pound heavier than she had been on the day they had married over thirty years ago, her tight black trousers and thin black cotton jumper effortlessly showed off her pencil thin figure and long shapely legs. Her eyes sparkled as she chatted away to her husband and son simultaneously, picking up the envelope awkwardly and placing it onto the mantelpiece, she dropped the shopping bags heavily onto the coffee table.

Even now he could still remember the first time they had met, she had been working behind the lingerie counter at Arnold's Department Store in the town centre, he had been shopping for a birthday present for a then girlfriend, pure coincidence, but then the path of true love often is he concluded to himself, his face a picture of joie de vivre. She had given up work after the birth of David's younger brother, Ben, before volunteering to work at one of the High Street charity shops when both of the boys had started school.

"Gosh! I need a cup of tea. Anybody else want one?" Calling out over her shoulder, she turned around, making her way to the kitchen, carefully meandering between the bags that had now over-spilled haphazardly and dangerously onto the floor.

"Oh, yes please, Mum," David shouted back, his eagerness to please his mother equalled only by his enthusiasm to quench his own thirst.

Like most adolescents he had stopped growing in his late teens, and, now thirty years old, was still not especially tall, just five feet seven inches, his shoulder length hair dark and parted in the centre, his goatee beard, little more than a tuft of hair on his chin, but sufficient to soften his hatchet face. He had a reputation for being confident, self-possessed, and sometimes a little smarmy, with a penchant for wearing suits with brown shoes and no tie, and possessing the annoying habit of shaking hands with everyone he met.

There had always been a shroud of mystery surrounding the means of his income, when questioned, he always responded in the same way, declaring nothing more than he ran a web-based business start-up company. He beamed at his mother as she handed him a piping hot mug of tea and two digestive biscuits, placing the belated elevenses onto the mantelpiece, he picked up the envelope and, stepping briefly into the hallway, balanced it on the stair bannister.

"Where's Ben? Does anyone else want a cup of tea?" Anna bawled from the kitchen, besieged by cups, saucers, and boiling kettles, fully submerged in the seemingly endless chores that made up her role as the self-appointed provider of family refreshments.

"I will!" Her shrill voice echoing in the hallway, Sarah brushed her handbag against the wall as she entered the house, closing the front door behind her. At twenty-five years old, she was very slim, very attractive, with dark shoulder length hair, an appealing face, baby-soft complexion, and blessed with the sort of personality that made her instantly loved by all around her.

Eighteen months ago, bored and at a loose end, she had decided to look for some volunteer work, very soon after that she was spending three shifts a week alongside Anna at the charity shop, the two of them finding an instant connection, very quickly becoming bosom pals, and quite inseparable. Removing her thick blue woollen coat, and folding it carefully over the bannister, she picked up the envelope, walked into the kitchen, and handed it over to her friend.

Taking the flat paper casing and kissing her friend on the cheek at the same time, Anna turned the envelope over, the front cover bore the frank of Michael Hickman and Associates Solicitors and was addressed to Ben.

"Ben come down stairs please, there's a letter for you here."

As if anticipating his mother's request and appearing almost immediately at her side, snatching the envelope, giving his mother a gentle peck on the cheek and flashing a smile at Sarah at the same time, he leant over, grabbed the black handled serrated edged bread knife from the wooden knife block sitting next to the kettle, and ran its blade along the seal flap.

Social media and internet shopping have completely altered the purpose of the postal service, letters, and other such correspondence, having long since disappeared in the digital era, the postage stamp, with its rich history spanning well over a hundred and fifty years, now rendered virtually redundant.

Letter boxes were now crammed full with small packages, their contents safely secured in light brown cardboard casing, firmly fastened down with opaque packaging tape, or delivery cards with the promise of even bigger parcels left with neighbours or hidden away discreetly, beneath up-turned flower pots or inside plastic creates, positioned cleverly behind garden sheds or dustbins.

Intrigued by this postal novelty, the four of them formed a mini scrum around Ben, bound as one, inter-locked together, a sold mass, their necks stretched out, eyes peering over, each vying for a best vantage point ready for the critical moment of reveal. The envelope successfully negotiated, and, to everyone's satisfaction, the Michael Hickman and Associates Solicitors headed paper pulled out from within matched the postage frank perfectly.

"That looks interesting."

Anna broke the silence, her arm draped over Sarah's shoulder.

"It's a letter from Michael Hickman and Associates Solicitors, it would appear that I need to make an appointment to see Michael Hickman himself."

There was not a great deal of interest in Ben's voice as he looked up from the piece of white paper he held in his hand, his jaded eyes adding weight to that sentiment.

A year younger than Sarah and six years younger than his brother, Ben was tall, towering over his elder brother, his round face, a complete contrast to David's thin angular lineaments, his jug ears more akin to those of Prince Charles than anyone present in the room at that moment. Very mild mannered, very well spoken, and extremely well read, his parents would have described him as easy going, always pleasant to anyone and everyone, his older brother would describe him as lazy and lacking in ambition, substantiating the case for the prosecution, he worked as a freelance reporter, always reluctant to be overtasked, and never in any danger of burning out, it suited him and he liked it.

"Wonder what that's all about? It could be something serious, there could be a problem somewhere, solicitors normally spell trouble."

Speaking as is from experience, Reg's voice was loaded with all of the caution and restraint of someone whose fingers had already been burnt. David frowned at his father, theirs had always been a strained relationship, an eldest son with little or no respect or regard for his parent. Sensing the inevitable tension, Sarah endeavoured to lift the mood.

"Or it could be something amazing, something that will change Ben's life, imagine if you've come in to a load of cash Ben, you'll be able to buy as many notebooks and pens as you want with that!"

Quite unable to match Sarah's enthusiasm, Ben re-read the letter once again, his forehead creased, his eyebrows all tangled up, his voice filled with resignation.

"I'll go there immediately after lunch."

Chapter 2
Monday

Well positioned in the busiest part of the high street, Michael Hickman and Associates re-opened after lunch at two-thirty. Arriving promptly, Ben stood at the doorway, nervously gazing into the reception area, and coughed, a vein attempt to attract the attention of the large lady in her mid-sixties, her skin as pale as her hair was silver, a pair of narrow blue florescent spectacles resting on the end of her nose, sitting at the reception desk.

If ever the efficiency of an office could be gauged by the tidiness of its reception desk, then this was surely the cream of the crop, for on the right-hand side were two light grey rectangular plastic post trays, stacked perfectly one on top of the other, on the left-hand side a bonsai tree, with its rich green leaves, planted in a white ceramic plant pot, the soil topped with stones, both of these framing a gleaming Apple iMac computer. Peering over her glasses, she spoke, her voice, crisp yet polite.

"Can I help you, sir?"

Ben's eyes scanned the room, sufficient in size, just, and very much adequate as the reception area for small high street solicitors, removing the letter carefully from its jealous protective sleeve, he handed it over the desk. Reading the contents quickly and efficiently, digesting only what was required, the receptionist looked over her glasses, and smiled.

"Ah yes, Mr Hickman told me to expect you, he will see you right away."

Following the finger at the end of the extended arm, Ben made his way towards the light brown door to the left, knocking over the bonsai tree as he edged his way around the desk. Looking over his shoulder as he entered the room, he smiled as he watched the elderly administrative assistant diligently picking it up again, scooping the dark soil and stones back into the white pot, before replacing it back onto the desk. Once inside the room he was greeted by Michael Hickman himself.

"Good morning Ben, and, how are you? Long time, no see, how's your father? We go back a long, long way you know, went to the same school together, in the same year."

His voice as crisp and polite as that of his receptionist, he talked much more quickly, multi-tasking at the same time, removing a thicker envelope from his desk drawer whilst directing Ben to the seat opposite his own. Frowning as he scanned the letter, immediately fully conversant with its contents, he turned his head, his silver hair high and tight, the longer strands doing their very best to draw attention away from the receding hairline, and removing his reading glasses looked up at Ben.

"Well, Ben, do you know a Mr Williams, a Mr Bill Williams? Well I suppose you must do, or at least must have done at some time, well, the poor devil has passed away, a few months ago in fact now, up in Ayrshire, south-west of Scotland, not very old either, late-fifties, good grief was that all, sad news, sad news indeed."

Raising his eye brows, his reading spectacles still in his hand, the right-hand temple tip in his mouth, he concluded, his voice slower and more deliberate, as if he were taking a breath in between each word.

"And you, Benjamin Johnson, appear to be the sole beneficiary of his estate."

Surprised by this new information, Ben was now sitting bolt upright in his seat, too flabbergasted to speak, his gaze fixed onto the grey filing cabinet just visible behind Michael Hickman's left shoulder, searching for a focal point from which his mind might trawl up the facts he was currently sadly lacking. No, he definitely did not know a Bill Williams, not when he was alive, and certainly not now that he was dead.

"What? I have inherited some money, is that what you mean?"

"Yes, you're a very wealthy man."

The solicitor smiled, reaching down to pull a large white envelope from a draw somewhere hidden beneath his desk.

"Here's a copy of the details, I've had it all prepared for you, you've quite an inheritance there my friend. Read through it, and come back and see me tomorrow. Oh, and make sure that you send my best to your father."

Wobbling on his feet and still too staggered to speak properly, Ben stood up, removed the envelope, thick with the enclosed wad of paperwork, from the solicitor's out stretched hand, tucked it under his arm, and, nodding his head, left the room. Passing the receptionists desk, he chuckled to himself, everything was back in order, the iMac resting perfectly in the centre, the post trays and the bonsai tree positioned on either side.

"Have a good day sir," the receptionist beamed back at him.

"You know, I think that I might just do that."

Ben could barely feel the pavement under his feet as he stepped outside and back into the street, the value of the estate having been written in bold print, four hundred thousand pounds, he was floating on air.

*****

"Who is, sorry who was, Bill Williams?"

His voice almost completely drowned out by the front door slamming shut noisily behind him.

"Bill Williams? Bill Williams? Bill Williams!"

Reg smiled, pleased but not immodest with himself, for it had only taken three attempts to answer his own question, his memory not as good as it once was, but still functional.

"Yes, yes, Bill Williams. Wasn't he that friend of yours Anna? Do you remember, all those years ago, Christ, it must be almost a quarter of a century ago now, he worked, no, I think he owned that posh wine merchants near Arnold's, now what was it called? What was it called? It's on the tip of my tongue. Yes, that was it, The Premier Cru Bottlehouse!"

The back of the chair creaked, the palms of his hands resting heavily down on its wooden frame, his head hovering over Anna's shoulders, there was nothing he loved more than reminiscing into the past, life's rich pageant recalled, old acquaintances not forgotten, readily brought back to mind, and all of that. Suddenly he shuddered, the smile abruptly leaving his face, an unexpected agitation, as if an unwelcome guest had entered the room, a spectre from a distant time, recovering quickly he managed to compose himself.

"Do you remember? Oh, you must remember, Anna. Every Friday night you would go there and pick up a nice bottle of wine for the weekend, you used to say that it was our little treat for me working away from home. Oh, come on Anna, think, think!"

Her conversation with Sarah sitting beside her now brought to an abrupt end, Anna gazed into the vacant space between the two of them seemingly lost in thought, and the more she ruminated, the more the colour drained from her face. Yes, she could remember, in fact she could remember Bill Williams very well indeed.

"When you were pregnant with Ben, well just before, I think."

Reg continued, his enthusiasm unabated by his wife's silence.

"He came to the house loads of times, in fact he was one of our closest friends around that time, he even bought you a present when Ben was born. Funny how we never saw him again after that."

Silence filled the room, engrossed in his own thoughts, as if all of his energy had been expended, his over exuberance exhausted, Reg went quiet, very quiet.

"Yes, I remember, I remember him, now."

Her voice barely a croak, her hand covering her mouth as she stared up at the ceiling, seemingly oblivious to everything that was going around her.

Holding his wife's hand, Reg studied Anna's face, willing her to calm herself down, all attempts to pacify her failing miserably. Suddenly he was distracted again, distracted by dark thoughts, dark thoughts and painful memories filling his mind, unwanted recollections from the past, announcing themselves in a place from which he thought they had been banished for good.

Instinctively he reinstated these uncomfortable, unnerving thoughts to the back of his mind, focusing, as he had so often done in the past, on more practical matters. Ben had definitely returned home from the solicitors with a spring in his step, he was, evidently, the bearer of good news, news that he could not contain for more than a second on his arrival home, eager to impart his new information with the rest of the family, news that might draw attention away from Bill Williams the person, and towards something with more universally approval.

"Oh Bill, my dear friend Bill, dead."

Anna stammered, her face red with weeping despite having managed to finally stem the flow of tears.

"Let me have that letter."

Holding his hand in mid-air right in front of Ben's face, shaking it vigorously, under his nose, Reg barked out his order. Meanwhile, sitting huddled up in her chair, her arms wrapped tightly around her body, Anna shivered, she could see Bill very clearly now, tall, his short silver hair parted to the side, his ears outsized against the rest of his face, but his smile, that smile, and that infectious enthusiasm, well, they more than compensated for any facial imperfections.

"Let me see, Bill Williams back in our lives after all these years, well I never."

Taking the envelope in his hand, Reg was, all of a sudden, introspective, his voice trailing off into a whisper. Armed with two fresh white man-sized tissues, his arm around her shoulder, Ben did his best to comfort his distressed parent whilst his father's eyes scanned the pages, reading the contents, muttering to himself and nodding his head.

Bill Williams was indeed dead, at fifty-eight, shame, too young really, following a short illness. He had never married, shame, again, and no family survived him, so, more than likely, he would have more than a reasonable sum of money in his estate, in fact there would probably be more than enough to make somebody very wealthy for a very long time.

In summary, his last will and testimony allowed for two options, the preferred choice was that Ben would accept the legacy in its entirety, and so inherit the whole estate. Should Ben choose to forgo his inheritance, then the money would be divided equally between two obscure animal charities and Cancer Research. His eyes fixed to the bottom of the page, having evidently reached the final paragraph, Reg suddenly froze, his hands unable to make sufficient purchase, the sheets of paper fell to the floor.

"Good God Ben! You've inherited four hundred thousand pounds, near as damn it half million quid!"

"I know that, Dad, I'm not stupid, but should I accept it? I've never heard of this Bill Williams guy. Why would he want to leave all of his money to me? Why would he possibly care about me for goodness sake?"

"There can be no question, four hundred thousand pounds, you must accept it, there's no room for sentiment with that amount of money, you'd be a fool not to."

His eyes, their pupils covered with metaphoric pound signs, wandered around the room, pausing at the tired and dated kitchen just visible through the doorway, before resting on the threadbare carpet under his feet, his hand quietly patting the arm rest of his tatty armchair. His legs stretched out in front of him, a smirk of satisfaction suddenly covering his face, handing the letter and envelope back to its rightful owner, the decision already made, they would be keeping the money, he was adamant about that, his mind not for turning.

Reading through the letter again, as if searching for a something new, but, in reality, the same words still telling the same story, Ben's mind was in turmoil. Accept the cash and he would have riches beyond his wildest dreams, an inexhaustible pot of money, wealth that defied all imagination, but was it really as simple as that? Questions were burning his mind, pricking his conscious. Why would this Bill Williams, someone he had never even met, want to make him such a generous gift? What about David? Why would Bill Williams want to miss him out? They were brothers, for goodness sake! It just didn't feel right.

Cursing his luck and desperately searching for a means of departure from his predicament, Ben knew that he needed to buy some time, acquire some breathing space, some room to think. Looking at his father, his voice filled with resignation.

"I'll go back and see Michael Hickman again in the morning,"

Squeezing her youngest son by the hand, and eager to shift attention away from her remorseful outburst, Anna knew that she had to act quickly.

Ordinarily Monday evening was a relatively subdued affair, the start of the working week, the excitement of the weekend already twenty-four hours past, all of this amounting to something relatively cheap and simple for tea, preferably followed by a reasonably well produced drama on the television at nine o'clock accompanied by a small glass of wine, before retiring to bed on the conclusion of the ten o'clock news headlines.

Well, today was going to be different, and she was going to make absolutely certain of that. This was not going to be just another Monday, the start of just another week, no, she would make sure that today was different, a special Monday, the start of an exceptional week, and exceptional demanded something more distinctive, more superior.

Jumping clean out of her seat, and grabbing Sarah by the arm, Anna snatched her handbag, and in an instance the two of them were speeding off into the hallway, picking up their coats, before hurrying out of the house, getting into the car and racing off to the supermarket. Steering the car carefully into the congested car park, her emotional recovery now almost complete, Anna managed a smile, quietly congratulating herself on locating a space reasonably close to the store.

Once inside, they battled their way through the busy aisles, bursting with early Monday evening shoppers, jostling their way through the store. First stop, the fruit and vegetables, positioned conveniently at the front by the entrance, a packet of chestnut mushrooms very quickly finding its way into the base of the shallow trolley, in the meat aisle Anna carefully selected three packets of sirloin steak, two pieces in each pack, six in total, whilst Sarah headed off to the frozen foods section, returning back to her shopping companion, eagerly waving a bag of frozen chips in her right hand and a bag of battered onion rings in her left. Re-united, they walked, purposefully to the wines and spirits department, picking up three bottles of French sparkling wine and four bottles of real ale, before heading off to join the queues at the checkouts.

Back home, huddled together in the small kitchen, the pair of them enthusiastically prepared the food. The chips, lying chaotically alongside the onion rings on a rectangular baking tray, heating up and turning a perfect golden brown in the nice warm oven, the pieces of steak adding to the excitement, their juices flowing, fat sizzling and spitting in the frying pan, the popping of the wine bottle corks augmenting this symphony of general good cheer, the aroma as fulsome as the anticipation of the good times to come. The both of them, no strangers to the house galley, yakked on incessantly, and by the time the food was prepared and ready for plating up, both were in incredibly fine fettle, and ready to make a good night of it.

The table set for five places, the four already present having already taken their seats, Reg was the first to raise his glass.

"A toast, everyone, a toast to Bill Williams, and may God have mercy on his soul."

Not a drop of wine had managed to find a way through anyone's lips, when all heads turned to the hallway, distracted by the sound of the door handle turning in the hall, the front door slamming shut.

"Ah, perfect. You're just in time, David, come and join us, your food's on the table. Tonight, we are having a celebration!"

Taking his coat off and discarding his black leather messenger bag in the hallway, David completely ignoring his father's beaming face, walked directly to where his mother was seated, leaning over, he gave her a loving kiss on the cheek. Nodding to his brother and smiling coyly at Sarah, before, finally, he turned to his neglected parent.

"And what might we be celebrating this time, Father?"

Chapter 3
Monday

Grimacing at the unwelcome plate of food on the table in front of him, two of his clients having cancelled their appointments that afternoon, and ten miles of roadworks with a forty mile an hour variable speed limit to contend with on his return journey home, David was not in an especially good mood.

Eating his food slowly, one parent sitting on either side of him, he listened attentively to his father's account of the day's events, his mother, now seemingly back on top of her game, chipping in with her own contribution when and where ever she felt was necessary.

Efficiently, and very quickly, they successfully furnished him with a concise, and yet thorough, account of the history of the life and times of Bill Williams, his relationship with their family, and Ben's subsequent inheritance.

His knife and fork simultaneously falling to the table, David continued eating, his teeth crushing and grinding the food in his mouth. Pausing, virtually all of the chips and the majority of his steak still lying un-eaten on his plate, he rose from his seat, for, finding both the food and the story increasingly difficult to swallow, he was incapable digesting any more of either one of them.

He had heard enough, more than enough, and was going to go down the pub, he needed some time to himself, with just a pint of beer for company, getting up from the table and out of his chair, he put his coat back on, and, without looking back at his family, left the house, slamming the front door behind him.

Probably no one's favourite pub, the Cross Keys would not have been David's number one choice of hostelry either, except that it was his local and the short distance from his house meant that he could leave his car safely parked up in the driveway and enjoy a couple of pints without having to concern himself with any unwanted attention from the local constabulary on his way home.

Making good use of the shortcut through the park, his destination just a brisk fifteen-minute walk from the house, but still a quarter of an hour, plenty of time for uninvited cogitation, and the more he deliberated over the information given to him by his eager parents, the more his head felt like it was going to explode.

Walking into the bar, five flat television screens, each permanently showing live coverage from Sky Sports, adorned the walls at the most advantageous points, each desperate to gain his attention at the expense of the other, next to one of those, a blackboard fixed to the wall next to the bar tempting the paying customer with pizza, steak and chips, and wholesome stews.

Shaking his head David's gaze fell upon the bar itself, much less attention was paid to the selection of beer, which, at best could only be described as standard; Doom Bar and John Smiths for bitter drinkers, Carling and Fosters for those who preferred lager, and a selection of bottled beers for folk with more modern tastes, or those who simply couldn't quite manage a full pint. Not especially spoilt for choice, he ordered a pint of Doom Bar, not his favourite, but more than acceptable.

Sitting at the bar, his leg tightly wrapped around a tall wooden bar stool, he made short work of the first half of his pint, lifting the glass from the polished wooden surface and finishing the second half in just one gulp, his thirst insatiable, his initial cravings satisfied, he turned to order a second pint, as he did his empty glass was immediately snatched from his hand.

"Another Doom Bar, gorgeous?"

Tanya's Welsh accent reverberated, filling the area immediately around the bar. Aged around forty years old, she was a single mother with an eighteen-year old and a four-year old, both boys. Neither chic nor sophisticated, but much to the pleasure of the punters gathered eagerly around her, she certainly bought a much-needed visual accent to the presentation to the bar area, brightening up the otherwise drab environment with her leopard pattern tops and tight leather trousers. Her Welsh accent was genuine, her face always fully made up, and as immaculate as her perfectly manicured fingernails, her long hair, dark and curly, always tied up over her head.

"Yes, please."

David mumbled, carefully avoiding the possibility of any eye contact, Tanya had a reputation, and it wasn't a good one, and he was certainly not in the mood for any of that. Moving away from the bar, and pulling out a seat from under one of the small round tables in the corner, he gazed at the grimy grey wooden panelled walls, each one covered in prints of movie stars and footballers, the photographs faded by the sunlight, their frames covered in dust.

The beer was doing its work, the alcohol penetrating into his brain, numbing his senses, calming him down, picking up one of the beer mats scattered on the table, Peters and Co. Crisps, wild thyme and rosemary flavour, he shuddered, his mind fixed on two very different matters, although each with its own distinctive and un-pleasant flavour, his mother, and the money.

Turning the beer mat over and over in between his fingers, and quietly muttering to himself, he slowly began to process the information he had received. Bill Williams had died and left all of his money to Ben, why would he do that? As much as he racked his brains he could not see any further than one explanation, he must have been related to Ben, and therefore, he must have been Ben's father, and if he was Ben's father then that must mean that, at some stage, he must have had a relationship with their mother.

Taking a sip from his pint glass he thoughts turned towards his mother, how could she have done that? How could she have betrayed the whole family in that way? Living a lie for the almost a quarter of a century. She, who he has loved unconditionally all of his life, whom he had placed on to a pedestal, elevating her above all others, well that illusion, built up over almost thirty years, had been completely shattered in thirty short seconds. Good grief, his father wasn't perfect, not by any stretch of the imagination, but, surely, even he deserved better than that.

Gritting his teeth, he considered the money, all of the evidence suggesting that Ben had inherited a small fortune, four hundred thousand pounds falling into his lap in the blink of an eye. Good God, Ben, who had barely lifted a finger, scarcely done a full day of honest toil, tucked up with enough cash to last a lifetime.

Sighing deeply, his head buried in his hands, spiralling into depression, his mind free falling, and with little pleasure, he ransacked his own memory, appraising his own life.

His money had not come easy, building up his business from scratch, wooing clients from anywhere and everywhere in the early years, getting himself off the ground, there hadn't been much dignity in that, he sighed to himself. Since then life had felt like one endless trawl, hunting out new business and new clients, more recently travelling further away from home, dragging his net further afield, even more time spent in the car, sitting in endless lines of traffic, his idle fingers

24

mindlessly drumming on the steering wheel, a small fortune spent on limitless packets of crisps and Extra Strong Mints. Off the road, and back in the office, he was shackled to the computer screen, the mundaneness of opening emails and attachments slowly driving him to distraction. It paid the bills, he re-assured himself, again.

His love life was a similar tale of boredom and tedium. Just two relationships came to mind from the past five or six years, neither of which were of any real significance, neither of which could be described as serious, both of which he had tired of long before they had got to that stage. In a perverse sort of way, he had always craved for someone like his mother, more recently, and even more intriguing, it was Sarah that was catching his eye, embarrassingly on more than one occasion she had caught him, his gaze fixed on her perfectly formed breasts, her shapely legs.

Shaking his head and feeling the red mist falling, he got up from his seat, God, how he hated his mother now. Finishing his pint, he stared at the framed photograph on the wall immediately in front of him, five black and white film shots surrounding a silver plague embossed with the number 007, he smiled to himself, *if only.*

Standing at the bar, he ordered a third pint.

"Cheer up, gorgeous. I'm on a break soon, I'll put a smile on your face."

Wearing a thin leopard patterned blouse, her cheap black, lacy bra clearly visible underneath, Tanya flashed a smile, he did his best to ignore her, not remotely interested in anything she had to say. In fact, since the events of the day he had started to develop a real distaste for women, they were after what they could get and couldn't be trusted, in fact, they made him sick.

Sitting back down at the small table, nursing his pint glass, his eyes once again drawn to the photo's adjourning the walls, James Bond, now there was a man who knew the right way to treat women, he mused to himself, taking his pleasure and moving on, shrugging his shoulders he picked up his pint and saw it of in just three quick gulps.

Getting out of his seat, and suddenly feeling very dizzy, he swayed from side to side, struggling to keep his balance, propped up by his knuckles on the table, an almost futile attempt to re-gain his composure, he eventually managed to negotiate the short distance separating his table from the toilets.

The door from the bar led to a narrow corridor, its dirty blue carpet, mottled with the stains of spilt beer, the drab mustard yellow walls corroded by the dampness, pretty grim in itself, but a brief and welcome respite from what lay ahead. Through a second door, the light brown floor tiles were wet, and a dreadful stench hung in the air. The four urinals, once white, were stained with a disgusting yellow tinge, in the single cubicle, the toilet seat broken in half, and left un-repaired for weeks.

Pulling a second paper towel from the dispenser, the hand drier hanging off the wall and covered in a crisscross of yellow and black tape, David finished drying his hands awkwardly, his hand-eye coordination virtually non-existent, his central vision having all but completely disappeared.

Amidst all of the confusion he could hear the door open and close behind him, and looking over his shoulder, still swaying impossibly from side to side, he saw Tanya standing, her back against the door.

"What the hell are you doing in here?"

He slurred as he threw away his spent paper towel into the bin, adding to the damp, stinking pile already overflowing onto the floor. Tanya smiled at him.

"Like I said, I'm on a break, and you look like you might need cheering up."

Shaking the last of the water from his hands, his head partly cleared for a second by the repulsion, David looked at her in disgust.

"Not by you, now go away and leave me alone, you shouldn't be in here anyway."

"Oh, but I am."

Striding forward, within a couple of seconds she was standing right in front of him, her leather trousers creased behind the knees, skin tight at the crotch, her large hooped ear rings clashing against her bare neck. Her arms resting on his shoulders, he could see the outline of her nipples through her leopard patterned blouse, she caught him looking, tilting her head to one side, she smiled, and stared at him, her eyes crazy with lust and power.

On the window sill above the urinal were three rolls of white toilet paper, arranged in a small pyramid, a miniature brass monkey, additional supplies, waiting patiently in the wings, ready to fulfil their role when required, for now spectators, sitting at their vantage point, watching as the cruel and sadistic events un-folded.

His vision now blurred, David felt totally disorientated, his head turned from left to right and right to left, desperately trying to locate the sources of the noises he could hear in his head, the things he thought he could feel with his hands, none of which could possibly be there. He could smell Tanya's cheap perfume as she pinned him, hard, against the greasy, grimy, tiled wall with her left hand, her arm stretched out, the full weight of her body against his.

"Didn't you notice that little bit of powder I slipped into your second pint David? Oh dear! What a shame!"

Completely paralysed, his mind unable to fully comprehend what was going on, David turned his head away.

"You men, you all think that you're God's gift, don't you? Well, you're not, you're nothing. I could have you anytime, anytime I want."

He could feel the heat of Tanya's breath, her lips touching his ear as she spoke. Barely able to support himself, somehow, he managed to summon up enough strength, enough force, to push himself away from the wall, and barge passed Tanya, knocking her over, staggering out of the toilets, his humiliation complete.

Stumbling back through the park, and feeling physically sick, David reached the swings positioned in the corner of the small children's play area. Retching against the yellow painted steel frame, his beer infused vomit covering the broken wooden seat suspended on a rusty chain, his head spinning, his body swathed by an un-controllable dizziness.

Bent over double, his head pounding, he started to think about his father. was this how he had felt the first time he had learnt of his mother's infidelity? Her cheating on him with that Bill Williams? She taking what she wanted, without any consideration for their marriage, without any consideration for him. In essence, Tanya had done exactly the same thing, drugging him up, forcing herself on him, mocking him to his face. Christ, a man would be chastised for just thinking of such a thing. Women, they think they can get away with anything!

It was almost pitch black in the park, his entire body overrun by a feeling of helplessness, what little energy that remained being sapped by an un-expected feeling of guilt, was he such an awful child that his mother had to seek comfort from outside of the family, was he so pathetic that scum like Tanya think that they can insult him the way she had just done?

Arriving at one of the abundant wooden memorial benches, positioned so thoughtfully and carefully along the tree lined path way that meandered through the park, the sporadic lighting provision allowing for some ophthalmic relief in the darkness, he sat down encasing his head with his hands.

For a quarter of an hour he rested there, his whole body shivering with the cold, the outside temperature being exacerbated by the alcohol in his blood, his head finally starting to clear, he got up, and trudged home.

Placing his hands gratefully on to the warm radiator, his fingers slowly coming back to life, and closing the front door quietly behind him, David could hear the laughter and the chatter coming from the living room as he stood in the small hallway. Sufficiently warmed up he poked his head around the door and scanned the room, apparently a detour had been made to the off licence, for there were five empty wine bottles scattered around the coffee table, the original estimate of three clearly insufficient for the celebrations that were to ensue.

Looking further around the door, he could see his father and mother sitting on the settee, chatting merrily together, without a care in the world, his father wearing the expression of a man who had invested all of his money in just a single lottery ticket and a Divine Providence had intervened allowing him scoop the jackpot all to himself.

Intrigued and surprised by what was happening before his very eyes, he gawped jealously at his brother and Sarah sitting cosily in the two arm chairs, for whilst Ben was gazing intensely into her eyes, all of a sudden, she was looking back at him, the pair of them seemingly captivated by the other's attention.

"Come on in, Son," Reg shouted across the room.

"Yes, come and sit down, David, we've just been taking about Ben's piece of good news," Anna echoed, getting out of her chair and fetching a wooden one from the kitchen.

Shaking his head, David remained in the doorway, he really wasn't interested in listening to his mother talk about Ben's piece of good news all over again, however much excitement that might have generated amongst all of those present in the room, in fact, he wasn't really interested in anything that was going on right now in that irritating little soiree. He smiled, a dark ironic smile, scanned the whole room one last time, rotated under the doorway, and climbed up the stairs and towards his bedroom.

Ready for bed, he picked up the small glass of water from his small, white, bedside table, and took a sip, getting the rehydration process underway. Work was cancelled for tomorrow, he mused to himself, well, certainly the morning appointments anyway. The glass fully drained, he got up and crossed the landing, arriving at the bathroom he poured himself a second. Holding the glass under the tap, the ice-cold water spewing out, and gushed to the bottom, he could hear Sarah's taxi pull up outside, followed quickly by the excruciating sound of hugging and kissing at the front door.

Despite wave upon wave of cravings and countless packets of mints, David had resisted the temptation of taking a cigarette for over five years, and before then, as a testament to a Government television advertisement campaign, he had never made a habit of smoking in bed, the dangers so graphically depicted on the small screen. However, after everything he had endured that day, this would have been one occasion when he would have been more than happy to expose himself to that risk, and, drawing on an imaginary cigarette, he fantasied of the predictable impact of the nicotine as it instantaneously found its way to his brain, and suddenly everything was just that little bit more bearable.

Holding his two fingers up to his lips, he thought about Tanya, he would be giving her a taste of her own medicine, and very soon, he smiled, as he deliberated as to how his revenge was going to manifest itself, the score with that little slut well and truly evened up. Taking another sip from the glass he sucked in his cheeks, pretending to blow smoke rings into the cold dark air, his cravings for a cigarette getting more intense by the second.

Shaking his head, and removing the illusory addictive distraction, his mind returned to his mother. Had he jumped to the wrong conclusion about her? He had loved her so much for all these years, and yet he was so quick to make assumptions about her past? Perhaps Bill Williams wasn't Ben's father after all? Ben had inherited his money, that didn't mean that he was necessarily his son, did it? He groaned as his head started to ache, grinding into his temples, and making him feel sick.

Pulling a packet of paracetamol from his bedside table, he pressed two out of the metallic blister pack, before eagerly taking them with the remainder of the water, his thoughts turned to Sarah. He'd always had a soft spot for her, actually he fancied her like mad, was his kid brother trying to muscle in with her now? He better not be!

Leaning in bed, his head resting on his elbow, he unlocked his phone with his thumb print before selecting the green square with the white speech bubble, and texting Daniel.

Chapter 4
Tuesday

Open for just two years, The Café Narino was one of those coffee shops best described as artisan; its cups as diverse in shape and size as they were in colour, the chairs and tables a showroom of different styles and designs, the rustic flooring of untreated wood, the walls littered with original paintings from local artists, all of this complimented by the coffee, with its unique aromas and fragrancies, hailing from territories not normally chartered by the big branded coffee shops.

Muttering under his breath, a full five minutes of inaudible chuntering, Daniel sat in one of the green leather chairs, quietly cursing his best friend. What could David possibly want that was so important? He mumbled to himself. Couldn't he have waited until this evening? Then they could have gone for a pint down The Cross Keys.

It wasn't the best pub in the world, in fact, it wasn't even the best pub in the town, but they sold a decent pint of bitter, and that Tanya was very easy on the eye too, Daniel smiled to himself, visualising Tanya, leaning over the beer tap, pulling his pint, wearing her lascivious grin, her leopard patterned blouse leaving little or nothing to the imagination.

Rolling his eyes as he acknowledged Daniel's presence, his face filled with fury, David strolled into the café and straight towards the counter.

"Two lattes please, an extra shot in one of them, no, actually make that two, and I'll have two flapjacks as well please."

Carrying his sturdy wooden tray, compete with the triangular soft, sticky treats lying on top of two stacked up light blue plates, he made his way to the end of the counter and picked up his drinks. Sitting down in the chair opposite to Daniel, holding his friend by the hand as he took a sip from his chipped red and white stripped china mug, his whole body visibly shaking.

Taller, and leaner, Daniel was the same age as David, and, having spent a decade at the same school, they cemented their friendship playing on the same rugby pitch, one at fly half the other inside centre, at school, club, and county level.

"So, what's up mate, what's the drama?"

Opening up the conversation, as cheerfully as he dared, and sat back in his seat, preparing for the barrage that would surely follow, for his part, David recounted the whole story, from the beginning, speaking slowly and deliberately.

"This bloke called Bill Williams has died, right, and left all his money to Ben. Now, it was a hell of a long time ago, but I can just remember Bill from back then, even though I was only five, maybe six. I can remember that he worked in an off licence, you know, one of those posh ones that only sold expensive wine, single malt whiskey, and imported beer, it's closed down now, but it was only about a minute's walk from Arnold's department store, Mum worked there, years ago, behind the women's underwear counter, she only gave it up when Ben was born. Yeah, I can remember when Dad was working away from home we always had a special tea on a Friday to celebrate, Mum always bought an expensive bottle of wine to have with the food, they must have tried a different bottle every week, she would show me the different labels."

David paused and took a sip from his latte, blowing across the top of the mug, his breath running over the surface of the milk froth, cooling it down, before continuing.

"Now, if my memory serves me right, about once a month Bill would come and join us for tea on a Friday, parking his posh car right in front of the house, I used to look at it through the window, but, you know, he was suddenly ingratiating himself with Mum and Dad, you know, the three of them suddenly the best of friends. Dad was still working away from home during the week when Mum fell pregnant with Ben. Christ what a rubbish time that was, all she did was moan about her bad back and her head aches, about ten years ago she told me that it had been a difficult pregnancy and she had given up work earlier than she had planned, which was convenient, as she could spend the summer with me, when I was off school once she had given up work, she was a completely different person. You know, I can still remember some hefty chunks of that summer holiday, happy times shared between me and Mum, really bonding together, cementing our relationship, well I had her all to myself, didn't I?"

Taking a bite of his flapjack, David looked up at the ceiling, the tear forming in the corner of his eye betraying his emotions.

"Only, half way through the holiday, things changed. It was almost as if the bigger Mum got with Ben, the more we saw of Bill, until it felt like he was around the house all of time, certainly every other day at least, helping Mum with household jobs, jobs Dad could easily have done at the weekend."

Pausing again, David took another piece of his flapjack, washing it down with a huge gulp of the hot, milky latte.

"Bill would even look after me sometimes, taking me out to the shops to pick up bits and pieces for tea, just the two of us, you know, if Mum was busy in the house and, of course, Dad was working away. Which he was, in fact, he was working away virtually all of the time, can't remember exactly where or why, I think it involved a new road on the other side of the country, something like that, perhaps that's why I can remember that time of my life so clearly, even though it was so long ago."

Wiping the last crumbs of his flapjack from his mouth David paused again, his mind completely submerged in introspection, his hands flat on the table. Caught off guard, surprised to think that he must have had some respect for his father at one time, and that perhaps their relationship had started to go sour when his father started working away from home on a regular basis, there had been no specific trigger, they had simply drifted apart, the father's absence having such an impact on the young son.

He sighed, a long heavy, sigh, his lungs completely empty, his eyes transfixed onto the shiny brass old factory style light fitting, suspended by a twisted link chain, six feet over his head, its light seemingly illuminating a pathway through his memory.

"The funny thing was that, over time, Bill and I started to really get on, although it did feel like he went right out of his way to make sure that we did. In fact, and I've never told you this, it was actually Bill who first introduced me to rugby. I remember him throwing that strange leather oval shaped ball across the park at me, and me throwing it back at him. I hated it at first, why couldn't we have just played football, like all of the other kids? But over time I got better at it, and, soon, I could throw the ball further, and more accurately, pretty soon, I was running with the ball under my arm, trying to dodge past Bill as he stood in between our two crumpled up coats, lying on the grass."

His hand to his mouth, massaging his lower lip, David paused again, as he struggled to chronicle the events, both happy and sad, of the past.

"I can remember the day Ben was born really clearly, God, how weird is that? It was a Tuesday, I think, and, Dad had already returned home, the project completed, just the loose ends to tie up back in the office. It was the half term holidays and I remember Mum had taken me to the park. I remember it so well because the circus always came to town during the October holidays, setting itself up in the park, and I always loved going to that. Me and Mum were just walking past the newly erected big top, you know one of those massive tents with red stripes, we had to walk carefully to avoid those big wooden pegs, hammered into the ground, holding down the guy ropes. Then, suddenly, Mum collapsed, falling to the floor like a sack of potatoes, in agony, complaining of severe pains in her stomach. A young couple in their mid-twenties out walking their dog had called Bill, using Mum's mobile telephone, and within ten minutes he was there, caressing her in his arms, supporting her head, I can remember feeling nervous, anxious by their closeness. Bill called the emergency services, and within minutes an ambulance was pulling up on the main road running along the side of the park, two paramedics running across the grass to where we were all stood."

"Good God, you never told me that before, your poor mum," Daniel uttered, holding his mug in both hands.

"Well, that was the first and, thank God, the last time I've ever ridden in an ambulance. Although I have to admit being quite excited at the time, you know, surrounded by gloves, needles, bandages, cardiac monitor, oxygen masks, all that equipment they need for keeping patients alive. Bill followed the ambulance in his own car, he must have dodged through the traffic to maintain contact throughout the journey, we were going pretty fast and they had the siren on as well. We got to the hospital and Mum was given a bed, me and Bill sat down on the two small chairs positioned on either side, staring at her, lying there, writhing in agony. Funny you see pictures on the news about crowded hospitals and patients waiting in corridors to be treated, and yet I can remember the three of us being by ourselves, five empty beds surrounding Mum's. Of course, everything was fine, the doctor came and told Mum to be patient and wait for the Ben to arrive."

"So, what's the problem then? No, hold on, don't answer that just yet, I'll go and get us a couple more drinks. Another latte? Extra shots?"

Staring into space, David sat nodding his head, taking off his coat and throwing it over the back of his chair, meanwhile Daniel got up, and headed towards the counter, stuffing his hand into his trouser pocket, he removed a ten-pound note from his pocket and ordered the drinks.

Quietly drumming his fingers on the wooden counter, Daniel looked across the seating area and gazed at his best friend keenly, they were going to be there for some time, he sighed to himself, that was for certain. He knew how close David and Ben were, and it would take a major upset to rock the boat sufficiently for those two to fall out. Carrying the mug laden tray in his hands, he returned to the table, nodding his head, more enthusiastically now, David took a sip of his drink and continued.

"I remember waiting for what felt like hours with Bill whilst Mum was laid up in bed, when Dad finally arrived all hot and flustered, saying that he had been in a meeting or something, and couldn't get away. Ben was born at five-thirty in the evening, I can remember that as if it was yesterday. I was watching Blue Peter on the small television at the side of the bed, it was one of my favourite programmes back then, and when the doctor had asked me to turn it off I had the worst tantrum ever. That's where that family joke comes from, you know, whenever I got angry, Mum and Dad would say that there must be a baby on the way."

"Well, well, I always wondered where that came from."

Daniel allowed himself a quiet chuckle.

"Then I had one of the weirdest experiences of my life. Mum had to spend the night in the hospital whilst, Dad, Bill, and I all went back to the house, just the three of us. It was the first time I had actually seen Dad drunk, proper drunk I mean. They celebrated with a bottle of single malt whisky, an expensive one which, Mum told me later, that Bill had bought with him. I went to bed, but could hear the two of them laughing and talking all night. Anyway, Mum came home with Ben the next day, Dad had driven to the hospital and fetched her."

Suddenly, very abruptly, David broke off from the conversation, picked up his mug and drained half of its contents in one long sip, replacing the mug quietly onto the table, he looked Daniel in the eye intently, and concluded with one last bit of drama to end his story.

"And then the funniest thing happened, we never saw Bill again, not a word, not a card, not a present, nothing, until now."

Daniel broke the silence.

"You said that Ben has come into some money."

"That's the whole point. We hear nothing from this Bill guy for the best part of twenty-five years, and then suddenly, bang, he's kicked the bucket and left his whole estate to Ben."

"How much?" Daniel enquired, his voice as soft and gently as he could muster.

"Enough, Christ, more than enough. But it isn't the money I can't get my head around."

"I mean, Ben is bound to share the cash with you, what with you two being so close."

Interrupting his friend, desperate to defuse some of the tension, it was a statement and not a question.

"To be honest with you, I don't want any of the stupid money, he's welcome to it, all of it, every penny. Besides, that's hardly the point, is it? The point is, well, I mean, why him? Why just him and not me as well?"

Shuffling around uncomfortably in his seat, his determination to be the voice of reason un-thwarted, Daniel tried to interject.

"Yes, I see what you're saying, but still."

"He knew me much better than Ben. In fact, he only saw Ben once, the day he was born for God's sake, he didn't know him from Adam. We used to go to the park together, he bought me ice creams and stuff. When Dad was away and he came to see Mum, he always fussed over me. Surely if he had no children of his own and wanted to leave the money to someone he would have left it to me, unless…"

"Unless what? Unless what for goodness sake? Perhaps he just felt a real bond to Ben as he helped out on the day he was actually born, nothing more than that. It's not the same as being at the birth itself, but just being involved can have a real impact on people, my dad told me that, he was involved in my birth right from when my mum's waters burst, in fact, he was even there when I was born."

David's retort was short, sharp, and to the point.

"Maybe you're right, but here's another idea for you to think about. What about if my mother had an affair with him and he was actually Ben's father?"

Daniel lent over the table towards his friend, tapping the table with his fingertips before leaning back into is chair again, his head cocked to one side, inspecting his friend's face, his own suddenly very serious. Sipping at his latte, miniscule sips barely worth the effort, he bought some time, precious time to think, as whilst his eyes were on David, his thoughts were on his younger brother, considering the pair of them, lining them both up side by side in his mind, he very quickly concluded that they had very little in common, in fact they had virtually nothing in common at all.

Physically, the differences were obvious, plain for all to see. Their height, their complexions, the shape of their heads, the size of their hands, and their ears, especially their ears. Scrutinising their personalities, he soon came to the same conclusion, they were very, very different. Ben totally carefree, living his uncomplicated life for the moment, in the here and now, without any real consideration, or concern, for the future. David the polar opposite, so serious about everything, always planning, always scheming, never leaving anything to chance.

Raising his cup to his mouth again, and slowly taking another mouthful of coffee, Daniel smiled, yes, they were very different, and were getting more different by the minute.

"Yes, that might be a possible explanation, but surely not?"

"Oh, come on mate. It can be the only explanation, you know that, and don't pretend that you don't. God, what am I left with?' A mother, who, like an idiot, I've pretty well worshipped all of my life, is actually nothing but a slapper, a slut, happy to open her legs to anyone and everyone, and then spending the next twenty odd years of her life, our lives, pretending that it never happened, everything just normal, whilst my pathetic father looked on."

"Don't you think you're getting a bit carried away here mate."

Daniel looked at his friend earnestly, shocked by his emotional outburst, but to no avail.

"Getting a bit carried away? You know what? I hate her, I really do. I already hated him, the useless waste of space that he is, and now I hate her, I hate her, and all of her kind."

Daniel held up his hands, pushing against the air with his palms.

"Look mate, calm down, calm down, come on, finish off your drink."

Nodding his head, and cupping his mug with both of his hands, his face filled with resignation, David slowly finished his drink. Daniel replaced his own empty mug onto the table, and looked at his friend.

"Look, mate, are you sure about all of this, I mean, really sure?"

David slammed his empty cup down onto the table.

"Okay, you tell me then, you tell me why Ben got all of the money."

36

Daniel shook his head slowly from side to side, finally meeting his friend's gaze.

"Okay, okay, let's say, let's just say that she had an affair, and okay, that Bill Williams, or whatever his name was, is Ben's father, well, come on, does that really matter now? It happened such a long time ago, what difference does it make now?"

Rubbing his face with his hands, David, his eyes black with fury, stared at Daniel, but his eyes were blind to him, he couldn't distinguish his features at all, all he could see were those disgusting toilets, and that disgusting Tanya pinning him against the wall, looking up at him, that sick grin all over her face. He hated women, all of them.

"It matters to me mate; it matters to me."

Chapter 5
Tuesday

Anna could barely feel the toes of her feet as she sat in the front seat of the car, they had just the one between them now, she having traded in her Mini Cooper when Reg retired. Rubbing her hands together vigorously, she turned up the heater, the leather seat freezing cold against her bottom and the small of her back.

Sufficiently warmed up, she pulled sluggishly out of the drive and, turning the steering wheel to the right, headed onto the main road. Her destination already very clear in her mind, somewhere where she could submerge herself into the past and re-visit those memories so abruptly bought back to mind, somewhere she knew that she would not be disturbed, where no one could find her.

Half an hour later, the gravel crunching under the wheels as she drew to a halt outside of the Royal Oak, she sat in the car, her eyes covered in a veil of tears, she didn't really understand why she was crying, she just couldn't stop herself.

Removing her black leather gloves and wiping the tears away, she gazed through the windscreen, almost a quarter of a century had passed since she had last sat in that car park, almost twenty-five years since the night when she had told Bill that it was all over between them.

Looking up the window of the room they used to share was still there, number forty-five, the second one from the end, on the top floor, two stories of double bedrooms housed in the building adjourning the pub, a middle-of-the-road overnight accommodation, no frills, no recognised hospitality standards stars or rosettes, just a bed for the night with minimal fuss at a minimal cost. Cagily she looked around the car park, checking the cars, looking for anything familiar, old habits always the most difficult to break, she smiled to herself, there was nobody about, and what if there were?

Her nervous steps treading lightly over the rock fragments, she lengthened her gait, negotiating the pair of wooden steps that led up to the front door and into the Royal Oak itself. Mercifully, the cloakrooms were still positioned on the left-hand side of the large, rather grand, hallway, a vase of beautiful bright yellow sunflowers sitting on the round table right in the centre, presenting the warmest of welcomes to the customers as they walked through before entering the lounge area.

Freshened up and ready to face the world, she opened the oak double doors and walked into the lounge, her eyes scanning the room, marvelling at all of the alterations since she was last there. The lounge had been totally transformed, at least one of the walls having been completely removed, the tables and chairs less cramped in the bigger environment, a dark wooden floor had replaced the carpet, the lighting reflecting off its smooth and glossy surface.

Bill would have approved, she smiled to herself, as she glanced over at the bar, her eyes running anxiously along the beer taps, seeking out that familiar red and gold plaque on the tap handle, yes it was still there, positioned at the very end now, but still there, so, yes, Bill would definitely have approved.

Another teardrop broke free and filled Anna's eye, Bill's voice, as clear as day, filling her head, a ghost from the past, happy times a long time halted.

"Pint and a half of Best Bitter please."

The young waitress, aged around twenty years old, slim, very pretty, her cheeks covered in ginger freckles, smiled confidently as she pulled a chair out for Anna at the table before handing over a menu. The service had definitely improved, Anna thought to herself as she browsed over the laminated piece of white paper headed simply, but sufficiently, Breakfast Menu.

Having mentally made her selection she lifted up her eye and surveyed the restaurant. As with the bar area, the whole space had been completely refurbished, and, again, very much for the better she concluded. Breakfast is breakfast, and the menu was of course predictable, and as with the waitress service, without any disappointments, the waitress skilfully wrote down Anna's order, scrambled eggs, with spinach, on harvest grain toast and a pot of tea, with skimmed milk, on her notepad, effortlessly keeping up with her as she spoke.

Re-arranging the cutlery on her table, for no other reason but for the want of something to do, she gaped at the sheer volume of customers that had descended on the restaurant that Tuesday morning, her mind working overtime, wandering

if any of the people sat at the tables that surrounded her were embarking in the same sort of secret rendezvous she had done with Bill, all those years ago?

Re-arranging the cutlery once again she examined some of the faces more closely, taking in more of the detail, scrutinizing each and every one. A furtive peek towards the door? An awkward glance over the shoulder? Perhaps the eyes locked too intensely with the conversation? All the tell-tale signs that perhaps an innocent breakfast for two might not be all that it seemed. She smiled to herself disappointedly, no, perhaps not.

Nodding her head in approval, Anna made a start on her spinach, removing her fork from her mouth she gazed at the green leafy contents suspended precariously between the tines and slots, and smiled again, recognising the subtle changes in the carte du jour, spinach was certainly not on the menu back then, she pondered, the concept of superfoods having still yet to be invented.

Not that the two of them ever enjoyed the pleasure of breakfasting together, she sighed, not once relishing in the delights of waking up in each other's arms, each evening having its own Cinderella ending, only with their white charges and delicate pink carriage turning back into four mice and a pumpkin long before the midnight hour.

Running her knife through the triangles of lightly buttered toast that had formed a buttress dam on the edge of the plate, supporting the spinach in preventing the scrambled egg from running off, she was suddenly conscious of a small hand hovering over the table.

"Mind if I have a sachet of your sugar, I don't appear to have any?"

Looking to her left, Anna could see a mild lady in her mid-thirties, dressed casually in black leggings and an olive-green jumper, leaning nervously towards her.

"Of course, have these," she replied, handing over two small light blue Silver Spoon branded packets of the sweet tasting carbohydrate.

'Isn't it lovely here, I haven't been before, have you?'

Anna smiled to herself, her intention had been to escape from anything in the way of human company, but now that it had suddenly presented itself, she was surprised by the warmth of its welcome.

"I have, but not for a number of years."

The hint of sadness of her tone did not go un-noticed by her new companion.

"Sorry, I'm interfering, I didn't wish to pry. Unless, of course, you want to talk about it?"

Anna gazed listlessly into the plate on the table in front of her, privately recalling her illicit rendezvous with Bill, all of those years ago.

The routine always the same, slick and safe, the crust of the toast crunching between her teeth, she mused, smirking quietly to herself. Two drinks, one taken downstairs with their meal and one taken up to their room, whilst the two drinks varied, fluctuating from grape to grain and vice versa, the room was always the same, number forty-six, on the top floor, as far away from the public gaze as was possible, whilst always booking it under Bill's name, using his credit card it hadn't really mattered for they were virtually invisible, an irrelevance to the people working there, staff turnover was high, and those who managed to stick it out for more than a month tended to work shifts, and so, inevitably, there was a different face sitting behind the desk in the dark foyer on virtually every occasion they came.

"Sorry, no it's fine, I've had some wonderful times here."

"He must have been very special."

Her new confident probed, gently.

Again, her mind drifted back in time, yes, he was special, and he made her feel special. Feeling a familiar tingle running down the full length of her spine, she pressed the palms of her hands down, hard, onto the table, as she recalled his sexual appetite, from the start it had been very obvious that he was going to be much more attentive than Reg had ever been, keener to please, putting her needs ahead of his own. But, was it love? Or was it just lust?

Suddenly a crumb of toast fell from her open mouth, her grin too big to house the contents of her breakfast, but the distraction was not enough to take her away from her musings.

Lust? Definitely, there was no doubt about that. But love? Yes, love as well, resting her head onto her hands, she looked up to the ceiling, towards the glorious heavens, tears welling in her eyes, yes, absolutely, love as well.

Leaning back in her chair, her eyes closed tight as if to take herself as far away from the here and now as was humanly possible, her mind journeying back a full quarter of a century, when, attracted by the bright lights and the promise of something new, she remembered how quickly she had covered the short one hundred yards that had separated Arnold's from the Premier Cru Bottlehouse on that cold opening night in December.

Nervously, she had pushed open the thick glass door and walked in, joining the throng of the equally inquisitive crowd that had already made its way inside.

Shafts of light beamed down from spotlights strategically located on the ceiling, illuminating the rich, dark, mahogany floor. There was no shelving, all of the stock being displayed in whole cases stacked straight onto the floor, the uniformity of these rectangular containers broken up by barrels, their light wooden staves held together by gleaming brass hoops, displaying single bottles resting on fresh, clean straw, inviting closer attention. In the corner, she had spied the cash register, tucked away, hidden from view, as if money were too vulgar a consideration, secreted behind a promotional display of Chateauneuf-du-pape, on special offer, but still twice the price charged at the local supermarket.

"Can I help you, Madam?"

A voice filled with enthusiasm called from across the other side of the champagne display.

"No, actually, let me show you around the shop first."

She had caught Bill's attention the very second she had walked through the door, immediately captured by her pretty face, her slim figure, so handsomely presented in her black leggings and tight black jumper, yes, he had spotted her straight away, and now he couldn't take his eyes off her.

Gently holding her at the elbow, he had ushered her around the shop, meandering through the displays. Heading straight to the French wines, they passed through the Burgundies; reds of Pinot noir grapes, whites from Chardonnay, then onto wines from the Languedoc-Roussillon Region, bold Merlots and Cabinet Sauvignons, before briefly pausing at the French Roses, available in every shade permissible; peach, mango, redcurrant, until finally, they stopped to browse the extensive range of champagnes; cases of Blanc de noirs adjoining equal quantities of Blanc de blancs.

Arriving at the tasting area, a large room positioned behind the main showroom, numerous bottles of wine scattered along-side rows of empty glasses, on the surface of a long wooden table, customers encouraged to help themselves, Bill had plied her with a delicious vintage red, and the promise of as much sampling as was required for her to become a wine connoisseur. Happy to oblige, in the weeks that followed she had quickly established herself as a regular customer at The Premier Cru Bottlehouse, her weekly excursions lasting longer and longer, sampling wine and chatting to Bill. On a Friday evening Bill would recommend something special for her to take home for the weekend.

Holding her cold cup in both hands, Anna drained the lukewarm tea, and poured herself another, totally oblivious of the person sitting next to her, her reminiscing continued unabated.

Within two months Bill was reciprocating, visiting her at the lingerie department virtually every day. There were plenty of similarities between selling wine and ladies' underwear, but certainly not enough to justify the hours they had spent together at her counter, he chatting away incessantly at the front, she listening intently from behind.

Smiling to herself as she recalled the chemistry they shared right from the start, the flirting in those early days, open, unconcealed, yet at the same time neither wanting to appear too keen, each holding back just enough to keep the other wandering, both bodies engulfed in a shroud of anticipation and expectation, the thrill of the chase, those feelings, so prevalent when she had been much younger, those feelings that she had managed to suppress for so long, re-surfacing once again.

Eventually, and effortlessly, they agreed to meet up at lunch.

"We might as well, we both have a lunch hour after all, why not spend it together?"

Her hand moving towards her neck, subconsciously running her fingers along her favourite gold double hollow curb chain, she smiled contently to herself, Bill had made it sound so easy, so natural, they were two friends, close friends, so, yes, why shouldn't they meet up for lunch.

For the following three months, they had met for lunch together at every opportunity, their relationship growing more flirtatious by the week, more eye contact, more touching, hugging, squeezing. She knew she was playing with fire, she knew that it had to stop, she knew that it wouldn't, it was too late.

Quivering, she recalled their first proper kiss, their mouths open, tasting each other for the first time, it felt strange, different to Reg, better, fierier, more passionate, more addictive. Once they had taken the plunge, they couldn't keep their hands off each other, and very quickly their relationship became physical, well as physical as was possible, with Bill's old Range Rover parked up inconspicuously, hidden away in the darkest, most secluded lay-byes they could find.

After three weeks of fumbling around uncomfortably on the rear seats, Bill had suggested that they might want to book themselves into a room somewhere. Taken by surprise, and with Reg working away, she had quickly hatched a plan, calling her sister, younger by two years, her own marriage already plagued with problems, her life a daily torrent of both mental and physical abuse, her husband having turned to drink following compulsory redundancy.

Happy to escape the wretchedness of her own home to spend an evening, or as many evenings as Anna wanted for that matter, looking after her precious little nephew, her sister had been delighted to oblige adding that she didn't need to be told a different story each time either, as whilst she was never completely convinced by the tales of late-night stock takes and staff meetings, she fully understood the situation and Anna had her sympathy.

Tugging at her gold chain, she recalled their first time in bed together. After enjoying a simple two course meal from the a la carte menu and a bottle of wine, they had left their empty glasses on the small square table, their napkins scrunched up into two balls of white cloth in the centre, taking her by the hand, his first sign of open affection in public, Bill had led her up the short flight of stairs up to their room.

Her eyes wandering around the walls, the shamrock green wallpaper in the restaurant was somehow reminiscent of the room they had shared, its green walls a brighter, mint shade, patterned with bright yellow flowers on leafy green stalks.

Once inside the room there had been very little in the way of awkwardness, she heading straight towards the shower, he getting un-dressed and into bed. Running her hands down her body she took a deep breath, exactly as she had done standing at the end of the king-sized bed, with Bill lying down, his head resting upright on the pillow, his gaze fixed on her bath towel, fastened up around her naked chest, wrapped tightly around her slim waist. Desperately stifling a giggle, she remembered Bill's gasp the moment she had let the towel fall slowly and deliberately to the floor.

That was how it all started, and that was how it carried on, getting more intense as they explored each other's bodies, discovered each other's minds, bringing all of their fantasies to life, right there in that same room, in that same bed.

Looking around and, as if awoken from a deep and pleasant slumber, her smile immediately turning into a frown, she turned to her companion.

"Yes, I've got some very happy memories here, but that's all they are, memories."

"Did it end well?"

Anna looked across the table, sucked the air in deeply and openly recalled her last conversation with Bill in the restaurant.

"Having a baby? How did that happen? I mean. Bloody hell!"

He had bawled, when she had told him of her pregnancy, sitting at the same table as she was now, their meal, with all its delicious prospects, drawing to its inevitable close.

"What do you mean, how did that happen?" she had replied, rolling her eyes, before continuing.

"We've not exactly been careful, have we? It can't be Reg's we don't really have sex anymore, you know that."

"No, okay no, we haven't, and yes, yes you've already told me that, but what do we do now?"

Bill asked, his voice quieter and calmer, re-gaining his composure as he finished off the last mouthful of his rhubarb crumble.

Screwing up her face, Anna recalled how resolute she had been.

"End it of course!"

The words had come out as a hiss, her frustration boiling over, as she had lent forward across the small square table, her face just inches away from Bill's.

"We have to!"

One thing that she had been quite clear about, right from the start of their relationship, was that she would never, under any circumstances, leave her husband, they already had a son, so that would be quite impossible.

Fifteen awkward minutes passed in silence after the bombshell had been dropped, neither wanting to resume the conversation. Eventually, Bill went to the bar to buy some more drinks, a pint of Best, in a jug not a straight glass, for himself and a half of Best, in a straight glass not a jug, for her, returning to the table his face filled with resignation, in silence they left their table, and went up to their room.

She had stuck to her guns, she absolutely had to, and that had been their last time in bed together, and standing at arms' length in the car park, Bill had made one last demand of her.

"Okay, okay, but I want to take care of you whilst you're pregnant, I want to see you every week, every day of every week if necessary, right up until the day the baby is born, and I want to see it, our child, if only just the once, but I must see it. You cannot deny me that. At least allow me that."

She had allowed him that, that one concession, saving her own marriage taking priority over everything else, and, true to her word, Bill saw his son Ben once, and only once, on the day he was born.

Desperate to maintain her composure, despite the two big tears that had already formed so inconveniently in her eyes, with more following, flowing in an unbroken stream, meandering very publicly, and embarrassingly, down her cheeks, Anna looked up anxiously, seeking the kind and caring face of her attentive neighbour. It was gone, and her temporary companion had gone with it, her seat tucked neatly under the table, her empty plate and cup arranged into a neat pile in the centre of the table.

Drying her eyes, Anna got up and paid her bill. At the front door, grabbing her keys from out of her handbag, she took one last look over her shoulder, and mumbled one last emotional good-bye to the Royal Oak and to Bill, closing the lid on that particular chapter of her life forever.

Chapter 6
Tuesday

Completely at a loose end, and with no appointments scheduled for the day, David had managed to successfully secrete himself in his bedroom until his parents and brother had all taken leave of the family abode.

In the queue at the convenience store a short hundred yards from his office, he waited patiently behind a pair of scruffy teenagers playing truant from school, their school ties stuffed in their trouser pockets, he smiled to himself as they scuttled away with their illicit supply of nicotine, and, taking a ten pound note out of his own wallet, exchanged it for a lukewarm latte in a cheap takeaway cup, a dry cheese and pickle sandwich, a packet of crisps, and a tabloid newspaper.

Sitting at his desk, the newspaper open, his laptop firmly shut, he tucked into his meagre lunch with minimal relish, reading about the seemingly outrageous exploits of celebrities who up until that moment he didn't even know existed, and the fallout from the weekend's football results in the ongoing battle for the dominance of the Football Premier League.

An hour later, and barely replete, he tossed the packaging and the paper away into the wastepaper bin and tapped his password into his computer, three and a half hours totally submerged in the toil and tedium of opening, reading, and deleting emails after that, stretching out his arms, he slammed his laptop closed.

His arms suspended at right angle to his body, his fists clenched, pausing for a second, his thoughts locked into the abyss into which he had been thrown, his complete reluctance to leave this cold, characterless, room, the cravings for just his own company intensifying. He didn't want to go home, he didn't need to be reminded how jealous he was of Ben and all of that money, or how much he had been let down by his mother, fallen so far from grace he could barely bring himself to think about her, and he certainly did not want to be reminded of how weak and pathetic his father was. Good God, he couldn't even go into his own local anymore, not after that episode in the toilets with Tanya.

Easing himself into the driver's seat, very soon he was pulling up at the supermarket car park. The security guard, standing at the front of the store, chewing gum, his shirt hanging out of his trousers, and looking as if only a major incident would revive him from his apathy, didn't give him a second glance as he ambled in, zigzagging his way through the busy clothing department and on to the café at the back of the store.

The contrast with Café Narino could not have been any greater, the identical tables, the matching chairs, the electronic menu board all pointing towards a big cooperative, its giant wheels turning relentlessly in the constant, endless search for grater sales and even more profit, swelling the coffers, satisfying the anxious shareholders.

Having dined there on numerous occasions before. and with a confidence born out of familiarity, he ordered fish and chips, with peas. The young man bringing over the food was probably better associated with the Café Narino than the supermarket. His heavily gelled hair dyed fluorescent dark blue, the right sleeve of his shirt rolled up to his elbow, revealing the words 'Stay Strong' tattooed onto his inner arm in bold black ink, a statement of intent, his very own personal mantra, survival in a troubled world that simply didn't care anymore.

Suitably equipped with a coordinating knife and fork, and pushing the small white dish of disgusting tartare sauce off his plate and onto the table, David set about satisfying his now ravenous appetite.

Back home, and rummaging through his coat pocket and pulling out his keys he inserted the largest of the bunch into the front door. The key had almost finished doing its job, when he stopped dead, his arm suspended in the air like a marionette, tucking the key back into the relative safety of his coat pocket, he buttoned up his coat, wrapped his checked woollen scarf around his neck, and turned towards the park and the Cross Keys.

Ten minutes later, leaning against the bar, quietly admiring the extensive range of spirits displayed in front of the mirrored wall, a vast selection of blended and single malt whiskeys, a range of gin that defied all comprehension, varieties of vodka and rum beyond the wildest of imaginations, all complimented with every type of mixer possibly available, his ruminations were interrupted by the familiar sound of the young barman's voice.

"Pint of the usual, David?"

"Yes please, mate, no, actually, make it two."

Carrying the two glasses over to the small round table in the corner, he smiled to himself, that would save a return trip in ten minutes, he generously applauded his own good use of time.

"Let's say that she had an affair, and that Bill Williams, is Ben's father."

Daniel's words had been ringing in his ears for most of the morning, taking a long drink from his glass, but failing miserably to wash them away, he returned it to the table, nearly half of its contents having disappeared down his throat. Scanning the bar, it was virtually empty, as empty and as meaningless as his own wretched life. He gazed at the mirror on the wall, its smeared glass embossed with the brewery's logo, his face was white, very white, but darkened around the eyes through lack of sleep and exhaustion. Resting his forehead on the table in between the two beer glasses, he closed his eyes.

A fierce debate raged in his aching head, pounding him into submission, as he mentally compared himself to his younger brother, noting that physically there was very little in the way of similarities, in fact on reflection, it could be argued that it would be difficult, on appearance alone, to even class them as brothers at all, emotionally, it was a similar tale of disparity, they were two people of very different personas.

Whilst all of that strengthened the case for an inconsistency in paternity, the evidence overwhelming, but, despite all of that, was his mother was really capable of having an affair with another man? Digging in deep, David, desperately searched for a way out for his mother, his hatred for her still tempered by the unconditional love he had felt for her right up until just a few days ago, but he was finding it increasingly difficult, if not impossible.

Leaving the dregs at the bottom of his first pint, he thirstily drank the first quarter of his second, before continuing his mental journey of his parents' relationship. He had never really questioned the solidity of their marriage before now, his perception having always been that his pathetic father had been incredibly fortunate in finding someone like his mother to spend the rest of his sad little life with. Suddenly it wasn't quite so clear cut, he had discovered things about her that he didn't like, in fact he had discovered things about her that actually repulsed him, to the point whereby he was inclined to feel that perhaps they were welcome to each other.

The torment continued, relentless and unabated, making his head spin. Was it really any of his business anyway? He was just one of the off-spring, nothing more than that, he had no idea what went on in their actual relationship, after all, unless appearances were deceptive, they seemed to be happy enough, there was genuine companionship, absolutely no doubt about that, but surely a marriage required more, a certain chemistry, a genuine connection?

The walls paper thin, and his bedroom being closest to theirs, he recalled those nights during his childhood, his pillow over his head, shutting out their noise, the sound of their love making, but what about recently? What about in the last fifteen years in fact? Had the romance all dried up, a dusty desert, bereft of all life?

Or was it just a marriage fuelled by contentment and compromise, two people living out their lives together, sharing the same space, the same existence? His mother, so fiery, so intense with her emotions earlier in life now happy to settle for what she has, her once inextinguishable flame of passion finally doused through guilt and remorse.

A pint glass appeared on the table in front of him.

"Hiya, David, you alright then? I thought I'd buy you a drink."

His eyes flickered, betraying his nervousness.

"Oh no, there's nothing in there, don't worry," Tanya continued coyly.

Immediately, the colour drained from David's face, still raw from the events of the previous night, still shaken up by what had taken place in the toilets, the arrogance in her suggestion of the power she had over him, the control that all women had over men, only the gratification of her sexual needs important, nothing else even a consideration, just like his mother all those years ago.

"Hi, Tanya, how are you?"

His voice as keen as he could manage, the forced smile let him down, betraying his lack of enthusiasm, despite the extra free pint of beer sitting on the table in front of him.

"Better than you by the looks of things."

His head bobbing up and down slowly, David quickly polished off the contents of his second pint and, reaching out for the third, he stared at the contents, running his finger up and down the side of the cold glass.

Her voice and its contemptuous tone, seething with rage his mind backtracked twenty-four hours, the beer tainted with drugs, she pinning him against the wall in those disgusting toilets, all fuelling his revenge, yes, he would pay her back, and ten times over.

Looking across at Tanya, he gently recounted the whole sorry tale, leaving out none of the detail, watching her face getting closer and closer to his own as the story unfolded, her gaze more intent, her interest matched only by her enjoyment in learning of his downfall.

"Fucking hell!" she exclaimed, when he had finished.

"So, your brother has been left all of the money and you've got nothing, nothing at all. Your mum must have had a relationship with that bloke all those years ago, she must have done, and your brother cannot possibly be your real brother, well not your full brother anyway. Fucking hell!"

Lifting his third pint glass up to his mouth he drank all of the contents in one single gulp, the liquid bloating his stomach, the alcohol mercifully dulling his senses. A logical conclusion, he rolled his sleepy eyes, and one that surely anyone with an ounce of common sense would arrive at should Ben decide to accept the money. Good God, if Tanya had thought that then, yes, definitely, everyone would.

As if awoken by his fury, he sneered as he thought about his mother. Her reputation would be in tatters, that was for sure, ruined, she wouldn't be able to leave the house let alone work in that charity shop, she would be in disgrace, and she deserved it. His father would look a right idiot, putting up with her for all those years, perhaps he deserved that too? But their family name dragged through the gutter, the whole family, including himself, what about his reputation? Muttering to himself, he looked at Tanya.

"What a mess, what a complete mess, and whose fault is it? My mother, my stupid mother who seems incapable of keeping her legs closed."

Slamming his empty pint glass onto the table, he stared at Tanya, burning with anger, his blood boiling over, the hatred he felt for his mother, that had been festering for the last twenty-four hours, was now spreading through his mind, an unstoppable cancer growing, flourishing in its vulnerable host.

Glaring at Tanya, his face filled with contempt, he could feel her hot sweaty little hand resting on his wrist, her other playing innocently with her hooped gold earring, her legs crossed, her skirt so short that he could see her cheap black knickers, he hated her, he despised all women, and revenge was a dish best served cold.

"What you doing now?"

His voice little more than a grunt, nothing given away.

"Going home, the children are at their grandmother's."

Squeezing his arm gently, Tanya looked down at David as she rose from her seat. Staring into her eyes, he recognised the look immediately, he had seen it in the toilets, condescending, lustful, shameless, suddenly he could see the outline of her nipples more clearly under her tight blouse, her eyes followed his as she caught him looking, again.

Fastened into their respective seats, neither spoke throughout the short, uneventful, journey back to Tanya's house, she pretending to concentrate on the busy road ahead of her, he pretending not to notice, neither having the inclination to break the silence.

Closing the door behind them, there was barely room for the two of them in the small, plain, hallway, less than a short stride away the steep carpeted stairway rose in front of them, barely an arm's width away, the glass door to the living room hanging immediately to their left.

He could feel her fingers around his neck, her lips pressing eagerly against his, her body pushing hard up against his own, her chest heaving, her breathing getting quicker by the second. Pulling her in more closely, his chin resting on her shoulder, David smirked quietly to himself. In the last twenty-four hours, he had learnt a very painful lesson, don't trust women, they just want what they can get, they let you down.

Suddenly his hatred for the fairer sex erupted into a blind fury, his teeth gritted, his face contorted in anger, he lost all control of his senses, his whole being driven by a force never experienced before, a craziness bordering on lunacy. Rage pulsating through his arteries, his strength Herculean, almost godlike, he grabbed Tanya by the left arm and spun her around, pushing her forwards, pressing her face, hard, against the wall, her right cheek brushing against the cheap yellow and blue striped wall paper, his left hand gripping the back of her thin neck, his right hand on the hem of her skirt.

"Let's see how much you like this, Tanya." He snarled.

Hot and sweaty through physical exertion, he took a step backwards, catching his breath, his left hand still on the back of Tanya's neck, still pressing her, hard against the wall. Giving her a final shove, he removed his tired hand, opened the front door, and left.

Looking down at the floor, her hair in her face, blood rushing to her head, Tanya reached out with both hands and pushed herself away from the wall. Turning to double check that the front door was closed properly, a waft of smoke filled the confined space of the hallway as she took a cigarette from the packet in her coat pocket hanging on the wooden stair bannister, and lit it, tossing her red disposable lighter back into the pocket.

Moving into the living room, for a minute she drew heavily on the cigarette, inhaling the smoke, taking in the nicotine, before discarding it carefully into the ash tray on the coffee table.

Exhaling the last of the smoke, she moved slowly across the room towards the fireplace, and, with her head tilted to one side, she looked at her reflection in the mirror, adjusted her damp knickers, straightened her skirt, and smiled.

Chapter 7
Wednesday

Sitting at the end of the bed, Reg struggled with his socks, his body stiff, his joints aching. his head felt fuzzy, he hadn't slept well, tossing and turning from the early hours of the morning, truth was he hadn't really experienced a good night's sleep since Monday.

Life had not always been quite as comfortable as it was now, he frowned to himself as he finally got one of his socks over the toes and past the heel of his right foot, neither of them having bought much, if anything, in the way of a monetary contribution to the marriage.

The perennial shortage of funds, compounded by the fiscal burden of bringing two young lads into the world, had weighed heavily, making moving house impossible and so, thirty years after their fairy tale wedding, they found themselves residing in exactly the same premises, having exchanged contracts in the very same week they signed the marriage register.

The house, a modest property in a small town in the south of the country, boasting a short but bustling High Street, just two pubs, a Leisure Centre, and an out of town Retail Park with a supermarket, itself adding its very own chapter to the woeful tale of financial insecurity, for in the past thirty years they had changed the kitchen only once, the carpets never, the meagre budget only allowing for superficial improvements, rooms freshened up with a lick of magnolia emulsion and cheap paintings to hang onto the otherwise bare walls.

Ben's legacy would change all of that, the tide finally turning in their favour he mused, pennies from heaven, pennies from heaven, a sardonic grin covered his face, enjoying his clever literal connection between Bill's death and the inheritance.

In the kitchen, just two plates of lightly buttered toast and two cups of tea separated husband and wife, sitting together at the small table, as they always did at eight-thirty every Wednesday morning.

"Everything alright with you this morning, Reg? You're very quiet."

Anna enquired, cutting her second slice of toast in half, they had been married thirty years, she could sense when Reg's mind was elsewhere, she could read him like a book.

"Everything is fine, just fine. Now, come on drink up, else you'll be late for work."

Skilfully evading the question, Reg motioned at Anna's half full cup of tea, obligingly she finished it off, and they both left the table.

Walking down the bustling street together, they held onto each other's hand tightly, dodging in between the other pedestrians occupying the crowded pavement, swinging arms everywhere, the hurried steps and pushing elbows of a local workforce so recently enjoying breakfast in the comfort of their own homes, now reluctantly bracing themselves for the day's work that lay ahead.

Their walk together terminating at the newsagents positioned conveniently in the middle of the fork in the road, they broke off, each going their own separate way, Anna towards the charity shop half a mile further on, and Reg a short ten yards into the newsagents, where he bought a copy of the day's paper and headed back to the house.

A second cup of coffee resting on the table in front of him, Reg carefully folded the paper over and let it drop to the floor, reaching out for the small, black plastic remote control, the television screen flickered to life, he hopped through half a dozen channels before turning it back off again, its jet-black screen offering little or nothing in the way of bringing any life into the room.

Stretching out in his chair, returning to his own private world of daydream and slumber, he closed his eyes and smiled, life as a retiree in modern suburbia, his troubles a million miles away. At a quarter to twelve he instinctively re-joined the real world, and, putting on his favourite brown corduroy jacket, left the house, locking the front door behind him.

Sauntering up to the bar he glanced at his watch, exactly twelve o'clock, perfect. With two pints lined up in front of him, holding out his hand, he reached out for his change, looking Tanya up and down, his face covered with distaste. He really couldn't stand the sight of her, she lowered the tone, her tasteless make-up, tight trousers, she was a bit of a tart, and she insisted on wearing those ill-fitting blouses all of the time, he counted the money in his hand, muttering to himself as he took the drinks over to the table near the fruit machine.

From the corner of his eye he could see three young lads in their early twenties playing darts, the taller of the three standing at the oche, his left foot running parallel with the faded white toe line, punching the air as the third of his darts joined the other two resting precariously in the precious red felt bed of the treble twenty, his two companions both raising their pint glasses, saluting the accomplishment.

Apart from those three, the bar was totally empty.

Making his way to the table, his own reflection looked back at him from the large rectangular mirror that hung on the wall, smiling he studied his own distinctive features, the eccentricities of his appearance certainly getting more pronounced with age. Typically, today he was dressed flamboyantly, in fact perhaps even more so than usual, a pair of faded brown checked trousers, paired up with a light blue shirt and a bright yellow, herringbone stitched, silk tie, the leather elbow patch on the right arm of his brown corduroy jacket flapping around at his elbow, the loose threads of its stitching tattered and frayed.

A familiar face appeared at the door, bolstering up the meagre numbers, Reg raised his right arm to acknowledge Stephen's arrival as the latter ran his hand along the bar, beaming as he paid Tanya the same compliment with equal enthusiasm.

His oldest friend, whilst the same age as Reg, a lifetime of excessive drinking and the inevitable onset of rosacea had rendered him with the unattractive appearance of looking permanently flushed, his face a bright red, almost scarlet, and bloated around the eyes and cheeks. The rest of his body had not been immune to the affects either, his bigger waistline carrying at least two stone more than that of his comrade, all of life's excesses having added a good five years onto his age.

Both retired they had happily settled into this Wednesday lunchtime routine, their assembly never later than midday, their departure never before five o'clock.

"Cheers, Reg."

Stephen raised his glass, eagerly taking his first sip, the contents of his mouth finding its way down into his stomach long before his backside found its way to the wooden seat of his chair.

"Cheers, my good friend."

Whether to enhance the senses or escape the possibility of being poisoned, the time-honoured tradition of clinking glasses was perfectly observed, Stephen's craving for that first taste of alcohol having not gone un-noticed, but remaining un-checked, as the two of them sat in silence for a minute, ceremoniously enjoying the first half of their first pints.

"Now what's this I hear about your Ben coming into some money?"

Stephen, looked up from his pint, his top lip all but disappeared under the foam of his beer.

"How did you know that?"

Taken by surprise by the unexpected irritation in Reg's tone of voice, Stephen hesitated in replying, his face filled with embarrassed.

"Cath told me. She was out shopping with a couple of friends of hers yesterday and they popped into the charity shop, you know, where your Anna works. She was talking to Sarah, you know, and she told her, only in passing like."

Gazing intently into his friend's face, his voice agitated and flustered, he quickly closed the conversation down.

"You know how they gossip in that place. You can't fart around here without someone discussing it over a second-hand copy of Little Women. My round?"

Picking up the two empty glasses, Stephen skipped eagerly over to the bar. Reg mused, his mind drifting listlessly backwards and forwards in time, glancing over towards the bar he could see Stephen flirting shamelessly with Tanya, his laughter exaggerated, words gushing out rather too quickly, his wandering hand touching her arm as he ordered the drinks.

It probably wasn't a surprise to hear that word was already getting around about Ben's inheritance, but still, only forty-eight hours had passed and his family was already the number one topic of conversation at the local charity shop, he certainly hadn't expected that.

Returning to the table, Stephen, placed the beer glasses carefully onto the wooden surface, and sat down. Leaning forward in his chair, and taking a sip from his pint, Reg took a deep breath, and started re-telling his story.

"Well, yes actually, he has, an old family friend passed away and he has left Ben rather a large sum of money. Too much money really if I'm honest with you, over four hundred thousand quid. Far too much for one person really, so, fingers crossed, we're hoping that he might want to share some of it out with all of us and we can finally sort the house out."

"Christ. How does David feel about it?"

Reg's mouth dropped, startled and by the question, surely the first thought would be that David would be delighted, wouldn't it? Undeterred and taking Reg's silence to be his cue to carry on, Stephen continued.

"I mean it seems funny that this guy has left money to just one of your sons. If you're leaving money to someone's children, surely you would leave it to all of them, with an equal share to each, in this case the fortune divided equally into two halves, you know, two hundred thousand each."

His face the piteous pallor of a cheap envelope, Reg mumbled into his beer, his garbled words almost barely auditable.

"Well, Ben will give some of the money to David, any brother would do the same, yes, of course they would. It'll all be fine in the end."

Suitably encouraged, Stephen continued the conversation following his own train of thought.

"I'm sure he will, yes, of course he will. Your two are very different, very different in many ways, and, yet, remarkably similar in others, and so very close to each other, they always have been, haven't they? No, Ben definitely won't want David to miss out. All of that is a given, but, surely, there are a number of other questions we need to be asking?"

"Like what?"

Reg demanded, raising his glass to his mouth, his face now a crimson shade of red.

"Well, firstly how would David actually feel about accepting money from Ben? He's the oldest of the two, he's always been the one who has been more financially astute. Let's face it, Ben hasn't exactly busted a gut in his rush to make his own fortune, has he? How's David going to feel about all of that money falling nicely into his brother's lap, when he has worked so hard building his own business? Awkward to say the least. And what about you? How do you feel about it all? You must have asked yourself why the money was left to Ben in the first place?"

"What do you mean? What exactly do you mean by that?"

Reg snapped, his patience seemingly running thin.

"Well like I said, why leave the money to just one brother, why not both?"

The impact of the last three words were not lost on Stephen, his voice trailing off as he watched Reg's face turn an insipid shade of pink in front of his very eyes.

"What are you trying to say?" he pleaded, his voice stammering and stuttering.

"All I'm saying is…" Again, Stephen hesitated.

"Come on, come on, spit it out."

Back sitting in the front seat of the emotional roller coaster, Reg's upset turned to anger, almost choking on his own rage, his voice was loud, too loud, he knew exactly what Stephen was going to say, he had been repeating the exact same words to himself, a hundred times over during the past thirty-six hours. He knew the truth and had done for most of Ben's life, but he wanted to hear it from someone else, overcome by a masochistic streak, he wanted to feel the pain, the pain of the truth.

With some reluctance, Stephen continued, "Well, generally people leave money to their relatives, don't they? We know that this Bill character had no family, so he couldn't leave any of his money there could he? What about David? He's his brother, for goodness sake, and yet he is left nothing, it's as if he didn't exist. And, whilst we're talking about it, what about you and Anna? If he was a family friend, then why not leave something to you two as well?"

Tears filled Reg's eyes, his brain registering what was being said, these were not questions, they were statements, statements of fact.

"You think that he might be Ben's father, don't you?"

His voice was barely a whisper.

"I don't know my good friend, but that is a possibility, you have to admit that, or at least consider it as a possibility, oh, for Christ's sake, I'm so sorry old chap."

Cursing his own lack of foresight in not setting up a tab at the bar, and placing the correct money directly into Tanya's outstretched hand in exchange for the beer, Reg successfully eliminated the requirement for any conversation, his eyes not leaving the grubby linoleum floor once as he slowly transported his prize back to the table.

For twenty-four long years, he had always been reluctant to meet the subject of Ben's paternity head on, preferring instead to a life of anger, torture and torment, wallowing in a pit of self-inflicted misery, but safe in the knowledge that his marriage would escape unscathed by the whole episode. Yet, here was his best friend, his closest friend and confidence, eager to talk about it, perhaps the time had finally come to stop making excuses, stop skirting around the edges, and finally confront his harlot of a wife over her infidelities all those years ago.

He put the pint glasses onto the table, and sat down, but first he needed to make sure he was one hundred percent certain.

"Okay. Let's think back. Over twenty-four years ago, God, that's such a long time. David would have been five or six, Anna was working at Arnold's, I was working on that development, remember on the other side of the country? I was away during the week, but back at the weekend, good grief, I was on that job for months, it paid well, we needed the money, you know how it is. Bill, him, he worked in that wine merchants, remember that posh place, all barrels of straw and chalk boards, well, Anna started bringing a nice bottle of wine home on a Friday evening, it was to celebrate my returning back home for the weekend. Well so she said."

Stephen looked up from his beer glass.

"Nothing wrong with a nice bottle of wine mate."

"No, no of course not, but other things have always niggled me about that time, and, well the opportunity was there if she wanted it, wasn't it, from Monday right through to Friday."

"Now, hold on, just because the opportunity is there, that doesn't necessarily mean that anything actually happened. Christ Reg, I only bought it up to, well, I didn't mean to open any wounds."

"I know you didn't, mate, but our marriage hasn't been perfect, we've had our ups and downs, you know that, you've helped me through sticky patches more times than I can remember, and you know that I'm very grateful to you for that. Well, and I've never told you this, too ashamed I guess, but I've always had my doubts, always had my suspicions, well, I'll tell you what, I'm going to sort this out, sort this out once and for all."

His face wan through lack of blood, his knuckles white through pinching his knees, Reg was not exactly a picture of health, and Stephen could barely look his comrade in the eye, as he sat back in his seat, watching him get up, push his half-filled glass to the centre of the table, put on his corduroy jacket, its centre vent irreversibly creased, fastened it up at the lowest of the three flat buttons at the front, and leave.

Chapter 8
Wednesday

Any couple over three decades into their marriage will understand the importance of the small pleasures in a long-term relationship, those routines however insignificant, however trivial, that mean so much. For Reg and Anna, the Wednesday morning ritual of waking up, sharing breakfast, leaving the house together before going their separate ways at the newsagents, so simple, so trivial in itself, and yet it meant the world to the both of them.

Standing alone on the pavement, Anna lovingly looked on as Reg disappeared into the newsagents, bearing right, she carried on the short half a mile walk to the high street, pausing at the flower shop, her favourite, her haven, her sanctuary in an all too often defective world.

Its window was as beautiful as it was stunning, bursting with flora of all descriptions; a bouquet of white roses bunched up with lilac freesias the first to catch the attention of her discerning eye, further along, another bouquet, again crammed with roses, pink roses surrounded by yellow chrysanthemums and vibrant iris, the trio completed by more pink roses, but arranged differently, this time with alstroemerias and gypsophilia. All three lovingly assembled and wonderfully displayed in light blue china olpe vases, carefully positioned on an old, weathered, wooden bench, along-side smaller nosegays and posies, enticing the customer into the shop with the promise of more of the same.

Reluctantly she dragged herself and her eyes away from the horticultural delight, and, ten minutes later, she was waving at Sarah, stood waiting patiently outside the charity shop, protected from the elements in her light brown thick winter coat, the shop keys in her gloved hand, her black leather handbag slung casually over her shoulder. Glancing down at her watch, it was twenty-five minutes past nine.

"Good morning, Sarah."

Anna smiled, squeezing her friend's arm.

"Morning Anna."

Sarah smiled back enthusiastically.

The door opened effortlessly as Sarah rotated the key in the lock, the high-pitched buzz and flashing red light emitting from the alarm panel issuing a sharp reminder for the passcode to be administered without further delay. Security measures negotiated, and safely installed into the shop, Anna and Sarah hung up their coats on the two brass coat hooks, secured to the wall via a rectangular piece of polished mahogany, in the small staff room at the rear of the store.

The trick to a successful charity shop is imaginative merchandising, creating a positive Aladdin's Cave of ornaments, knick-knacks, trinketry and curios. Figurines and collectables displayed in a glass display tower, their prices hand-written on plain white rectangular tags, gift wrapped but without the expense of any wrapping paper, the showpiece table-top display of cups, saucers and other items of general bric-a-brac thoughtfully laid out on a green cotton tablecloth, row upon row of bookshelves, crammed full with books of all genres, hardbacks, paperbacks, old and new.

With a steady stream of donations arriving on a daily basis, by cleverly filtering the new stock and rotating the old, it was possible for Anna and Sarah to completely transform the shop from one week to the next. Standing in the middle of the shop, her hands on her hips, Anna surveyed the emporium, her experience at Arnold's was invaluable here, the merchandising techniques she had learnt working the underwear department readily transferred to books, records, gifts, as well as clothing. Sarah had been a good pupil, keen to learn her trade, together, they made a good team.

By ten-thirty, the regulars were starting to drift into the shop. A man in his mid-fifties, tall, slim, always smelling of fresh coffee, and always saying good morning, before making straight for the small literature section, two black bookcases, three shelves each, six in total, carefully positioned alongside of each other resting on top of the deep wooden ledge of the shop window. His eyes drawn in by the well-worn volumes, paperbacks and hardbacks displayed together, their spines creased through wear, their pages made dry through the passing of time, on most occasions he would have a rummage through the shelves and buy nothing, on all occasions he thanked them both for their time and left with a smile.

A lady in her late sixties, as always, protected from the elements in her blue quilted jacket, a pale green silk scarf wrapped tightly around her neck, strode purposefully towards the white plywood box located next to the cash register. For a full five minutes, she thumbed her way through the selection of old vinyl records, always careful so as not to crease their delicate sleeves, Anna smiled, she couldn't remember the time when she had actually bought one of those old LP's, but she did like to have a natter.

The doors flung open, Anna glanced up, carefully replacing the vintage Monopoly set back onto its freshly dusted shelf.

"Mother, we need to talk, and we need to talk right now."

Yelling at the top of his voice, and marching straight past Sarah, completely ignoring her, Ben barged into the shop, his face bright red, looking as if he were fit to burst.

"Okay, Ben, calm down, calm down, just let me put the cloth and polish away."

Straightening out the box, the word Monopoly, its classic white writing standing proud against the red background on the side, Anna turned to Sarah.

"I'm just going to take Ben out the back for a cup of tea and a chat, you'll be alright here by yourself for a few minutes, won't you?"

Rolling her eyes, Sarah nodded.

The stock room, its walls lined with both galvanised steel racking and traditional bookcases, a proper mish-mash of wood and metal, in various heights, depth and colour, was small, and over-subscribed.

This was the hub of the shop, this was where the donations were collected and sorted. Whilst all contributions were gratefully received, sadly at least one in five of the offerings are often in too poor a condition for sale and have to be discarded, mercifully, and at the other extreme, the condition of other goods is such that they are put aside for sale on internet trading sites. The remaining items rest on the shelves, products for sale, gathering dust, waiting patiently for their turn to be selected for display on the shop floor.

Squeezed in the middle of all of this was a small table, its tiny surface crammed full with an old electric kettle, a single pint carton of semi-skimmed milk, a box of tea bags, and an un-opened packet of plain chocolate digestive biscuits on a small white plate.

Placing a consoling arm around her troubled off-spring, Anna motioned him to sit at one of the two grey plastic chairs that surrounded the table. Still standing, gazing through the steam of the boiling kettle, she sighed, a nervous sigh, matching the nervous ache in the pit of her stomach.

She wasn't surprised to see him, she wasn't surprised to see him at all, she had been expecting that he would want to talk to her, ever since he returned from the solicitors on Monday morning. Yes, she had been waiting for Ben to come and talk to her, in fact, she was waiting for the whole family to come and talk to her.

"Now, Ben, how are things with you? Is everything alright?"

Putting her hand on his shoulder, she gave it a reassuring squeeze. Crumbs of biscuit fell to the table as Ben opened the packet and removed the top one, broke it in half and put it into his mouth. They weren't his favourite, he preferred milk chocolate, but perhaps a sugar rush might make him feel better, it didn't, and he put the half-eaten biscuit back onto the plate seeking solace in a sip of tea instead.

"Is everything alright? Well, of course, everything is not alright. For Christ's sake. My head's spinning, I don't know what to think, I don't know if I'm coming or going right now."

Sitting down on the chair next to him, Anna took his hand, holding it gently in her own she gazed at him, wanting, as she had done so many times before, to take away his pain, knowing that, on this occasion, that it would not be possible. Her voice was as soft and comforting as she could manage.

"Okay, okay, tell me what's on your mind, take your time, nice and slowly."

"It's all this money business."

Ben blurted, the words coming out much more quickly than he had wanted.

"I've got so many questions buzzing around in my head, and they all need answering, I just don't know where to start."

"Well, let's start at the beginning."

Her voice was soft and gentle, encouraging her son to open out his broken heart.

"Okay, let's start with why me? Yes, that's my first question, why me?"

Her heart sinking, she allowed Ben to continue talking.

"Why have I inherited all of that money? I mean why just me? Why not anybody else?"

Still Anna sat, motionless, her mouth wide open, no words coming out.

"Although I think I already have an idea as to the answer to that question."

His voice suddenly filled with menace, Ben stared into his mother's eyes, and, wasting no more time, cut to the chase.

"Is Bill Williams my father? Is Bill Williams my father? God, I can't even bear to think about it, let alone say it, and if I accept the money I might as well say it, I might as well shout it out from the roof tops, tell the whole world, that my mother slept with somebody else, got pregnant, and I'm the product of the whole sordid affair. It's not true is it mother, Bill Williams isn't my father, is he? Please tell me that he's not, you would never do that to Dad, would you?"

Anna's eyes fixed themselves onto the table, it's dark wood soaking up her gaze, dulling her mind, allowing her some temporary respite, it didn't last long, for Ben continued.

"And what do I say to David? I mean I can't start to imagine what he must be thinking right now. If I turn the money down, that'll be an end to all of the questions, the whole thing was a big mistake, no one need know any more? But that won't be the end, will it? I mean, how can it be? I'll want to know more, David will want to know more, it will never go away, not ever."

Sadness, anger, bitterness, betrayal, so many emotions filled Ben's voice, and Anna could hear them all. Taking a deep breath, she took the plunge.

"Why don't we take each question one at a time? See if that helps?"

It felt like a totally inadequate thing to say, but she had to start somewhere.

"Okay."

Sighing heavily, Ben looked up from his empty cup, finally making proper eye contact with his mother. Fit to burst, chaos, turmoil, muddle and mayhem, four vast armies scrapping it out with each other in a gruesome, bloody fight, his mind the battlefield, panic and confusion taking over, his thoughts running blindly in all directions.

"So why do you think you got the money and not David?"

Anna got straight to the point, there was little use in delaying the inevitable.

"My heart tells me that it is because he was present at my birth, I remember you telling me that years ago, my head is telling me something else."

Studying Ben's face, Anna's heart felt like it was about to explode, she could see the pain in his eyes, she could feel the pain in his heart, she could feel something else too, a rage, a rage so intense it threatened to blow their relationship apart, she could not, must not, allow that, taking a deep breath, fighting back her tears of self-pity, she let him continue.

"People only leave their money to family members, right? Well, that's what normally happens anyway. So, if Bill was a normal sort of person, and we have no reason to suspect that he wasn't, then that would mean that I am part of his family, his family as well as my own, and that would mean that he was my father, my biological father."

Ben's eyes were fixed to the floor as he spoke, only looking up as he repeated the last three words.

"My biological father."

Slowly raising his head, now he was staring at his mother, straight into her eyes, they were sitting opposite each other, less than two feet apart, she could not avoid his stare, the rage of earlier now manifested itself into disgust, revulsion, hatred.

"Oh Ben, my darling Ben."

Anna did her best to meet his stare.

"Well, Mother, what have you got to say, I need to know the truth, tell me the truth now."

Quite unable to keep still, Anna wriggled around uncomfortably in her chair, the palms of her hands sweaty, her mouth bone dry, her salivary glands gone on strike, her vocal chords seemingly joining them at the picket line, for when she opened her mouth, no words came out.

"Come on, Mother, I have a right to know the truth."

The packet of biscuits fell over, half of its contents spilling onto the floor, biscuit crumbs and chocolate everywhere, Ben's mug lay on its side, the last of its contents spilling over, a milky brown lake forming in front of him, as his fist smashed onto the table top.

Taking a deep breath, bracing herself for what was surely to come, Anna was shaking uncontrollably, she felt physically sick, but knew that she had to soldier on, she had gone too far to stop now.

"Okay, alright, okay. Yes, Bill is your father, your biological father."

Tears flowed down her cheeks, an endless river of relief, of liberation, the guilt, the millstone that had hung around her neck for the past twenty-four years, the sword of Damocles that had dangled so precariously over her head all of that time, now disappeared, vanished in an instance.

At last, at last someone else knew the truth, her wretched secret finally out into the open, but had she really wanted that someone to be Ben? Leaning

66

forward, she wiped the spilled tea onto the floor with the back of her fingers, just something to do, something to occupy her idle hands.

A strange feeling of inner calm had taken over, as if she had taken the plunge into the icy water, her body adjusting to the temperature, and was now treading water, waiting to start the swim through the rapids, and eventually, hopefully, towards more serene waters ahead.

Ben sat in silence, his face white, his eyes opening and closing as he breathed in and out through his nose, his elbows on the table, his head in his hands. His mother's revelation had not come as a surprise, he had spent the last three days mulling things over, visiting and re-visiting every scenario, and, at every turn, he came to the same conclusion, Bill Williams was his father, he had to be. Anna grabbed hold of his hand.

"Oh Ben, I am so sorry, so very, very sorry, although I do feel better now that I've told someone."

The last words had barely left her mouth, when Anna knew that she had said the wrong thing, snatching his hand from hers, Ben leapt out of his seat.

"You feel better. Well, I'm so very glad to hear that. You stupid cow, you stupid little cow. Do you really think that anyone is going to give a damn how you feel? No one is going to feel sorry for you. In fact, I'd be surprised if anyone will want to know you once this gets out. Jesus Christ!"

The lump formed in Anna's throat made it so tight that she was barely able to swallow, staring into her son's eyes, all she could see was hatred, pure hatred, she looked at him, her own eyes pleading with his, she held out her hand, an olive branch hanging in the air.

"I didn't mean it like that Ben, you know that I didn't. I know what I did was wrong, it was just me and your dad, well, we, oh, what's the point, there is no point in trying to explain, trying to make excuses, but there were reasons, you need to understand that, at least try and understand that. I had hoped that it would stay a secret, I don't know why, I just hoped it would. I had planned to tell you at some time, try to explain what happened and why, you have to believe that I did, I just didn't know when."

"Well, I know all about it now, thank you, Mother, Christ you're pathetic."

Pushing her hand away, the table vibrated as he shoved his chair against it, the unloved piece of furniture falling over onto its side, his empty mug bouncing twice before smashing into a thousand pieces on the floor, the broken china crunching under his feet as he stood up, he barged past Sarah, his shoulder slamming against her delicate frame, he knocked the bunch of flowers she was carrying clean out of her hand, its petals scattering all over the floor. Closing the door behind him, he sprinted into the street, and, without looking back, kept on running.

Chapter 9
Wednesday

The humdrum of his life plummeting to new depths, his very existence becoming positively mind-numbing, David dragged himself into the town centre, wandering aimlessly up and down the High Street, pointlessly looking through shop windows, crossing the threshold on one or two occasions before retreating to the relative safety of the pavement once again.

Having lived there all his life he knew each and every shop intimately, which cafe served the best latte, which shop sold the cheapest birthday cards, where he could get the day's paper late in the afternoon, in fact he knew everything he needed to know about this miserable, depressing place he had the privilege to call home.

Standing in front of the counter at the newsagents next to the bank, he gazed at the young man putting the twenty-pound note carefully into the till, the last time he had stood at the same spot was the last time he had bought a packet of cigarettes, five long years ago. The shop itself was exactly the same, its off-white walls lined with newspapers and magazines, the light grey linoleum floor seemingly permanently covered in muddy footprints, the young man was a spotty teenager back then, the eldest son of the family that had owned the business for years, now a young man, he stood proudly behind the counter, the next generation taking its turn.

Attached to his fingers through static electricity, he shook his hand vigorously, removing the cellophane from the packet as he walked out of the shop, and discarding it into the bin immediately on the pavement outside. Putting a cigarette into his mouth, it felt strange and yet familiar at the same time, he coughed as he inhaled, his irritated body ejecting the unwanted chemicals invading its lungs and airways, the smoke scattering into the air as it dispersed sharply from his mouth.

Town was busy, the national obsession with shopping still un-abated, the hustle and bustle of the High Street, still alive and kicking despite the internet explosion and the unwelcome advent of on-line shopping, crowds of people still packing the pavements whilst an endless trail of delivery vans congested the roads.

His coat fastened up against the cold, David yanked the half-finished cigarette out of his mouth, took one last draw before tossing it on to the ground and pressing his foot over the smoking remains.

Suddenly he was aware of a kerfuffle in the distance. Someone running, sprinting almost, like a bat out of hell, their arms flying about all over the place in a most un-gamely fashion, propelling them forward, zig-zagging their way through the hordes of people, themselves with their shoulders hunched up, their hands thrust deep into their pockets, allowing him as much space as was humanly possible.

Whilst David recognised Ben immediately, he was completely at a loss as to what he was doing in town right at that very moment, and more importantly, why was he charging down the road like a steam train, causing maximum chaos and inconvenience to those around him?

His eyes still blinded with rage, Ben, wasn't quite as quick to identify his brother, and did not do so until David had lengthened his stride sufficiently enough to have placed himself between his younger family member and the pavement in front of him.

"Hold on there, my good friend."

His voice bellowing through the crowd, he intercepted his younger brother, grabbing him by the arm.

Dropping his hands onto his knees, Ben grabbed David's arm, he bent over double, desperately trying to catch his breath. His eyes were just beginning to focus now, he had already recognised his brother's voice, instinctively holding out his hand, he placed it into his brother's, and the two warmly shook hands.

"David, what are you doing here? Why aren't you working? Is everything alright?"

The next five minutes were spent with each explaining their own presence to the other, before David finally put his arm around his brother's shoulder as they turned towards the park gates.

Conversation flowed easily and effortlessly as the two of them walked through the park side by side, pausing they stopped at one of the wooden benches that lined the pathway. Made in teak and beautifully proportioned, the bench was infinitely more superior and imposing than those around it.

Brushing away some dead leaves and sitting down, Ben read the small brass plaque attached to the back-frame. *In loving memory of Doreen, May 1920–November 2015.* She must have been very much loved by all of her family he mused to himself, admiring the craftsmanship, vigorously rubbing his hands together, his body cooled down after the exertion of earlier.

David reached into his jacket pocket, pulled out another cigarette, and, cupping his hand to shield the flame from the elements, lit it up.

"I thought you'd packed that in," Ben commented, raising his eyebrows in surprise.

"Actually, do you know what, I'll take one, I've always wondered what it's like."

David strongly shook his head, relenting only after much persistence on his younger sibling's part, the naked flame of his new lighter finally igniting the dried tobacco, tightly rolled up in its thin white paper casing. Hesitating, his brother held the nicotine stick away from his mouth before sucking awkwardly on the filter, coughing and spluttering as the smoke found its way into his lungs. For a minute, the two brothers sat on the bench side by side in silence, both genuinely enjoying the other's company, both pretending to enjoy their cigarette.

"So, tell me again, what were you doing in town?"

Not entirely satisfied with his brother's earlier explanation, David continued with his gentle interrogation.

"As I said earlier, just doing some shopping," Ben replied coyly, nervously returning his cigarette to his mouth. David smiled, and continued.

"This money's a funny old business, isn't it?"

David was skirting around the issue, Ben had known that immediately, he had also known his brother long enough to know that there was a point to every question he asked, and that they would arriving at that point very shortly. Not waiting for his brother to reply, David carried on.

"I've struggling with it all Ben; I'm not going to lie to you. I've hated you, I've loved you, I've been jealous of you, I've felt sorry for you, Jesus Christ, every emotion you could possibly imagine."

Gazing thoughtfully at his brother, Ben took another draw from his cigarette, a veil of smoke filled the air space between the two of them, a positive smog when added to the smokescreen of deceit, each desperately trying to hide the truth of their intentions from the other.

"Where is your head now David? What are you thinking?"

He had to tread carefully, Ben knew that. Firstly, he knew that David idolised their mother, to him she was perfect, she could do no wrong, so the idea that she might have had a baby by anyone other than their father, would not be something he would be able to comprehend, let alone willingly accept. Secondly, as is often the case, there had always been a degree of sibling rivalry between them, would he be able to accept his younger brother's new-found wealth? Leaning forwards, he threw his cigarette end to the floor, grinding it into a pulp with his foot.

"You know you can have as much of the money as you want, I won't need even half of it."

David exploded. "I don't want, or need, your charity, thank you very much. I've survived without it for the past twenty-four years, I'm sure I'll cope with out it for the next twenty-four as well. No, I'm not interested in taking any of your money, what I am interested in, however, is how the hell you got hold of it, I'm very interested in that indeed."

Not daring to look at his brother, Ben looked down into his lap, playing with his hands, David puffed away vigorously at his cigarette, the white cigarette paper now all but disappeared, the filter burning his lower lip, too hot to handle he spat it out and onto the ground.

Without turning his head, Ben gazed at his brother through the corner of his eyes, David was not happy, and, after twenty-four years of virtually living in each other's pockets, he knew it.

"What are you trying to say? What do you mean by that David? What other things are you concerned about?"

Trying desperately to mollify his brother, Ben played things down.

"What I'm saying is that I would rather that you didn't accept the money, none of it."

Ben persevered with the pretence of being confused.

"What do you mean? Don't accept the money. Why on earth not?"

"Well, obviously, if you do people are going to start asking questions, you know awkward questions, embarrassing questions. Questions like why you got the money and I got nothing."

"So, what if they do?"

Ben retorted, sticking to his guns.

Staring at his brother, David raised his eyebrows. What was he going on about? Either he was missing the point completely, or he was deliberately trying to be as annoying as the circumstances would allow.

"What if they do? Are you fucking joking or something, you stupid idiot? Don't you think the whole thing might get more than just a little bit embarrassing?"

"Why? I don't see what you're getting at, really I don't."

Playing the fool was getting almost impossible now.

"Oh, for God's sake, shall I spell it out for you? They'll be asking whether Bill was your father, they'll start questioning the fidelity of our mother, our family name will be dragged through the mud. That's what people are going to be asking, that's what people are going to be thinking, you idiot. Christ it's bad enough that we have our doubts about our mother's behaviour without letting the whole world know about it, at least if you turn the money down we can keep the whole disgusting mess between the family, just the four of us."

Taking another cigarette from his jacket pocket, and taking a long pull, David waved the dense cloud of smoke away from his face as he quickly exhaled, looking across at his younger brother, he sighed heavily, they were in this together, he knew that, he needed to calm down, he knew that too.

"It's a bit late to be worrying about that now, isn't it? Don't forget that Sarah was at our house celebrating on Monday night, and you know how much she and Mum gossip in the charity shop.

David looked at Ben as he spoke, nodding his head in agreement before muttering under his breath.

"Do you think that Bill could really be your father, Ben? Do you think that Mum, our mother, could have had a relationship with somebody other than Dad?"

The question was rhetorical, he knew the answer, he just wanted to hear it from Ben, masochistically re-igniting the fire of his anger and hatred for his mother and father.

Kicking away the leaves at his feet, Ben was incapable of looking his brother in the eye. He knew the truth, their mother had told him, whilst they sat huddled around that table in the tiny little stock room in the charity shop, but did that give him the right to tell his brother? Surely that duty lay firmly with her?

Suddenly his thoughts turned to their father. If he told David the truth, he might confront him, Good God, they didn't see eye to eye at the best of times, this might shatter what little affinity was left in their fragile relationship, and leave them with nothing. Of course, on the other hand, their father might already know, he might have always known, and what if he did? Had he discussed it with their mother?

Sitting on the bench, his head in his hands, Ben's head was starting to ache, the more scenarios that came to mind, the more difficult it was for his mind to line them up into some sort of order.

In any event, his parents' marriage had been nothing but a charade, and a charade tainted by a tale that anyone with a penchant for gossip would lap up with positive glee. David was right, accepting the money would serve only add fuel to the fire, stoking it up into a toxic inferno, potent enough to tear the family apart. Looking across at his brother, he shook his head.

"I don't know David, and, to be honest with you, I don't want to think about it, any of it, it's just too depressing. Anyway, if Mum did have a relationship with somebody else then surely that's between her and Dad. We're just the children, we're not part of that side of their relationship, are we? And, let's say that she did, we can't turn back the clock, now can we? We've got different dads, I don't know, is that such a big deal? We're still the same two people, aren't we?"

Turning his head, suddenly lost in introspection, Ben re-read the inscription on the bench, and wondered whether Doreen's family had been any happier, less complicated, than his own. Completing the arithmetic, he quickly established that she had been ninety-six when she had died, a ripe old age indeed. He smiled to himself, an idyllic mental picture already forming in his mind of that perfect summer's day, she sitting at the head of an old wooden table, in a picturesque meadow, the gentle murmur of a stream in the distance, knee high grasses invaded by creeping buttercups and white clovers, the rays of the hot sun against her wrinkled, weather-beaten face, surrounded by her family members, the old and the very young, all of them demanding her attention, craving her approval, the fruitfulness of a long and happy life.

His musings were abruptly halted by David's outburst.

"I mean, what have I got? A mother so easy she'll sleep with anyone who's happy to recommend a bottle of something red on a Friday night, a father who is so weak that he carries on as if nothing is happening, and a brother who quite frankly couldn't care less about the whole affair, just as along as he gets his hands on the dirty money."

"It's not like that."

Ben protested.

Cursing his bad fortune under his breath, David's patience had finally run out, the conversation was over, the whole episode too much, and past the point of no return. Shaking his head, he stood up, he deserved better than all of this, he was better than all of this.

He was better than Tanya, he'd already proved that, lacing his drink with her little sachet of white powder, taking advantage of him in his weakened state, oh yes, he had already paid her back for that little episode. He was better than his pathetic father, standing by whilst his disgusting mother gallivanted around with, with some guy who worked in the local off license for God's sake. He was better than Ben, money or no money, he had dreams and ambition, what did Ben have? Nothing. To hell with women, to hell with his family, to hell with them all. He got up, glared at his brother and snarled.

"Ben, a word to the wise, mate, think very carefully about what you do next."

Pulling out another cigarette from his jacket pocket, he strode off, engulfed in a thick veil of smoke.

Chapter 10
Wednesday

The front door was still shaking violently in the doorframe casing long after Ben had finished hurtling through, leaving Sarah frozen to the spot, shivering and in shock.

How could he have possibly been in such a hurry that he couldn't even say good-bye? How rude! Rubbing her chin with her fingers, her eyes raised up to the ceiling, she quickly re-gained her composure, scanned around the shop, checking that it was empty before firmly closing and locking the door.

Looking like Armageddon, the stock room was in disarray, one of the chairs keeled over on its side, a lake of spilt tea and broken biscuits all over the table, crumpled balls of spent tissues on the floor, and sat amongst all of that, her body slumped forward, her head resting on her elbows, Anna, seemingly inconsolable, sobbing her eyes out.

"Christ, Sarah, what have I done?"

The question was rhetorical, Sarah knew that, and, for now anyway, it would have to remain that way, at least until after they had finished work anyway.

"Let's talk about it over a drink tonight, shall we?"

Taking a dry tissue and slowly getting up from her seat, Anna dabbed her eyes and wiped her nose.

The eight-hour shift felt more like an eternity, with Anna wanting time and space to herself, and Sarah more than happy to oblige.

Wednesday was by far the quietest day of the week, the majority of the shops on the High Street closing a mid-day and the charity shop itself not significant enough a draw to keep the crowds from the comfort of their own homes. Today had felt like the quietest Wednesday ever, and, looking up at the clock, Sarah was relieved to see it was coming to an end.

"Meet you at the Cross Keys at seven-thirty?"

Sarah asked casually as she set the alarm at closing time, the final extended, three second bleep, indicating that the panel was set, and it was time for them to both go their separate ways.

"Yes please."

Turning away from Sarah, and in no rush to go anywhere in particular, Anna stood admiring the recently installed decorative wrought iron park gates on the other side of the road, mentally complementing the craftsmanship, before crossing and walking through the park entrance. Alone, she spent the next hour pottering around, looking approvingly at the neat grass verges, the rectangular flower beds, and the old pavilion, its grand ornamental structure a brilliant white backdrop behind the perfectly manicured bowling green.

Feeling nauseous, she sat down on a bench, her eyes filled with tears. In talking to Ben that morning, she had opened her very own Pandora's box, started a chain of events that could surely only lead to one place, disaster and despair, now she had to tell Reg and David.

Not a sound came from the house, neither David or Ben having arrived back home yet and Reg was snoring happily in his favourite seat, comatose in an alcohol fuelled sleep. On tip toes, she crept into the kitchen, silently she buttered two slices of wholemeal bread, inserting a slice of smoked ham and a spoonful of mustard in between them. The sandwich in her right hand, its bread flapping over almost spilling the contents on to the floor, her handbag in her left, and as quiet as a mouse, she left the house, silently closing the door behind her.

Tanya was probably the person in the world that Anna detested the most. She hated every little bit of her, her tight trousers, the see-through blouses, her cheap jewellery, her make-up every shade of tart, she was disgusting.

At the bar, having successfully avoided making any meaningful eye contact, she stuck to the task in hand and ordered three double gin and tonics, one for herself now, and two for the table. Smiling to herself as she walked away from the bar, ordering a gin and tonic wasn't as straight forward as it used to be, still, she stuck with what she knew, just a classic London Dry Gin, nothing fancy, nothing aromatic added to make it taste any more flowery, no rhubarb or ginger, no pink grapefruit or even pomelo, just the traditional pungent aroma and juniper flavour, just gin, in its purest form.

The trio of beverages safely lodged in between her two hands, she located a table in a quiet spot, far away from the darts boards and the pool table, somewhere with some privacy. Placing the empty glass on the table, her whistle sufficiently wetted, she looked up and, spotting Sarah, enthusiastically waved at her friend, motioning her over, her hand hovering over the two remaining glasses and tonic water bottles on the table.

"What a day!"

Sarah exclaimed as she sat down, the air draining from her lungs as her bottom hit the seat of the chair. Living on the other side of town, the Cross Keys was a good three quarters of an hour walk from her house, she had invested that time wisely, trying to establish the best course of action, sadly, as she pushed open the pub door and caught sight of her friend, she was no closer to a solution than when she had set off. Anna was having some form of crisis, there was no doubt about that, she had never seen her so upset before today, raised voices in the tiny stock room, tables and chairs crashing around, floods of tears, she would need to tread very carefully, very carefully indeed.

"What a day indeed!"

There was little or no energy in Anna's voice, her eyes tired and drained, sensing the mood, Sarah allowed time for them both to finish their drinks before rising form her seat.

"My round. Same again? Doubles? No, what about double Doubles?"

Watching her friend as she approached the table with her drinks laden tray, Anna could feel the warm glow of the alcohol in her bloodstream quickly making its way to her brain, loosening her tongue sufficiently to allow for conversation.

"You've never been married have you Sarah?"

Sarah's elbow almost slipped off the table, she had been expecting an explanation, not a question.

"Good God no, and to be honest with you, I've not even come close yet. Sure, I've had a couple of serious relationships, but neither of those worked out, in fact neither lasted more than about six months."

Anna could read the disappointment on her best friend's face like a book, but that could wait for another day, another session of double gin and tonics, something to look forward to, she chuckled to herself, a brief respite from the harshness of her own current reality.

"Take my advice. What, my advice? For God's sake, what am I talking about? What do I know about all of that kind of stuff? Jesus Christ Sarah, I've completely screwed up my life."

As she spoke, and almost mid-sentence, she picked up her glass, half of the contents disappearing in an instance.

"Tell me what's happened. Take your time."

Blowing into her hand, in short quick breaths, Anna grimaced as one of the ice cubes in her glass inevitably found its way into her mouth, temporarily freezing the back of her throat. Taking another sip from her glass for Dutch courage, and a deep breath to further steady her nerves, she started at the beginning and told Sarah the whole ignoble story.

"Bloody hell, Anna! But you and Reg, well, I always thought that you two looked so happy together."

"We were, we are, we always have been, oh I don't know, it's too late now, everything will come out, that's if Reg doesn't already know, of course, and then everything will be ruined."

"Now just hold on, just hold on Anna, let's take this one bit at a time. What have we got? You cheated on Reg, not great, but I'm sure you had your reasons for doing that, they always say that the affair is the symptom not the cause don't they. You had a son by your lover, admittedly that's not ideal either, but it's not the end of the world, he's twenty-four years old now, that's a lot of water running under that particular bridge, for Christ's sake."

Gazing into Anna's face, she concluded that she looked in better spirits; suitably encouraged, she continued, "In a perverse kind of way, it's a good job Bill's dead. I know that sounds horrible, and easy for me to say as I did not know him, let alone sleep with him, but in a practical way it helps, at least there can be no further speculation in that direction, that chapter is well and truly closed."

"You make it sound so easy."

Taking hold of Sarah's hand, Anna could feel a smile creeping across her face, if only she'd known Sarah back then perhaps she wouldn't be in this mess now. Sarah spotted the smile immediately and decided to strike for home.

"So, Anna, that was the past, we can't change any of that, so, what are we to do for the future?"

A vacant look across her face, Anna gazed into space, Christ, if she knew the answer to that question, she probably wouldn't be sitting here now drowning her sorrows in double gin and tonics.

"I've got to talk it through with Reg first, I have to. After that I've got to tell David, I can't let him find out from somebody else, although I would imagine that he has worked it all out for himself anyway."

"You're right, you have to tell Reg first. Although he will almost certainly already know of course, you will definitely have to consider that?"

Running her tongue over her lips, Anna took another drink from her glass.

"I have, and a thousand times before now, during the affair, after the affair, when Ben was born, every one of his birthdays for the past twenty-four years. No, I don't think he knew then and I don't think he knows now, well not until this week anyway. Damn, he'll work it all out now, won't he? It's obvious what's happened, isn't it? I mean leaving all that money to Ben, what the hell was Bill thinking about? Why couldn't he just have given some to David? He knew David just as well, he used to take him to the park, he used to play with him all of the time when Reg was away. If he had just given David a little bit, a token gesture, nobody would have batted an eyelid. You idiot, Bill, couldn't you have given just a little more consideration when you wrote that stupid, fucking will."

Shocked and stunned, Sarah stared at her friend, never had she seen Anna this worked up before, and she had certainly never heard her swear.

"If he knew, or had just an inkling, then surely he would have confronted you with it years ago? Or certainly before now anyway. How has he been since Ben went to the solicitors? Have you had a chance to speak to him since then?"

Anna shook her head.

"I've managed to avoid him up until now, so I don't really know how he is, and I've certainly not had a chance to talk about it with him. I went out by myself yesterday, and Reg was out with Stephen today, nothing strange about that of course, it's Wednesday after all, although he has obviously got pretty drunk as he was fast asleep when I got home this evening, he didn't see me come in or leave the house. Hopefully he'll still be asleep when I get home, or better still let's have a few more drinks so I haven't got to worry about it."

Another double gin and tonic for the worse, Anna swayed as she attempted to get herself up and out from her seat. Taxis booked she helped Sarah out of her seat, the two of them edging their way clumsily towards the front door. Tanya was flirting with one of the regulars, stroking his hand as she pressed a pound coin's worth of change into the palm.

"Good God, does she ever give it a rest?"

Anna nudged her friend as they staggered past, almost knocking her over. In the car park, two taxis waiting in adjacent spaces, each as equally unsteady on their feet as the other, they kissed, parted company, and went their separate ways, Anna promising to talk to Reg in the morning and report back to Sarah as soon as she had.

Still feeling the effects, Anna's hand shook as she gently turned the key and opened the front door, it was quiet and all of the lights were switched off.

"That you Anna? Are you home now? Where have you been?"

Raising her eyes to the ceiling, Anna sighed a deep sigh. She always knew when Reg was drunk, his voice was slower, there were more pauses, his levels of concentration at breaking point just forming the words.

Placing her coat onto the bannister, she trudged up the stairs towards their bedroom, pausing, nervously at the door. Slightly ajar, she could see Reg through the gap, lying, naked, on top of the bed clothes, a half empty bottle of single malt whisky on the bed side table, an empty whisky tumbler sitting next to it. Following his gaze, she could see that he was watching one of the pornographic DVD's he kept hidden away at the back of his wardrobe, she hated those films, and he knew it.

"Come to bed then."

The drunken smirk on his face making her feel sick, Anna shivered, and nervously got un-dressed, naked and vulnerable she lay on top of the bed beside him, and praying that the alcohol may contain some mystical anaesthetic properties that might numb away the pain, she closed her eyes, the room spinning, the movie playing out in the background, a fitting and repulsive soundtrack for the depravity of the moment.

Trembling, curled up as tightly as possible into a little ball, she sobbed, and through the tears that filled her eyes she could see the film had ended, the white text of its meagre credits running down the black screen.

Snivelling quietly to herself, she lay there in silence, and questioned whether Reg had actually been making love to her or just fucking one of those girls he'd been ogling at on the television. She felt cheap, as cheap as one of those tarts in the movie, baring all, degrading themselves for money, bereft of any sense of common decency, and perhaps she was.

Chapter 11
Thursday

Too afraid to move, her body lying perfectly still in her bed, Anna stared into the darkness, turning her head to her left, she studied the form under the duvet lying beside her, Reg was sleeping like a log, his back bent up right against her arm. Gritting her teeth, she turned over to her right, screwing up her eyes she looked at the digital clock sitting on her bedside table, its red LED numbers luminescent in the darkness, it was half past seven.

She grimaced, her mind and her memory both appearing to awaken simultaneously, as she recalled the nightmare of the previous night. Perhaps she hadn't deserved it after all, surely no one deserved to be treated the way that Reg had the previous night, how could he show her so little respect? He was drunk, he was obviously angry, but even so, it was her body, how dare he violate it in such a way.

Shivering uncontrollably, she tucked the bedsheet under her chin, it was cold, bitter cold, suddenly an anger, an uncontrollable rage, was sweeping through her whole body, her eyes wide open, she was fully awake and fortified with a renewed vigour. She was certainly not going to lie there feeling sorry for herself, last night, last night, for Christ's sake, alright, she hadn't actually fought him off, she hadn't actually said that she didn't want to have sex, but she hadn't given the go ahead either, she hadn't encouraged him in any way.

As she slowly got up and pushed herself out of the bed, she caught a glimpse of herself in the full-length mirror next to her wardrobe, still naked, still venerable. Rubbing her eyes, she looked again, no, she wasn't venerable at all, she was slim, slim and alluring, slim, alluring, and desirable. In the shower, she closed her eyes as the water pounded onto her naked shoulders and the heat soaked into her body, pumping a dollop of shower gel onto her hand, she vigorously washed herself down, massaging away the tension and the pain.

Drying herself off, she reached into her underwear draw and pulled out a black lacy bra and matching panties, putting them on she felt sexy and seductive. Her confidence restored, the rest of her clothes, jeans and a sweater, she put on as quickly and quietly as possible before pulling the bedroom door to, and making her way downstairs.

Glancing at her watch, she tutted to herself, she wasn't working today so there would be no excuse to leave the house, she would have to stay put and face the music. Running her tongue along her dry lips she put the kettle on, perhaps that harmony would have a more melodic feel to it after a cup of tea, her dehydration certainly would.

Piping hot tea gushed out of the spout of the tea-pot, her hangover so bad it felt like there was not enough room in her skull for her brain, her hands and her eyes seemingly incapable of working together in lining up the china funnel of the tea pot with the cup on the table.

Tilting her head towards the ceiling, she pricked her ears, listening out for the inevitable banging and crashing that normally accompanied Reg when he woke up late, especially after an evening of over indulgence, a few too many drams of the sacred usquebaugh, the ill-named water of life that can leave even the burliest of men feeling at death's door.

Sitting at the small table, Anna finished her tea, silently got up, and with a steadier hand, poured herself a second cup. Pulling the chair from under the table, Reg sat down opposite, as if by instinct, programmed by years of routine and ritual, she got out of her seat and poured him a cup of tea.

Only the kitchen clock broke the silence, ticking in the back ground, ticking and tocking, tocking and ticking, synchronising itself with their thought patterns, the naked emotion, the entrenched attitudes, almost impossible to shift with so many unanswered questions, so much doubt. Carpe diem! Seize the day! Both knew that this was the time, the time to talk, and to talk properly. In reality, neither was able to break the silence.

Reg sighed, his elbows firmly fixed on the table, his right hand holding his cup of tea, his left cradling his chin, his bottom shuffling uncomfortably from side to side as he went over everything in his own mind. He deeply regretted last night, drinking beer all afternoon down the pub with Stephen, having a nap, and then breaking the seal of a bottle of single malt the minute he had awoken from his slumber, the hair of the dog that bites you, was never going to be a storyline with a happy ending.

Wincing painfully, he could picture himself lying naked on top of the bed, all of a sudden there was Anna, standing at the door, his poor, unfortunate wife, arriving at just the right time for him, and almost certainly the wrong time for her. Poor, poor Anna, the poor thing.

Taking a long sip from his cup, the hot liquid now flowing freely down his throat, the combination of the caffeine and wetness bringing his brain back to life, his mood changed, old wounds opening up, evoking memories of a darker time.

Slamming his cup onto the table, adrenalin pumping through his veins, his body was suddenly engulfed by inextinguishable flames of anger.

Poor thing? The poor thing? More like she deserved it, the bitch, yes, she had that coming to her, and for a long time now. She has certainly game for it in the past, and she wasn't too fussy where it came from either. All those years ago whilst he was slaving away on the other side of the country, earning the extra money they so desperately needed to build a decent life for the two of them, she was busy copulating with that Bill Williams, taking advantage of the empty house. Did she know that he knew? Well today she might just find out!

His anger sapping what little energy he had, and calm once more, Reg smiled as he gazed at Anna across the table, still unable to take his eyes off her even after all of these years. She was still very attractive, her shoulder length brown hair, dyed but that was understandable, her face, more heavily made up, and not completely free of a few wrinkles, still very pretty, defying her age, with her eyes sparkling now as they did when he first met her all those years ago.

Of course, back then, she was even more striking, her captivating eyes, the dark strands of her hair left unbound to tumble down over her shoulders, her slim hour glass figure, her breasts, waist, and hips all perfectly proportioned, but now, even now, she could still turn the heads.

Suddenly his body tensed again, stabbed by anger, yes, Bill would certainly have found her attractive, there was absolutely no doubt about that. Who wouldn't? Who didn't? She couldn't resist him, his attraction to her gleefully reciprocated, eventually leading to something more emotionally intimate.

His working away during the week would not have helped, and, sometimes his work took him away for months at a time, but when he came back on the Friday, Anna was always waiting for him with a nice bottle of wine, chilled with the glasses ready on the table. Within an hour they were both naked in bed, like a pair of teenagers, fuelled by their hormonal surges, making up for lost time on a Saturday night after the long week at school.

Sex with Anna had always been amazing, she liked being in control, it was all about her, and what she wanted, Reg stifled his smile with a sip of tea. The smile quickly turned to a frown, as he pondered as to how he had ever imagined that she would have been able to suppress those urges whilst he was working away.

He shook his head vehemently, she had David with her, for goodness sake, he would have been five years old, requiring far too much of her attention to allow time for such deviations from family routine, and her maternal responsibilities. Surely, she would never have left him alone in his bedroom, amusing himself with his playthings, whilst she frolicked in their bedroom with her own? So how did she manage it? More importantly, why?

Closing his eyes, Reg tried to concentrate, his mind imprisoned in a time capsule hurtling backwards and then forwards through time, never stopping, never pausing, tearing to and fro across the past twenty-five years. A quarter of a century had passed, all confrontation carefully avoided up until now, perhaps this was the moment? Perhaps the time had finally come to find out the truth, but was he ready for what that truth might bring with it?

Casting her eyes briefly over her husband's closed eyelids, Anna studied his face, what exactly was he thinking? The situation was not entirely alien, he would be feeling guilty about his behaviour in the bedroom last night, there was no doubt about that, sitting there in silence, his shame catching his tongue.

He wouldn't be apologising, she knew that too, it wasn't the first time she had come home from an evening out with friends only to be subjected to that sort of porn and whiskey fuelled sexual abuse, and, a wry smile appearing on her face, she had to admit, that on some occasions she had actually enjoyed it. However, like now, on the occasions when she hadn't, he would have known that, he would be feeling sorry for himself, he would be feeling very guilty, but there would be no apology.

But what else was he thinking about? The events of the past four days will have posed so many questions, questions that will have been posed before, on numerous occasions, but, surely, never satisfactorily answered, surely too many loose ends, like an untied shoelace trailing onto the ground, fraying at the ends, or, worse than frayed, perhaps completely broken? He must be thinking about

Bill, Anna concluded. Was he Ben's father? Christ, he must have asked himself that question a thousand times before now. Or had he?

Draining her cup, she kept it at her lips, a screen to hide behind, she and Bill had been careful to cover their tracks, leaving not a shred of evidence, hiding all signs of their blossoming relationship. David delivered, still in uniform, straight from school to her sister's house, the obliging family member delighted of her nephew's company, Bill never setting foot in the house on the same day Reg was due back home.

Every Friday, having collected her wine from Bill at the wine merchants, she had always given Reg what he wanted, he must have thought her keen, what with all that enthusiasm, the bedsheets freshly cleaned, he wouldn't have, couldn't have, guessed, that it was Bill's face she saw when she closed her eyes as she writhed around on top of him. Nor would he have noticed the contraceptive diaphragm, carefully in place for just the night, protecting her from his seed, so desperate she was to have Bill's, and only Bill's child.

No, they had definitely left no concrete evidence of their nefarious activities, no trail that would have given Reg the certainty he would have needed to question her fidelity, her commitment to their relationship, their marriage. Satisfied by her own train of thought, Anna got up from her seat, picked up the two empty cups from the table and headed towards the sink. Looking over her shoulder, she smiled at Reg.

"You were a bit keen last night."

Reg lowered his eyes and, looking down, replied, "Yes, yes I was."

Anna looked into Reg's tired eyes. "Never mind, perhaps Ben will give us some of that money he's got coming to him, then we can buy a bigger bed, and have even more fun."

Reg looked at Anna. He knew exactly what she was doing, they had been married too long for him not to. She had opened the door for him, this was his chance, he just needed the courage to take it. He kept thinking about what Stephen had said yesterday, if he could piece it together then anyone could, soon everyone would know what he had known for twenty-four years, his wife had had an affair, and his youngest son was the product of that affair. Now it was time to confront her. Carpe diem! Seize the day!

His head aching, his tongue stuck between his dry lips, his hangover was getting worse by the minute, his mental strength broken beyond repair, another seed of doubt planted in his shattered mind. Would he really be any better off confronting her now? He had tolerated the shame, the embarrassment for all of these years, why was it so important now? They had both played the part of both the knight and the knave though out their marriage, so why did it all need to be so principled now?

David and Ben were both adults, they wouldn't be living at home for much longer, and who would want to at their age? No, very soon it would just be Anna and himself sharing whatever was left of the family home. Shouldn't he be looking forward of the future, the bright future they had planned together, a new adventure, the next chapter, just the two of them. Leave the past exactly where it is now, in the past. Putting his hands flat palms down on the table, Reg mused, there were two options, there had always been two options, have it out with, or let the sleeping dogs lie.

That was the case now, and had been the case for the past twenty-four years. Reg could feel his strength being sapped away by the second, his body and mind engulfed in pain, nausea and lassitude. Getting out of his chair he stood up, and joined his wife, the pair of them standing side by side at the sink.

In any event Ben was his son. He had been there for him the whole of his life, he was his dad, his proper dad, did it really matter if he was his biological father or not?

Opening up this wound could prove toxic to their marriage, he could lose everything, both Ben and Anna, Lord knows he had lost David years ago. No, leave things as they are, nothing has changed, the money might raise a few eyebrows, but with whom, and for how long? No, leave things as they are and it'll all work out fine in the end.

Staring at the freshly washed mug, the excess water dripping onto his cold hand, running through his red fingers and onto the floor, suddenly, he could feel the dark mist falling again.

No, Ben was damn well not his son, twenty-four years ago, his wife had started an affair, and got pregnant, pregnant by Bill, Ben's biological father, Ben's real father. She chose to do that, seemingly unable to remain faithful whilst he was working away, it was her decision, it was her choice, well, she could go to hell, and take her bastard son with her, he hadn't turned sixty yet, he still had time to make a fresh start of it, perhaps move somewhere new, perhaps find someone else.

The tears welling up in his eyes blinded him as he applied the tea towel, gently dabbing at the porcelain of the mug. He was tired, the whole episode having left him totally drained, completely burned out by the chronic stresses of a marriage tainted by falseness and unfaithfulness.

He was too old for all of this, too old and worn out for any of it.

"Yes, a new bed would be nice."

He mumbled, resting his arm on Anna's shoulder, "Very nice indeed."

Chapter 12
Thursday

Its shoulders covered in a film of dust, the old, tatty, light blue dressing gown had been hanging on the back of his bedroom door for over twenty years. The door itself was littered with football picture cards, his meagre pocket money stretching to just one packet of five a week, now a collage of faded photographs, the faces frozen in time, their careers long since over, the white borders tinged yellow through age and direct sunlight.

The white wooden window sill still bore a dark yellow burn mark, those teenage years spent smoking Benson & Hedges King Size, leaning as far out of the open window as was humanly possible, almost toppling out onto the lawn below, frantically waving his hands, ushering the smoke out into the night sky, liberally spraying the room with air freshener before cleaning his teeth.

Sitting up in the bed, David scanned his bedroom, rubbing his drowsy eyes with the back of his hands, how he hated those football stickers, that old dressing gown, both constant reminders of how he had fallen short over the years, the realities of a life never quite matching up with his ambitions.

Turning his head, he could see his face reflecting clearly back at him in the glass of his bedside clock, he could barely recognise himself, his eyes had turned black, jet black, his eyebrows pulled down together, his lips shut tight. He couldn't really identify with how he felt either, there was a sense of greed that was alien to himself, but it was nevertheless an exhausting craving for money; money, power and dominance; dominance over everyone and everything around him. Couple all of that with a sense of arrogance; a sense of arrogance that both excited him and scared him half to death. He felt invincible; dangerously invincible.

Standing in the shower, he recalled his conversation with Tanya the previous evening, the temperature of the water increasing in the same way the excitement in her voice had intensified, as she had told him about Craig, an old friend, someone she had known for years, someone who could be trusted, who was setting up a new website and was looking for someone who could inject some cash into the project.

The water was getting hotter and hotter, leaning his head backwards, it flowed through his hair, down his face, and along the sides of his nose, closing his eyes he recalled the thrill that call had given him, like sitting in the front seat of the rollercoaster, the rush of excitement, the exhilaration, so much so that when he had finally put the telephone down, his hands had been shaking like a leaf.

Turning the shower control dial the water stopped immediately, he paused, placing his wet hand on the glass door, confidently counting his blessing, this was exactly the sort of thing he was wanting to get involved in, a silent partner, financing the deal, a new dimension, taking his business to the next level, the sleeping giant was finally waking from its slumber.

Either the traffic was quieter this morning, or, with this new zest for life, his foot had been resting heavier on the accelerator, in any event he was very quickly in town and pulling up into the car park.

Allowing the doors of the Café Narino to close behind him he cursed quietly under his breath, for looking at the long line of the people standing in front of him, it felt like all of those people ordinarily driving on the roads had left their cars at home and joined the queue at the counter of the Café Narino instead.

The young lady at the till was no more than sixteen years old, wearing a baggy dark brown jumper, a fresh coffee stain soiling the leg of her faded denim jeans, it had been a busy morning, and she looked very hot under the collar. Taking his change and moving down the counter, David picked up his order, a latte with an extra shot complete with a blueberry muffin, from the end, before finding a seat and sitting down.

Frowning as the rim of the piping hot cup scolded his lips as he raised it to his mouth, he persevered, and taking a sip of its contents, he surveyed the café, inspecting each table in turn, smiling to himself as he quietly past judgement on the people gathered within.

In the middle of the seating area, a group of women, six in total, all in their mid-twenties had joined two tables together and were huddled awkwardly in the confines of a space that was simply too small for them all, three sharing a settee designed for two, their handbags stuffed down the sides of the cushions, the other three sitting on wooden chairs opposite, leaning over the low table in the middle, itself over flowing with cups, saucers, and empty plates. Parents on their way home from the school run, an opportunity to extend the school gate conversations, one final natter before returning home to the dull realities of the cooking, the cleaning, and all of those other mundane tasks that make up running a home.

On the next table a couple and a single man, the three of them all in their late sixties, at a stretch early seventies, sat chatting away, two newspapers, a tabloid and a broadsheet, carefully folded over on the corner of the table, three mugs and a tea pot in the middle. The single man, his checked shirt creased at the front, his hair more than just a little unkempt, perhaps recently widowed, meeting up with the other two for some much-needed company at the start of another lonely day.

On the other side of the café a younger man, around forty years old, with short, mousy brown hair, his left ear pierced, and wearing a green parka coat, gazed intently at the traditional Staunton wooden chess pieces set up on the board in front of him, playing both sides by himself. David mused, a budding grandmaster maybe, sitting behind the black pieces, polishing up on that crucial opening theory, ready to conquer the chess world.

Lamenting his own lack of prowess on the chequered board, David turned his head towards the door, just as a man in his mid-forties, his right arm heavily tattooed, wearing grey tracksuit pants and a grey sweat top, strode confidently in, slamming the door behind him.

Following the man with his eyes, watching him place his order at the till, the same young lady, her face redder and more flustered, her brown jumper discarded and folded over the back of a chair, still busy writing down the orders and taking the money, David quickly concluded that he was a close enough match to the description Tanya had given over the telephone.

His purchases made, the man turned away from the counter, his eyes scanning the room, visibly filtering and eliminating the images as they worked their way around the four walls, in and out of the tables in an anti-clockwise direction.

Tilting his head as his eyes rested on David, and within five seconds of that he was striding confidently towards where David was sitting, his black Americano and croissant on a plate safely on the table, he extended his hand.

"David?"

"Craig?"

Craig's hand felt hot and sweaty in his own, adding even more suspicion to intrigue to the episode, and for two long silent moments David sipped at his drink, sizing up the stranger sitting opposite to him. Finishing his last mouthful of croissant, Craig opened the conversation.

"So, Tanya tells me that you're a man who might want to make an investment?"

Taking a sip of his coffee and slowly returning the cup back onto the table, David looked straight into Craig's eyes, gently nodding his head, before slowly picking his cup back up to his lips again. He had been desperate to keep the upper hand, and for a split second, he had been caught off guard, Craig's forthrightness taking him by surprise. His composure returned, he re-joined.

"I might be, tell me what you've got to offer."

The adrenaline was rushing through his body like an electric current running through his veins, sitting in his chair, surrounded by risk, hazards, potential pit falls at every turn, he was buzzing, living life on the edge at last, almost immediately he was getting impatient.

"Come on, what have you got to offer me?"

Encouraged by David's enthusiasm, Craig wasted no more time, getting straight down to business.

"Alright, no point in beating about the bush, here's the deal. I'm setting up a rough sex website, you know, where men treat women as an object, a play thing, it can be role play or for real, doesn't matter, subscription only, yeah okay, a bit seedy, but who cares? It's all above board, just couples uploading their videos and sharing them within the website community."

Leaning forward, he added with a grin, "Talking to Tanya, it sounds like it could be right up your street."

Feeling the blood rushing to his cheeks, David drained his coffee cup, how much detail had Tanya gone in to? Had she told Craig about that stupid encounter in the toilets? Looking at Craig's expression David concluded that, no, it didn't look like she had. Recovering quickly, he shrugged his shoulders nonchalantly.

"I give it to her the way she likes it, she's got no complaints."

"Good lad."

Craig replied, with little or no emotion in his voice, "Alright, let's say that I might be interested. What do you need from me? Where do I fit in?"

Leaning back in his chair, and at the same time desperately trying to look as dispassionate as he could, David could feel his mind racing with the excitement of the concept of rough sex, and his own raging personal vendetta against women.

Leaning forward on his chair, Craig stretched out his arms, and picked up the empty coffee cups and plates. Putting them onto the table next door, he returned his hands on to the table, pressing them down against the shiny wood, and looked at David, his stare intense, his eyes fixated on David's face.

"Okay. There's going to be some start-up cost. I know a guy who designs websites, in fact I've already given him some money up front, he's already made a start on it, I'll text you the URL. He'll need more cash though of course, you know to design the site, cover the costs of hosting, marketing, any security we might need, you know that sort of thing, plus maybe a grand a year in monthly subscriptions, but that's it."

"So how do we make any money out of it?"

His attention fully captured, and the internet not totally alien to himself, David tested Craig's credentials. "Loads of ways. First off, they'll be the subscriptions from our members, plus we could sell advertisement space, my mate told me about something called affiliate marketing, where we endorse a product and if someone buys it from the site we get a cut of the money. Fucking hell, we could even just accept donations off the people using the site if it really got going. You just need to invest some of your own cash into the project, and leave the rest to me. You should start seeing a return on your investment within six months, guaranteed, no risk, no worries."

His voice oozed with confidence, fuelling David's appetite for power, that sense of greed; greed, arrogance, and invincibility he had felt in his bedroom earlier he had felt in his bedroom earlier, he caught his reflection in a mirror, his eyes were as black as coal, his misogynistic tendencies, recently so prominent that they over shadowed all other emotions, taking full control of the situation. He lifted himself up, his hands on the arms of the chair, and leaning forward, glared at Craig, their faces just inches apart.

"How much?"

Craig didn't flinch, his self-assurance making David feel more than a little uncomfortable.

"Fifty-fifty, five grand, in cash, each."

Gently rocking backwards and forwards on his chair, running his sweaty fingers over his dry lips, David caught his breath. There was little more than five and a half thousand pounds in his savings account when he had checked earlier that morning, the product of three years of hard slog and toil, the money ring-fenced, ear-marked for a deposit on a brand-new car.

Mentally, he mulled over Craig's proposition, it sounded good, it sounded exciting, but it was risky and with more than just a suspicious nature about it.

Immediately his thoughts turned to Ben and his legacy, all of that money for doing diddly squat, his parents, his pathetic father, his sad tart of a mother, looking up at the ceiling, his mind suddenly crammed full with faded football stickers and old dressing gowns, faded football stickers, old dressing gowns, and Tanya. In a flash, his decision was made.

"Okay, I'm in. I'll have the money for three o'clock."

They shook hands and, without looking at each other's faces, immediately got up from the table and went their separate ways.

Pulling a cigarette out of the packet in his pocket, David swaggered out of the café and onto the street, the smoke instantly filled his lungs as he took a long and heavy draw, standing motionless on the street corner for a second, he smiled to himself. He had successfully negotiated the deal, made the investment, now he just needed to sit back and reap the rewards. The first steps to making some serious money, fulfilling the potential he always knew that he had, taking his business interests to the next level, setting himself up properly. The smile soon turned into a big smirk covering his whole face. His whole body succumbing to this new sense of power, this sense of invincibility.

The car was cold and he shivered as he sat in the driver's seat, fumbling for his keys, eager to switch on the ignition and get the heating system up and running, his foot pressing on the accelerator, the warm air was soon meandering through the vents, warming his face and his hands. Driving along the road, his feet now piping hot, but the adrenalin rush was well and truly over, a sense of reality making an unwelcome return.

He probably wouldn't be sharing too many details of the website with too many people, he mused, probably best to keep those particular cards very close to his chest, it wasn't illegal, no, definitely not illegal, but certainly more than a little immoral and with more than a sense of depravity about it. If anyone asked him where the extra money was coming from, he would restrict his response to as little detail as possible, say nothing of the website, just say that his business was going well and that he had picked up some more clients.

Parked up outside of the house, everything successfully squared up, David took his mobile phone from out of his coat pocket, and selected Tanya's name from his list of contacts, pausing, his fingers hovering over the screen, he wondered if she would still be interested in him after what happened last time.

A wry smile covered his face as his attention turned to Craig's new website, of course, she would be interested in him, why wouldn't she be? Her response was almost instantaneous, no, she wasn't working that evening and yes, she would see him and could he meet her at her house around eight o'clock, oh, and had he managed to see Craig yet?

Pushing the front door open, he could hear his father and mother sniggering and guffawing in the living room, what a pair they were, he cursed under his breath, his leather bag crashing onto the floor at the foot of the stairs, and getting more and more distasteful by the minute. How could two people be so oblivious to what was going on around them? He considered, hanging his coat up, both of them so wrapped up in their own contemptible little worlds, not caring about what other people might be thinking.

Bracing himself, ready to walk into the living room, he continued with the character assignation. How and why had he put up with the pair of them for so long, he simply did not know. Well, things were moving on nicely for him now, and he would soon be out of their hair. Good God, he had neither the time or the patience for either of them anymore, they were pitiful and they were welcome to each other.

Entering the living room, his mouth quickly contorted into a sneer, for there was Sarah, looking very much at home, sitting very comfortably in the chair in the corner of the room.

"Sarah's staying to have tea with us David. Had a good day?"

His mother's cheerful, chirpy voice cutting through him like a knife through butter, he flinched as she rushed over and flung her arms around him, shuddering he furiously pushed her away. Christ, when was she going to get the message? When was she finally going to realise that he didn't want anything to do with her? What was she thinking? Was she hoping everything would just be brushed under the carpet?

Good God! That bloody Sarah, that bloody fucking Sarah was there again. Keeping his mother at arm's length he stared at the ubiquitous guest more closely. If he didn't fancy her so much surely, he would hate her guts; but he did fancy her, he fancied her like mad, Christ! What he would give just to get inside of her knickers. Just once.

Shaking his head, the fantasy once again becoming reality, anger and frustration taking back over, for God's sake, she might as well make a clean breast of it and just move in. Jesus, he needed to get out of there, and get out of there fast.

"I think I'll skip tea thanks. I'm off out tonight, I'll get something then."

The bannister shook from side to side as David climbed the stairs heavily two at a time, and, within fifteen minutes, he was closing the front door behind him having showered and attired himself in a pair of designer indigo denim jeans, a navy-blue woollen sweater, and rather too much aftershave.

The brakes screeched as his car drew to a halt in the car park at the Cross Keys, his mobile phone, dislodged from its haven on the passenger seat by the excessive pressure on the brake pedal, lay face down in the floor, leaning over, he picked it up, rolling his eyes as he glanced at the clock, it was not even six o'clock, and his stomach was rumbling, instinctively and pointlessly he looked at the clock again, he wasn't meeting Tanya for almost another two hours. With time to kill, he texted Daniel.

Fifteen minutes later, and patting down his unruly wet hair, Daniel joined David at the table, leaning forward he fastened his shoe lace.

"Got here as quickly as possible, I'd only just got home from the gym, usual? I'll fetch them."

David nodded playing pointlessly with his phone as his friend went to the bar and ordered two pints and rump steak, chips, mushroom and tomatoes for the pair of them.

Belching quietly as he shovelled up the last three chips and put them into his mouth, David put down his knife and fork, and arranging them carefully together, as if in some form of victory ceremony to celebrate his empty plate, he picked up his glass, leaving it hovering in front of his lips.

"Tell you what mate, I've got to get out of that house, it's driving me mad. I haven't stopped thinking about what you said, you know about that Bill being Ben's father and all of that. You're probably right mate. I asked him about it yesterday, he didn't think that it could be possible, but he's got no reason to tell me the truth, has he? I mean, why would he? What with all that money involved."

"Have you had chance to talk to your mum yet?"

Daniel asked, pushing his plate into the centre of the small table, immediately filling the vacated space in front of him with his pint glass. They'd helped each other out so many times in the past, been there for each other when the chips were down, money, women, work, health, anything and everything.

"To be honest with you mate, I couldn't give a damn about her anymore, in fact, I can't stand the sight of her, or my dad, in fact, to hell with the pair of them. Actually, do you mind if I come and stay at yours mate. Please, I've got to get out. Get as far away as I can from those two."

Daniel looked at his friend. He could see the desperation etched on his face. He finished off his last mouthful of beer.

"Of course, mate, whenever you like."

"Thanks mate, now I'm off to see that Tanya. I'll text you."

"That's right, mate, you text me."

Chapter 13
Friday

Rubbing the sleep from out of his eyes, David glanced across at Tanya, lying next to him naked in the bed, the bright yellow duvet a crumpled mass on the floor, her frame, trimmed and toned, a testament to the hours spent in the gym, working the weights, crunching the stomach muscles, she was fast asleep, breathing lightly, her bosom moving up and down in perfect unison with each breath.

On a decent run it was around a quarter of an hour from the Cross Keys to Tanya's house, last night it had only taken David ten minutes, and, having parked his car next to hers, he pressed the doorbell, immediately she was there, in her dressing gown, opening the door, ushering him in with a grin on her face.

"Just the two of us tonight, I'm afraid, Mum's got the children."

David had followed her eagerly through the front door and into the living room. During the proceeding hour, they regaled themselves of the entire alcoholic contents of the fridge, vis-à-vis four cans of Budweiser and a bottle and half of Chardonnay wine. Sitting on the inadequate two-seater sofa, David's hand wandered onto Tanya's knee as he described his meeting with Craig, encouraged by the excitement in her eyes, the closeness of her body, her slim waistline, her lean flat stomach, he left out none of the details, adding to the erotica wherever possible. As the conversation intensified so did the levels of titillation, until the mutual arousal had reached a point whereby neither party could resist the temptation of moving into the bedroom any longer.

His head sank into the soft pillow, itself laced with her sweet scent, as he turned away from Tanya, and lying on his back, his legs stretched out, he allowed his mind to drift, meandering through his life story so far.

He was thirty years old, late twenties might have felt better, but you can't turn back the clock, he ran his own business, and had done so successfully for six or seven years now. Today he had taken things to the next level, investing his entire savings into a new venture, a new business, a business in which he was an equal partner. It was a risk, he knew that, but lots of people took risks, businessmen thrive on risk taking, the business world being completely reliant on the people who are prepared to take those risks, that was life, that was business.

Facing Tanya again, he could feel the electric charge returning, his whole body tingling with excitement, yes, all of the money he had saved up was gone, every penny of it, but then millions of people went about their daily lives with nothing in the bank, that really wasn't so unusual, in fact, it was perfectly normal, normal and, in a way much more exciting.

Closing his eyes, his thoughts turned to his parents, and immediately he could feel his body growing tense and a torrent of blood running to his head, he was completely ashamed of the both of them, they were a complete embarrassment, in fact, he hated them both, and wished them both dead.

Suddenly he could see Ben's face, appearing from nowhere, almost forcing its way into his thoughts, desperate not to be forgotten, not to be missed out. He sighed, a long, weary sigh, he loved his half-brother, no he loved his brother, yes, brother, for goodness sake, probably more than anyone else in the world. Only six short years separated them, living in the same house all of their lives, their bedrooms just feet apart, clothes handed down from one to the other, it would be impossible not to.

Lowering his eyes, he looked across at Tanya, now turned over and facing him, her cheek resting on the slim fingers of her small dainty hand as she slept. He smiled, she was very different from his previous girlfriends, but she had a pretty face, a fabulous body, and was incredibly good fun, especially when she'd had a few too many drinks.

His eyes blackened, a leer replacing the smile, no, actually, what he enjoyed most about the relationship with Tanya was the juxtaposition of the roles they played, his being the dominant part, hers the submissive, the both of them seemingly enjoying the power dynamic in their own way.

Adding to the excitement, the power play appeared to extend outside of the bedroom and into their daily lives, with Tanya appearing to gain real pleasure from serving him his beer at the Cross Keys, content to palm off her offspring with her mother to allow him even more of her attention, yes, he was in control and he liked that, he liked that very much. he closing his eyes, his mind drifted back to the previous night.

His head suddenly heavy with dressing gowns and football stickers he thought about his own bedroom, the winds of change were blowing, and blowing a real gust, he wouldn't be spending a single night more than was absolutely necessary in that particular dormitory. Christ, why has it taken him so long? How will his parents react, he pondered, he couldn't wait to see the look on their faces when he tells them, he might even tell them why as well, really rub salt into the wounds.

Slowly, he lifted himself off the bed and headed, naked, towards the shower.

*****

The steam rose up from the piping hot teacup resting on Ben's stomach, and, making its way up into his nostrils made his nose twitch. Turning his head, he gazed drowsily at the clock on his bedside table, fully awake for almost an hour now, with neither his body nor his mind quite ready to face the outside world, he had already completed the journey downstairs into the kitchen, made himself a cup a tea, only to head straight back upstairs and into bed.

Blowing across the surface of his drink, he pondered over his brother's absence last night, taking a sip of the hot aromatic liquid, before moving the cup away from his mouth, pressing it against his chest, enjoying the warmth through his pyjama top.

In fact, David had not really spent much time at all in the house these past few days, he deliberated further, his mind immediately becoming crowded with different scenarios. He took another sip of tea, as if to steady his nerves, Christ, it had better not be that Tanya, he cried out silently to himself, she has a terrible reputation, a real man eater, snaring her victims, using them, and then spitting them out when she had finished. Putting his mind at rest, he concluded that David wouldn't be so stupid as to get himself involved in her, and had probably stayed at Daniel's after a few pints too many at the Cross Keys.

Outside the sun was rising, the shadows slowly disappearing from the bedroom ceiling, strips of light invading the topside covering, he continued to sip his tea, praying that the purity of its flavour might be complimented by the presence of some or other seemingly magical properties that in turn might ease his troubled and confused mind. This time last week everything was so much less complicated, and yet in five, just five short days, his life had been completely turned upside down.

Looking around his bedroom, he rolled his eyes, nothing had changed, nothing ever changed, a mixture of childhood relics, teenage memorabilia, all fighting for legroom with his more recent purchases in the small cramped space that had been his bedroom for the past twenty-four years. Not exactly the billet of someone filled with drive and ambition, someone continually fighting for top spot, second best never an option.

The self-condemnation grew legs as he reflected on the mediocrity of his life since leaving school six years ago, his folder of achievements laden with certificates and qualifications, everything pointing towards a promising future. He enjoyed his work, it was interesting and he got to meet lots of interesting people in lots of interesting places, but it was freelance, with the disadvantage of no guaranteed income, some weeks, in fact most weeks, there was no income at all.

Good grief, no wonder he hadn't got around to leaving home yet, he simply couldn't afford to. Well, he jolly well could now, he smiled to himself, with the contentment of someone with both the means and the way, the money changing everything, now he could afford to get his own place, and finally say goodbye to his wretched bedroom, the family home with all of its shackles and fetters forever.

There was just one problem, David had told him in no uncertain terms not to accept it, it would cause too many problems he had said, and, on the one hand, he could see where he was coming from, awkward questions would certainly be solicited, the entire family placed under the microscope, for closer scrutiny, but for how long? In a couple of months, certainly no more than six, no one would be remotely interested in any of it, leaving him with the money, free to spend the rest of his life a wealthy man.

Rubbing his chin, his eyes sparkled as he marvelled at the endless options, his head giddy as they whirled around in his mind, all of them jostling for poll position, three or four ideas had already taken their places at the starting grid; moving out of home, buying a house, or even an apartment, there were plenty for sale in the area, and he could afford to take his pick of them.

Perhaps, in time, he would rebuild his relationship with David, surely it would improve when they finally stopped living inside of each other's pockets? Christ, if only it were that straight forward.

Sighing heavily as he contemplated the fact that he hadn't even accepted the money yet, and already it was causing some major complications in the family. The rift between him and his brother, seemed to be getting wider by the day, of course they had fallen out before, and on numerous occasions at that, but not like this, there was a real venom in David's voice when they had shared that park bench the day before yesterday, he had never spoken to him like that before, thank goodness, but was he right in what he said?

Would their family really generate that much interest?

What would the cashier at the supermarket checkout be really thinking, as she smiled making just the right amount of eye contact, lifting up the customer divider, and passing the first item efficiently across the scanner? Would her idle speculation be around what might be on the tea table that evening or something more sinister surrounding that disgraced family everyone was talking about?

Or the regulars gathered, early doors, at the bar at the Cross Keys, leaning on their elbows, one hand covering their mouths, the other tenderly cradling their precious alcohol infused trophies, would they really be more interested in gossiping about the paternity of the younger of the two sons than the density of the collar foaming on the top of their pints?

How would his parents feel?

Could his mother possibly continue working at the charity shop with her reputation in tatters, not knowing whether the customers perusing through the racks of second-hand clothing were more concerned about the quality of the cloth or the odium of the assistant working behind the counter?

They had always enjoyed a special closeness, and of course he understood why now, but, was right this moment really the best time to be leaving her alone, left to her own devises?

What about his father? Such a mild and unassuming man, suddenly finding himself in the centre of a paternity row, his retirement plans shattered into small pieces and scattered all around him? His resilience was also going to be put to the test very soon, surely, he too would know the truth very shortly, if, in fact, he didn't already do so.

An increasingly familiar dull ache was forcing its way into his stomach, making him feel more and more nauseous. How did he feel? All of a sudden, he had a different father, someone he never actually knew. That in itself had been a shock, but, even more surprising, was how quickly he had adapted to that particular change of circumstances, and how very little of his time spent hankering after more of the details surrounding his entry into this world.

The sands of time running unrelenting, his alarm clock doing its job of work, he closed his eyes, an uncomfortable tension running right the way through his body, his head starting to throb, and groaned as he reluctantly lifted himself out of bed.

*****

Sarah winced, the first sip of her hot chocolate scolding the tip of her tongue, putting her cup down onto the table, she thought about Ben and what Anna had confided in with her yesterday. How must he be feeling about those unwanted revelations from his past, his whole life completely turned upside down.

It wasn't even half past eight, still very early, and everything was quiet at the Café Narino, three members of staff quietly busying themselves behind the counter, an equal amount of customers in front, everything was calm, everyone relaxed.

Chuckling to herself, her eyes rested on the empty space in front of the counter, in an hour's time, there would be three times as many customers as there were numbers behind the counter, that vacant space suddenly filled with a long queue of men and women all craving their morning caffeine fix, all satisfying their social media needs on their mobile devices whilst they waited patiently in line.

A young couple, in their late-teens, were just taking their seats on to the bright red loveseat, snuggled together side by side, their knees in constant contact, two lattes sitting on a blue tray on the table in front of them. They were smiling and giggling to each other as they chatted away, at every opportunity they seemed to be touching each other, him running his hand along the length of her arm, she casually placing her hand into his, her finger-tips making just the very slightest of contact with his. He gazed into her eyes keenly, penetrating her with his love, a new love, bursting with freshness and clearness, the just starting out love, a love burning with fierce desire and passion, that would not, could not be extinguished.

Tilting her head to one side, holding her mug of hot chocolate to her mouth with both hands, her lips pursed, blowing across the surface of the steaming hot, frothy, liquid, Sarah smiled. Closing her eyes, suddenly and very much to her surprise, Ben's face appeared, smiling back at her.

Vigorously, shaking her head, she desperately tried to remove the image, but it kept coming back, forcing its way through the ether of her mind. Both intrigued and disturbed by its persistence, she found herself reluctantly conceding that perhaps she was finding herself increasingly more attracted to him, spending more and more time thinking about him, her daydreams increasingly filled with visions of the pair of them, together, each enjoying the simple pleasures of the other's company.

Stopping dead in her tracks, her childish fantasies cut short, she slammed her mug onto the table, what a stupid idiot she was! Ben, with his life filled with misery and mirth, wouldn't be remotely interested in her, in fact, the longer her mind rested on that particular scenario, the more the likelihood of anything coming to fruition diminished.

The hot chocolate gave her a much-needed sugar rush, urging on her imagination, but her feet remained firmly on the ground, the timing, even when the dust finally came back down to earth, settling onto the dry barren land that was her life, was wrong, all wrong. An eligible young man has the good fortune to find himself bestowed with riches beyond his wildest dreams, when, suddenly, coming from out of the woodwork, there she was, buzzing around him like a bee around the proverbial honey pot, it was almost shameful.

Another sip and reinvigorated even further, the mental landscape took another dramatic turn So what! People were welcome to their own opinions, she really couldn't care less, her affections for Ben had been intensifying for weeks, no months, now, long before that stupid brown envelope had fallen through the post box less than seven days ago.

Shuddering, a cold chill running right through her body, she remembered how Ben had shoved her out of the way as he stormed out of the charity shop, incensed, a murderous look in his black eyes. He had every reason to be fully justified in his anger, she knew that now, but she had never seen him like that before, like a raging bull, charging blindly at the matador's red flag, snorting and bellowing, destroying everything in its path, good grief, was he even capable of returning her affections?

A full hour had past now, the remainder of her hot chocolate stone cold, grimacing, she slammed the cup down onto the table. Looking across at the red snuggler, she could see that it was empty, the young couple had gone, all of that tenderness, fondness and devotion, so prevalent just a few feet away less than an hour ago, now completely disappeared, and with it, perhaps, any hope of her finding love for herself.

Was that to be her destiny, a lonely old spinster, twenty-five years old, working a handful of days a week as a volunteer in a charity shop, living at home, her lifestyle bankrolled by her deceased father.

Chapter 14
Friday

Stretching and yawning, each foot impulsively following the other, Ben tip-toed slowly down the stairs. Working freelance certainly had its advantages for a young man in his mid-twenties, not being at any one's beck and call, no one breathing down his neck twenty-four hours a day, demanding their pound of flesh, bombarding him with texts and emails, no he could generally come and go as he pleased, living his life at his own pace, by nobody's else's leave.

Walking into the kitchen, he lent over, and carefully avoiding the kitchen gadgets and utensils lined up on the window sill, pulled back the net curtain. He knew that his mother and brother would both be at work, but what about his father? The empty space in the front drive, a perfect rectangle of dry tarmac, surrounded by more of the same, but wetter, darker, made damp from the heavy rainfall of the night, was evidence enough to suggest that he was elsewhere.

Putting on his blue anorak he quietly left the house, closing the door behind himself. Ten minutes later he was clutching a copy of the day's paper, browsing through the back page, standing behind an elderly couple in front of the counter at the newsagents. Both well into their eighties, each proudly wearing their wedding ring, tarnished and dis-coloured through years of continuous use, celebrating the longevity of their marriage, years of love and devotion. Forcing his eyes away from the tabloid, Ben gazed at them, their identical grey coats totally practical, both warm and showerproof, their matching walking sticks crafted beautifully out of natural wood, her arm locked into his, additional stability in the event of her thin fragile legs failing her, and smiled to himself, not for one second could he imagine his own parents surviving into their twilight years in such harmony.

Sarah's legs tingled, the blood once again flowing freely at the back of her knees, as she stretched them out in front of her. Leaving her coat draped over her seat she walked awkwardly to the counter. A young man in his early twenties prepared her second hot chocolate, his long hair, tied back behind his head, his ginger goatee beard hanging precariously over the cup in his hand, his arms covered in tattoos. Everything he needed was close to hand, miniature skyscrapers of saucers behind him, and next to those a small army of coffee cups and mugs, of all shapes and sizes, were lined up, ready and waiting to be called up for duty. She watched him busy at his craft, steaming the milk for a good thirty seconds, vigorously pumping a handful of pumps of syrup mocha into the empty mug, before finally adding the steaming milk.

Balancing her cup confidently in her right hand, Sarah reached out her arm and picked up one of the tabloid newspapers from the rack fixed to the wall, and, sitting down she opened it up.

Staring back at her, the photograph of a celebrity couple, recently married after a whirlwind romance, two pages covered in beautiful photographs telling of a wonderful fairy tale wedding, no expense spared; an idyllic beach setting, excited guests, pictured in the private seating area on the seafront, the men dressed in gleaming white tuxedos and black trousers, the women clad in an assortment of floral and pastel colour dresses, the powdered pieces of dead coral of the white sand beach a perfect carpet for their tanned bare feet, the happy couple gazing into each other's dizzy eyes, seated in their exclusive beach suite, the patio doors open, the sun setting into the sea behind them.

Holding the newspaper at arm's length, she stretched out her legs, closing her eyes, she could see Ben smiling at her, again, the edges of his face illuminated in the darkness of her mind.

In the kitchen, the air simultaneously filling up with steam from the freshly boiled kettle and smoke from the freshly toasted bread. Ben held the butter dish in one hand and a knife in the other, quickly and efficiently, he buttered the two slices of toast, before pouring the boiling water into the tea pot. Sitting down at the table, his mouth filled with both tea and toast, he laid the paper down flat on the surface in front of him, and turned over the first two pages.

Another celebrity wedding, he murmured under his breath as he gazed inanely at the open pages, as if for respite, he immediately turned the paper over to the back page and the reports of last night's football matches, another upset in the Premier League, the manager seemingly incapable of sufficiently motivating his players to put in a decent shift in front of the restless home crowd.

His inquisitiveness getting the better of him, he skimmed through the sports section before returning back to the wedding article. Chance would be a fine thing! Sighing to himself, he cursed his life of solitude before folding the paper over and finishing his tea.

Desperate to lift his spirits, he wandered into the living room, looking at the empty chairs his mind wandered back to fun and frolics of Monday night, his mother and Sarah proudly serving up the tea, whilst his father made short work of the bottles of ale, their laughter getting more raucous with every unit of alcohol consumed.

Suddenly, as if out of necessity, his eyes were drawn back to the chair where Sarah had sat, he could see her clearly now, her pretty face, filled with smiles and pleasure, her eyes beaming. He sat down, squeezing the arms of the chair tightly, his fingers turning white, his breaths getting heavier and deeper.

Draining the last of the sweet chocolatey contents from her cup, Sarah sat back in her seat, the round of her back sinking into the soft leather, looking at her watch she suddenly sat bolt upright in her seat, as if rudely awoken from a melancholy dream. Placing her empty cup into the centre of the table, and putting her coat on, and marched purposely through the front door and out into the busy street.

The twenty minutes had passed slowly in the dull, gloomy living room, Ben, still unable to detach his gaze from where Sarah had sat, leaned forward uncomfortably in his seat, his head in his hands. Suddenly the dulcet tone of the doorbell filled the air, cursing his bad luck, he removed his gaze from the vacant pew, the doorbell sounding out yet another reminder that someone was waiting outside, the caller was persistent, he smiled to himself as he got out of his seat.

Reluctantly leaving his chair, he made his way into the hall, peering through the glass he could see Sarah standing outside nervously looking to the ground, her body swaying from side to side. Almost immediately he stepped back from the door, cursing his bad fortune again under his breath. What was she doing here? What could she possibly want?

Closing his eyes, his mind flashbacked to the charity shop, the image was crystal clear, him charging towards the front door like a heard of stampeding cattle, barging past her, practically knocking her clean off her feet, not stopping to acknowledge her presence, not even stopping to apologise for his lack of courtesy.

Groaning out loud, he crouched down, his back pressing, hard, against the door. His mother was working today, it was Friday, and she often worked an extra shift on a Friday, Sarah would have known that, so she definitely hadn't come to see her.

Taking a deep breath, he could see her outstretched arm, reaching up to the doorbell, different scenarios filled his aching head, ideas bouncing around frantically like a rubber ball trapped within the confides of his cranium. Perhaps she had come to take him to task over his rudeness in the charity shop, she could hardly be criticised for doing so, could she? No, she was far too mild mannered, too forgiving, to have given it a second thought. So, what exactly was it that had bought her all the way from her house, ringing his door bell at this time on a Friday morning? What exactly did she want?

Nervously, his hand shaking, unsettled through both anticipation and ignorance, he slowly turned the handle, and pulled the wooden door towards him, exposing his head to the elements, the drizzle falling lightly upon his mop of hair as he stuck his head through the door. With the warmest smile he could muster, he greeted the young lady, thoroughly impatient through increasing dampness, standing on the doorstep, moving to one side, he allowed her room to walk past.

"Oh, hi, Sarah, fancy seeing you here this morning, what a pleasant surprise, please, please come in."

Their bodies brushed against each other awkwardly as Sarah passed and entered the hallway, looking over her shoulder, she gazed into Ben's face, unable to tell if he was being sincere or not, there were no clues in his tone of voice and if there was anything to be gained from analysing his body language, it was too subtle to warrant remark.

Having committed herself, the threshold well and truly crossed, there was no turning back, and putting on her bravest face she skipped further into the house, taking off her fawn woollen trench coat, the waist belt hanging loose, having worked itself free from the confines of the inadequate loops, the light brown leather buckle falling lightly to the floor, she gathered it all up in her arms and handed it over to Ben.

"Hi, Ben."

There was little or no awkwardness in her voice.

"I just thought that I would pop in and see you, what with the other day…"

Frozen with embarrassment, Ben's shoulders dropped, his face a crimson red.

"I'm really am sorry about that Sarah, it was just, well I'd had some bad news, that's all, still no excuse."

His voice trailed off.

Gently squeezing his hand, she did not press any further, she was fully aware that he had been the recipient of some unexpected and un-savoury news, she knew that the burden of this news would be laying heavily on his shoulders, but if he could just open up his heart to her, trust her, trust her enough to discuss his feelings with her, maybe this could be the catalyst, the start of something more than just friendship.

Gazing at Sarah, Ben could feel his heart thumping in his chest, she looked so handsome in her dark blue pleated skirt, her simple, white blouse opened at the neck, carelessly revealing the shape of her round, firm breasts. Suddenly he felt a yearning, an unforbidden temptation, composing himself quickly he motioned her into the living room.

"Would you like a cup of coffee, Sarah?"

She flashed a smile back at him.

"Of course, it's a damn sight cheaper here than at the Narino."

Ben busied himself in the kitchen, grabbing two of the best white mugs from the cupboard, the jar of instant coffee from the window sill, and some milk from the fridge. Within five short minutes he was standing in front of Sarah, a tray, complete with two steaming hot drinks and a plate of ginger biscuits, firmly held in place in his large hands.

Sitting in exactly the same seat as she had on Monday night, Sarah looked very comfortable, drinking her coffee and nibbling at her pungent, spicy, biscuit. Ben was more anxious, sitting in the adjacent chair, glancing across nervously, looking at her through the corner of his eye, desperately trying to read her mind.

She had been quietly going about her business as he had stormed out of the charity shop, she would have seen his mother reduced to tears, drying her red eyes in the cramped little stock room, and she would have consoled her, of course that went without saying, an arm around the shoulder, words of comfort and encouragement, but how had his mother responded? The two of them were very close, but did that closeness extend as far as discussing family business, personal family business?

Crossing her legs, her skirt rising up her leg, the pattern of her black woollen tights stretched and distorted at the knee, Sarah started on a second biscuit, seemingly oblivious to Ben's turmoil.

Catching sight of her shapely leg, Ben blinked his eyes and shook his head, refocusing his attention on the question, quickly concluding that, actually, the answer was irrelevant, he had been very rude to her, and he owed her an explanation, and, at that moment, decided to tell Sarah everything.

Taking a deep breath and speaking much more quickly than normal, he recounted the whole story, every sordid little detail, as he spoke he could hear the words flowing more readily than he had anticipated, looking Sarah intently in the eye, he searched for a reaction, a hint of what she might be thinking, she returned the compliment, gazing into his eyes as he spoke, her face calm and comforting. Ben allowed himself a brief smile, yes, she had forgiven him, in fact, more than that, she appeared to have taken his side.

Inappropriately, he found his gaze wandering back to her well-formed pin, perhaps he might find love one day, perhaps that love was closer at hand than he thought. He quickly dismissed those tactless thoughts, force-marching them to the back of his mind. If she had even the slightest of intention in that direction, anything resembling any sort of uncontrollable urge to be with him, then that would surely be apparent by now, after all their paths had crossed on numerous occasions, virtually every week for that matter, plenty of opportunity for a relationship to blossom, if that was the course fate intended.

Sarah looked at Ben, studying his face as if scanning the pages of a book, skim reading the words thrashing around in the turbulence of his mind. He had recounted exactly the same story as his mother had done the day before, no details left out, no stone left un-turned, in short, he had told her everything.

The crumbs of her biscuit fell to the floor, her head tilted to one side, her eyes thick with worry and apprehension, that must have been a harrowing experience for him, a wretched story to convey, she thought to herself, mentally digging deeper into Ben's emotions, perhaps he had reached the end of his tether, the whole episode weighing so heavy and so intense, he was finally broken by it all, the thoughts and perceptions of others of little or no concern? What about his pride? Surely to goodness he must have some pride?

Sarah could feel a loud and lengthy argument raging in her mind, her brain mentally battling it out with itself. Yes, of course he had his pride, she concluded quietly to herself, and it wasn't his fault that his mother had an affair, it wasn't her fault that her husband had driven her to it through his lack of attention, his lack of loving, and understanding, making their marriage almost impossible to stomach, virtually forcing her into the arms of someone else, smiling to herself she recognised her loyalty to her friend, yes, there was only one side to that particular story!

Yes, he had his pride, but he had also had two days now to sort it all out in his head, put it all in some kind of order, and Ben wasn't the kind of person to harbour a grudge, she knew that. No, he would soon get things back into perspective, apply some logic to the situation, it certainly didn't feel like the sort of upset that was going to last long into next week, let alone forever.

Finishing her coffee, Sarah tried to put herself into Ben's shoes, her parents had been happily married right up until the death of her father, three years ago from pancreatic cancer, yes, they had been very happy, she was sure of that, and had no reason to think otherwise. On his death, her father had left the both her and her mother very well provided for, neither of them would suffer the incumbency of any form of employment again, his business wound up and a small fortune deposited into the bank.

Sarah smiled to herself, no, Ben was fine, just fine, gazing into his eyes, she could feel a warmness running right through her body, she took his hand, and gave it a squeeze.

Instantly they both stood up. Ben rested his hands on to her arms, holding them just above the elbow, he could see her chest moving in and out, up and down, as she breathed more heavily. Suddenly her arms were around his neck, her fingers running through the hair on the back of his head, he could feel her firm breasts pressing against his chest. He looked down at her face, her eyes fixed on his, burning with passion, a fire raging uncontrollably, flames of lust and desire inviting and enticing him closer. Their lips touched, he could smell her perfume, taste her breath, he could feel her tongue chasing his, finally he heard a small groan as the two tongues collided, the contact sweet and delicious.

Chapter 15
Saturday

Moving around restlessly in his bed, the alarm clock bleeping incessantly at him from the bedside table, his heart sank as he put the pillow over his head in a futile attempt to try and escape the ear-piercing shrill. Finally capitulating, he reached out and silenced the noisy timekeeper.

Midday, and the morning had positively dragged itself by, David was still in bed, hung over no doubt, Ben mused to himself, sitting up in bed, recalling the racket of the previous night, his older brother crashing about downstairs at just turned eleven o'clock, a combination of leaving the lights switched off so as not to wake up the house, and that good intention thwarted by his inebriated body's inability to negotiate the furniture scattered about around him, staggering and stumbling at every turn.

His parents were both at home too, and had spent most of the morning in the living room, in his father's case, every day was the same in the life of a retiree, and his mother very rarely worked on a Saturday, those shifts generally being taken up by children from the local Independent School, looking smart and feeling proud in their Windsor knotted ties, striped blazers and polished shoes, putting the hours in, ticking the boxes in their quest for that coveted Gold Duke of Edinburgh Award.

Yes, the family unit, once a safe haven, once renowned for its bliss, rapture, and time spent in common enjoyment, now seemingly dysfunctional, conflict and misbehaviour the accepted norm, and whilst its members' bodies were scattered all around the house, their minds were very much elsewhere.

Suddenly his phone vibrated, a text appeared on the screen. "*What are you up to today?*"

Sitting himself up on his bed, and slowly pressing the home button on his phone, Ben read the text for a second time. He didn't recognise the number, under normal circumstances he would have discarded it without a second thought, and just as he was putting the phone back onto the bedside table he looked at the text for a third time, pressing the message box with his index finger he replied, *"Who is this?"*

Almost instantaneously his screen flashed again. *"Sarah, silly!"*

Sarah? His feet crashed to the ground as he jumped up and off the bed, his dormant body exploding into life, as if ignited by an electric current, his arms the metaphoric jump leads, his mobile phone playing the part of the battery. The text a complete surprise, he sat, slumped on the side of his bed, his eyebrows distorted, his aching head resting between his hands, a pain in the very pit of his stomach, he must have ruined it, ruined everything, as he had on so many occasions before.

Suddenly he stopped, as if awakened from a nightmare, no, no he hadn't, he hadn't ruined anything. Looking at his phone, he thought about the previous day, recalling the events one step at a time. A second kiss, more intense and passionate, had followed the first, and then a third. Within minutes they were both lying on the settee, their naked bodies entwined, hugging, kissing, the curtains were drawn, virtually all light excluded from the room, their clothes scattered all over the carpet, like a teenager's cluttered and chaotic bedroom.

Ben held the phone in the palm of his hand, running his fingers along the side, yes, she had been as keen as he, telling him how two years of celibacy had left her feeling frustrated, graving sexual attention. In the end, they had both shared an equal amount of desire for each other, their bodies aching through sustained abstinence, sexual excitement built up quickly and very soon they were lying quietly in each other's arms, their bodies completely exhausted and spent.

Through years of texting, his thumbs moved effortlessly across the qwerty keyboard, within seconds three words appeared on the screen. *"Not a lot."*

Immediately he deleted them, the letters disappearing from the screen, his fingers hovering over the calligraphical characters, so neatly displayed in their little white boxes at the bottom of the screen, his heart thumping. Yes, she had been just as keen as him, she had wanted him just as much as he had wanted her.

"Not much! You busy? Do you fancy meeting up for a coffee?"

That sounded better, more information, but not too much, certainly no hint of guilt, and something she could respond to if she wanted. Feeling very pleased with himself, any anxiety quickly replaced by a confident swagger, and firmly pressing the white arrow in the green circle, he put the phone down on the bedside table.

Standing up, and suddenly feeling very agitated, he paced up and down, backwards and forwards around his bed, towards the window, towards his bedroom door. In an ideal world, he would have liked to have asked her out for a drink, a proper night out, on a proper date. But he didn't want to appear too pushy, too eager, take it slowly, one step at a time, he smiled to himself, anticipation and excitement flooding through his body.

"That would be great, half past one at the Narino be okay?"

Sarah's response had been almost immediate. A shiver ran down Ben's spine. He was buzzing, buzzing with the sort of excitement he had not felt for a long time.

"See you then!"

His mobile phone bounced up and down on the bed, as he threw it down, cursing himself under his breath for allowing so short a timescale, his over-excitement getting the better of him. In an instant, he was in and out of the shower, dressed, and closing the front door him, standing on the doorstep, fastening up his coat buttons, the wind biting at his ears.

In a vain attempt to keep warm, Sarah stamped her feet on the ground, standing outside the Café Narino, exposed to the elements, chilled to the bone, her eyes fixed on the pavement, shielding them from the bright sunlight finally breaking through the clouds, she lifted her head looking for Ben.

Sitting firmly on an emotional roller coaster, she didn't quite know how to feel, on the one hand, she simply couldn't wait to see him again, on the other, she was more than a little apprehensive, quietly cursing herself for being so forthcoming on the settee the previous morning.

Christ, what was she thinking about? How stupid she had been. Perhaps that was why he was so keen to meet up with her again, see if she was capable of keeping her knickers on for more than five minutes, Good God, he was a man after all. Suddenly she felt cheap, cheap and easy.

When a friendship between two people moves onto becoming a relationship, the course of events can often take a different path to that of two complete strangers connecting for the very first time and starting to date. Things might progress more quickly, common ground already established, it would be more than acceptable to omit some stages of the traditional courtship process, less of an obligation to observe subtlety and caution.

Desperately trying to keep a hold of that thought she squinted, her eyes blinded by the sunshine, the first strong rays of the late morning, gracefully warming up the space around her, she could just see the shadows of a pair of arms frantically waving in the air, waving back at them, she beamed, watching Ben approaching, getting nearer and nearer, finally taking the plunge, all of her reservations banished, she immediately locked her arm in his, and, in unison, they walked into the cafe.

Allowing herself a cheery little grin as the two of them joined the queue at the counter, and for a brief moment, she stared at her feet, mentally justifying the course their relationship had taken thus far. Smiling to herself, her gaze fixed to the dusty wooden floorboards, so far so good, she concluded, fast forwarding herself into the here and now, although she had not planned to have sex with Ben, well not before their first actual proper date anyway.

Her eyes sparkled as she raised her head to see Ben staring at her, his eyes totally fixated on her, her and nothing else. Turning her head, the smell of his cologne filled her nostrils she leant forward, and kissed his warm cheek, immediately he tilted his head, just a fraction, but enough, their eager lips met, suddenly she was not aware of anything that was going on around her, just the texture of his lips, the taste of his mouth, startled, she could feel the tip off his tongue seeking out her own, after the briefest of contact they pulled away from each other.

Smiling to herself as she turned away from Ben and faced the counter once again, the barista, a young lady in her twenties, with a metal guitar badge attached lopsidedly onto her blouse, one of the regular crew, her blonde hair now shorter, styled in a Pixie cut, grinning at her enthusiastically, totally oblivious to what she had just witnessed, no inkling of the significance of that brief and yet passionate kiss.

She had served them both before on numerous occasions, knew their drinks and how they liked to take them, but she had no idea of how the two of them had ended up together this morning or anything of what had gone on between the two of them in the past twenty-four hours, with pudding served up long before the main course had even left the oven.

"Hot chocolate and a latte this morning, Sarah?"

"Yes please, and, for a change, we'll have two muffins as well please."

Ben smiled at Sarah. Her brown hair trapped in between her coat lapel and her scarf, her slim shoulders, again, she was wearing a short skirt, allowing him clear sight of her shapely legs, her face beaming. She had given off all the right signals all right, and he had picked them all up. She looked gorgeous, stunning, looking around the café, and much to his satisfaction, he concluded that there was nobody else there in her league, he thought to himself, as he rested his left hand on her shoulder, and whispered in her ear.

"Tell you what, Sarah, I'll go and grab us a couple of seats, somewhere quiet, you bring the drinks across, okay?"

Sarah nodded enthusiastically as she watched Ben walk over to the corner of the café, picking out two of the leather arm chairs tucked away in the corner, out of the way, it would be nice and quiet there, they could talk properly. Yes, he would have his usual latte, and she would have her regular hot chocolate, but that was where the normality ended, this morning was different, very different indeed.

Arriving at the table, carrying a tray laden with the drinks and two raspberry and white chocolate muffins, Sarah allowed herself a wry smile, as she sat down, acknowledging her little piece of extravagance.

"So, how on earth did you manage to get hold of my mobile phone number?"

Ben opened the conversation, leaning back on his seat, breaking a piece off his muffin, the question wasn't just an ice breaker, he was genuinely intrigued. Taking a sip of her hot chocolate Sarah paused before answering.

"Anna gave it to me, after you stormed out of the shop, just in case I wanted to give you a call, a mother's intuition, I guess."

For the next two hours, they sat, sunk into the soft brown leather chairs, gazing across the small round table at each other, the plate smeared with raspberry jam, sprinkled with sugar crystals, and two empty mugs, a testament to how engrossed they had been in each other's company.

Both had been keen to avoid the subject of money and paternity, and, mercifully, that topic did not come up in conversation anyway, Ben preferring to focus on his work and his ambition, or rather lack of ambition in that department, Sarah chatting about her mother and how they were more like sisters than mother and daughter.

Nothing too deep and meaningful, nothing too heavy, not that any of it really mattered, the point was that they could talk, they could talk very easily. Yesterday they had ratified that they were physically attracted to each other, today they had ratified that they could hold a decent conversation with each other, for now, and at this stage of their relationship, that would do.

Playing with his empty cup, and watching the lunch time rush getting underway, Ben could feel his phone vibrating in his pocket. Frustrated by this unwelcome interruption, and rolling his eyes as he took it out, he looked at the screen, it was a text from his mother.

"Where are you? Please can you come home straight away."

Holding the phone out at arm's length, he allowed Sarah to read the text. She scanned the message without passing comment, the expression on her face giving nothing away, but she knew that it must be something very important. She had told Anna that she was meeting Ben that morning, she hadn't told her all of the details as to exactly what had happened in the front room of the house, but she had made a strong indication of her intentions with Ben, Anna had been thrilled, the thought of one of her sons forming a relationship with her best friend appealing very much. No, there was no way that Anna would have done anything to jeopardise Sarah's chances of getting together with her youngest son, so it had to be something important, and Ben needed to leave immediately.

Standing outside the café, they hugged each other, tightly, it was as if just holding was not enough, both craving the safety of being cocooned, wrapped in each other's arms, melted together into one.

Ben gazed into Sarah's eyes, he had not experienced the bond he felt now for as long as could remember, a mutual bond of love and devotion, a mutual desire and commitment, a mutual attraction, he had found his soulmate, yes, he was in love, and he was deliriously happy. Sarah, her arms still locked in his, gazed into Ben's eyes, as if magnetised by the thoughts she could read behind them, and felt exactly the same.

"I'll text you," smiled Ben, finally releasing her and standing back at arm's length.

Sarah smiled back, squeezing his hand tightly before letting go, they set off in opposite directions, both of their arms suspended in mid-air, as if handing over an invisible baton, each allowing the other to set off and carry on with the next leg of their lives.

Standing in the hallway, unfastening his coat, Ben called out to his mother.

"Hi, Mum, I'm back, everything alright?"

Pink blotches covering her otherwise waxen white face, despair filling her eyes, his mother crept into the hallway. She hugged her son, clinging onto him as if her life depended on it, her red nose snivelling as she pressed it against his shoulder.

"What's wrong, Mum? What's the matter? Where's Dad?"

She lifted her head, her bloodshot eyes gazing into his own, and replied, her voice barely a croak, barely auditable.

"Your dad's gone out with Stephen. Please stay here, Ben. I don't want to be by myself. I just couldn't bear it."

Chapter 16
Sunday

Looking up at the ceiling, her mouth dry, and her head pounding. Anna put on her woollen dressing gown, its patch pockets still stuffed full with last night's dried up tear-stained tissues, and made her way gingerly down the stairs and into the kitchen, her hand shaking uncontrollably as she reached over to place a highball glass under the cold tap. A glass of water and two paracetamols to the better, she sat down, her head resting on the table, her eyes closed, recalling the events of the previous afternoon and evening.

Ben had stayed with her for an hour and a half in the afternoon, and what a grim hour and a half that must have been, she filling the house with gloom, the wretchedness of her life, all hope now abandoned, his consolation, a nervous hand gently placed in to hers, very welcome, but not making the difference she had hoped that it would.

The evening had not improved after Ben had left, for she had sat staring at the television screen, eating a breaded ham sandwich with homemade hot mustard piccalilli, not exactly a feast fit for a king, by seven o'clock she had opened a bottle of Pinot Noir, an hour and a half later she was battling with the corkscrew, frantically opening a second.

Reg hadn't come home until gone eleven, tucked up in bed, the walls and ceiling wafer thing, she had heard him as he struggled taking his key out of the front door, falling over, resting at the foot of the stairs, the carpet finally deadening the sound of his raucous footsteps. She shivered, the cold water finding the shortest course down her throat, sitting back in her chair, she quietly moaned to herself, the glass returned to the table, her hands covering her eyes, shielding them from the morning sunlight as it forced its way in through the gap in the net curtains.

Reaching out for her glass of water again, she sighed, her family breaking up in front of her very eyes, both physically and emotionally, the dead cells of her relationship with Bill had grown into a tumour, a malignant tumour that was now invading the lives of everyone, spreading to every family member.

More effort was required she concluded to herself, and, resting her hands on the table, she pulled herself up from the chair, climbed the stairs, un-dressed and got into the shower. Once out of the shower, she stretched her arm out through the steam, and grabbed one of her favourite fluffy white bath towels from the radiator, and dried herself down, picking out some underwear from the drawer, she glanced across at Reg, fast asleep, as if in a coma, turning over, lying diagonally in their bed.

She smiled painfully to herself, sharing a bedroom with Reg was like sharing a carpenter's workshop, with every breath the sound of a saw ripping through the grain of the wood, the grumbling, grating sound of his snoring that had been a part of her life for the past thirty years.

In the living room, caressing her cup of tea, the rages of her hangover finally soothed by the steady flow of liquids and hot buttered toast, humidifying and fortifying her parched body back to life, she sat, alone, listlessly thinking. Suddenly she jolted, rudely aroused from her lethargy, she muttered to herself.

"Christ, is that it then. Thirty years of marriage, two children, and what am I left with? An empty house, an empty relationship, and an empty cup of tea."

Smiling at the irony, put her cup down onto the small round table, and stared out of the window. The stairs vibrated under heavy footsteps, the brief silence that ensued broken by Reg's voice calling from the hallway.

"I'm just off to get a paper."

Listening to the front door closing behind him, Anna nodded her head, she knew exactly what that meant. He was off to get a paper, and he would come back and spend the next two hours pretending to read it. A loveless, empty relationship, void of conversation, in fact void of any form of intercourse.

Letting out a long, deep, heavy sigh, as much filled with discontentment as it was frustration, she looked at her watch, it was almost eleven o'clock, another pointless, motiveless day was quietly passing her by. Shaking her head vigorously she jumped out of her seat, her body suddenly refreshed and strengthened by an unseen force, an invisible source of energy.

No, she was not prepared to sit by and let everything she had worked for all of these years implode into the abyss, she was going into battle, battle to save her marriage, battle to save her family. Five minutes and a very successful conversation with the very efficient lady at the other end of the telephone, she had successfully secured a booking for a table of six for half past one at the London Road Inn.

Scrolling down her list of contacts, she continued with her work, texting furiously, an individual invite to each person, that should do it she smiled. She had just finished texting Sarah, when she heard the front door opening.

"Thought we might have lunch at the London Road Inn today love," she called out.

"That sounds nice," Reg replied, his voice unenthusiastic and non-committal, his attention evidently more focused on filling the kettle with water than on listening to what his wife had to say.

You could have heard a pin drop, the two of them sitting side by side in the car, Reg his hands stuck to the steering wheel, his eyes fixed onto the road, Anna's were closed, her mind, mercifully, a million miles away. The hour drive to the London Road Inn was going to feel like a lot longer than that she thought to herself, turning her head towards the passenger's window, totally preoccupied in her own meditation.

How could things possibly be so different to the way they were just seven days ago? Why did Bill have to leave all of that money to Ben, just Ben, why couldn't he have shared it out equally between the both of them? She'd asked herself that question a hundred times now, and was still yet to arrive at a satisfactory answer.

Ben had come home to see her yesterday, but had only stayed for about an hour or two, having left very shortly after that to re-join Sarah. They'd obviously spent the rest of the day and night together, in the privacy of each other's company, at least some good had come from all of the turmoil, a small consolation she mused, allowing herself the smallest of smiles.

What about David? He had moved out on Saturday, he needed his own space he had told everyone, as if that would solve all of his problems, put everything right, nevertheless he had moved into Daniel's apartment, and would be staying there for the foreseeable future.

The car turned sharply into the car park, Reg battling with the steering wheel, having missed the right hand turn as he had on so many occasions before, rudely awakening her from the sanctuary of her musings. She looked across at her husband, not a word had been exchanged between the two of them for the past hour, perhaps their own marriage had reached its own journey's end as well.

Waving his key fob in mid-air, Reg locked the car door and followed Anna across the tarmac, politely holding the door open for her, ducking under his arm, she entered the pub.

The London Road Inn was a grand old building, almost five hundred years old, and resilient enough to have survived a number of different guises in its lifetime. Originally a manor house, before being converted into a very exclusive and expensive Prep School, then, much later in its history, renovated back into a much-adored family home by a merchant banker who, exhausted by twenty-five years of burning the candle at both ends working in the City, had taken early retirement. For the past decade, it had taken up the position of a pub and restaurant, filled with nooks and crannies, private dining areas, a library, as well as outside terraces and gardens, its character and numerous complimentary reviews on the internet attracting patronage from both near and far.

Anna had booked the long table in the library, comfortably seating up to eight people, surrounded by floor to ceiling oak book cases on two sides, providing an antiquarium to the considerable number of leather-bound hardback books that covered the shelves.

Walking ahead of Reg, Anna ran her hands along the shelves of the book case as she turned into the library. Her eyes sparkled as she thumbed through a vintage copy of The Tenant of Wildfell Hall, Anne Bronte's second and final novel. With no inclination of familiarising herself with its contents, despite there being more than a small degree of comparison with those and the tale of her own life, she just held it to her nose, and simply enjoyed the earthy, woody smell of its tainted pages.

Her face, a picture of pleasure and happiness, was filled with satisfaction, this had long been her venue of choice for special occasions, and whilst today was not extraordinary in that there was no birthday, no anniversary to celebrate, the bonds that kept their family together, so fragile and delicate at the very best of times, were in desperate need of solidification and if that wasn't a special enough occasion to warrant such a luxurious setting, then surely it would be almost impossible to find one that was.

Sitting diagonally opposite to each other, Ben and Sarah had already staked their claim at the table, their coats carelessly discarded over the backs of their chairs, two glasses of red wine in front of them. Acknowledging their presence with little more than a nod, and squeezing Anna's arm, Reg headed off into the direction of the bar, Anna seized the opportunity, rushing across to the table, and taking up the seat next to her youngest son.

"Thank God you two are here," She exclaimed, her voice filled with relief.

His face turning so crimson it could almost have been better described as purple, Ben smiled sheepishly, his body half turned away from his mother, he could barely bring himself to make eye contact. Last night he had shared her bed with Sarah, it was her breakfast table he had sat at this morning, drinking her coffee, enjoying her freshly baked croissant, gazing into her eyes not his mother's, and it felt awkward, it felt embarrassing. Anna could sense her youngest son's discomfort.

"Lovely seeing you two looking so happy," she said, leaning across, and giving Ben's arm a gentle, re-assuring squeeze.

There was little in the way of purchase on the polished dark wooden surface, and Reg's elbow slipped ineptly as he leaned over and ordered a pint of bitter and a soda water. He had already taken the executive decision that Anna would be driving home, and that he would be needing an anaesthetic of alcohol to help him through the afternoon. Placing Anna's drink clumsily in front of her, a quarter of its carbonated contents spilling out and flowing across the table top like a narrow stream of effervescent lava, he made his way to the other side of Ben, and sitting down, he took a long sip from his pint glass.

Taking a breather from guzzling his beer, he caught sight of David, striding confidently in to the library with Daniel struggling to keep up behind him. David paused, his mind quickly digesting the seating plan, allowed Daniel to catch him up and take the seat next to his mother, seating himself at the very end, a safe distance from both of his parents. Anna and Sarah shared a menu, their excited fingers jabbing at the luxurious laid paper, whilst Reg gazed miserably into his pint glass, which was already empty.

"Drink anyone?" he called out across the table as he got up from his seat.

"I'll have a pint please, Dad, and one for Daniel too."

Approaching the bar, Reg rolled his eyes at the queue of people waiting to be served. Taking his place behind a large man, in his late sixties, with thin grey hair and black framed spectacles, his eyes scanning along the beer taps for a second time, his enthusiastic gaze once again coming to a halt at the Flowers Bitter, a nice pint, dark, flat and very quaffable he muttered to himself, holding a twenty-pound note in his right hand. Turning his head, he looked over his shoulder, his eyes resting on his family, what a shame his own life wasn't as agreeable as the beer, he muttered under his breath, exhaling heavily in a long depressing sigh.

His torment continuous for a quarter of a century, the knowledge that his youngest son was actually that of another man, but the love for the women he had married making confronting the truth unthinkable, but the money had changed all of that, now everyone would know, could he live with that?

By way of escapism he had spent most of Saturday playing golf with Stephen after which the latter had helped the former drown his sorrows at the Club House, the perennial Nineteenth Hole, but there was no getting away from it, he couldn't bury his head in the sand forever, his face filled with resignation, he returned to the table with a tray of drinks.

Handing the drinks out to the eager recipients seated around the table, their arms stretched out like the branches on an oak tree, and fixed his gaze onto Anna. His own wife who had sought her sexual pleasures with another man, he being unable to give her the satisfaction she wanted, she casting the net further afield, trawling liquor shops for gratification, Christ, wasn't that shame enough for any one?

His eyes ran up and down her slim legs in their black leggings and knee length boots, past her waist, her tight black jumper excepted the slimness of her midriff, the fullness of her breasts, he could feel himself stir, the insatiable lust that has existed throughout their marriage, yes, despite everything, he still found her attractive.

But was that enough? He was in his fifties, with two good decades of life still ahead of him, did he really want to spend those with her? Quietly growing old and frail together, supporting each other through the twilight years. Did that sound as appealing now as it did when they first got married, their whole lives ahead of them?

Sitting down, he took a large mouthful of beer, licking his lips, and breathing a heavy sigh, no, he wouldn't walk away, he couldn't walk away, he had too much to lose, and besides, he still loved her, despite everything, he still loved her. Leaning over he touched Anna's hand.

In the back ground the prelude of Bizet's Carmen was streaming through the restaurant. Temporarily intoxicated by the music, Anna was nodding her head vigorously to the fast and playful time marking, at each symbol clash her eyes resting on a different member of the party in turn, her family, her friends.

Unexpectedly she found herself mulling over Carmen, was she really any different from Bizet's femme fatale? She was married to Reg, of course she was, but aside of that had her behaviour really been any different, any better? She smiled to herself, thankfully she had not stirred up enough jealousy to meet a similar end, well not as of yet anyway.

Reg's hand felt warm and sticky, there had only been the slightest of contact, more than enough for her to recognise the intended sign of affection, but, with all that had passed between them, had she got the energy, the strength left to reciprocate? It seemed likely that Reg knew all of the details: What had happened, when it had happened, and with whom it had happened, if they were to survive the pair of them would have to live with that, there was no turning back now after all. The unpredictability she was finding more difficult. One minute he seemed happy, content with what they had, holding her hand, looking at her with the affection of old, next minute he was forcing himself on her, in a passionate rage fuelled by half a bottle of scotch.

The icy chill, so evident in their relationship on so many occasions before, had reached sub-zero temperatures that morning, the truth was they hadn't exchanged a word between since leaving the house, and now, all of a sudden, he was touching her hand, wanting to be husband and wife again. Making a personal inspection of herself, Anna ran her eyes down her own body, she was wearing her black leggings and black jumper, and why, because she knew that they flattered her figure, she knew that Reg liked her in that outfit.

A tear welling in her eye, she realised that she loved Reg, he was her husband, so, of course, she loved him, she always had and always would. She could feel the sexual tension as she looked deeply into his eyes, running her fingers around his palm. No, the marriage wasn't over yet, they would survive this, she would make sure of it.

Scanning the rest of the occupants sitting around the table, her eyes lit up as they fell onto Ben and Sarah, the both of them head over heels in love with each other, a shimmer of light amidst all of the darkness. Holding her gaze, she mused, ever since she had become friends with Sarah, she had secretly hoped that one of her boys would manage to win her heart. She was especially pleased that it was Ben, yes, he would treat her better than David would, she told to herself quietly through her own thoughts, for some reason she had some real doubts about how David might treat a girl, he just seemed to be the sort that might be inclined to take more that he was prepared to give in a relationship.

Rotating her glass of soda water between her fingers, she frowned as she recalled the disturbing rumours about David and that Tanya from the Cross Keys, glancing across at her eldest son, she concluded that that would keep for another day.

Focus on Ben and Sarah, she told herself, yes, he would make a perfect husband for her, and she a perfect wife for him. She looked again at Reg, would their story have a happy ending? She hoped so, they had invested some much time and energy into their marriage, but only time would tell.

Ben had always been the more sensitive of the two brothers, and that split second of physical contact between his two parents did not pass him by. He smiled to himself, his mind running at a hundred miles as hour, processing what he had seen and what it might mean. Was that subtle touching of hands an attempt to resuscitate their love for each other? Was it that their marriage might survive this latest crisis? He hoped so, after all if there was to be a wedding, he would want both of his parents there, sharing in his happiness together, taking their places of honour at the top table, side by side.

Turning his head, he looked at Sarah, his face star-struck, hypnotised by her smile, in the past thirty-six hours he had not been able to get her out of his mind, his brain processing emotions that where both new and exciting, taking hold of her hand he squeezed it, drawing her more closely to him, he hugged her tightly, he wanted her near to him now, and forever.

Turning his attention to Daniel, Reg beamed as he shook him keenly by the hand.

'Thank you for taking David off our hands'.

'My pleasure, Mr J, my pleasure,' Daniel replied with equal enthusiasm.

Unable to take his eyes off Ben and Sarah, his lips so tightly closed there was a danger they might turn blue, scowling at the pair of them, David surveyed the scene from his vantage point at the head of the table, his arms stretched out on either side, his fingers drumming on the polished wood.

So, they had got it together, the pair of them, he silently fumed to himself, his own personal obsession with Sarah taking over, consuming his entire body with unwelcome sexual urges, yes, he had quite fancied trying his luck with little miss goody shoes, see if he could knock the halo from off her head. She would keep, he would get his chance with her, maybe sometime in the future, and, when he did, he'd show her a good time, that was for sure.

Looking his brother up and down his thoughts were not as convivial, overshadowed by a sense of jealousy and envy, unfamiliar, alien contemplations previously not experienced through their normally close relationship. The money and now Sarah, both were starting to grate on him with equal infuriation.

With a similar amount of distaste, he switched his gaze over to his mother, covering her with his scorn, he could see exactly what she was doing, wearing that outfit to try and win his father back, she knew how much he liked her in it, it would probably do the trick as well, he was always so proud of her slim figure, God, he was such a loser, he tutted to himself.

Suddenly his mind drifted back to the previous evening, and a big smirk covered his face. A trip to Tanya's house late in the afternoon had proven to be more opportunist than he could have possibly hoped. Good fortune on his side, her sister having taken the children out for the day, allowing Tanya's sordid little mind a free reign.

"Let's make a film for the website, please let's make a film for the website."

The sound of her voice, high pitched through over excitement, echoed in his head as he took a large sip from his glass, sloshing the beer around in his mouth, a vein attempt to extinguish the fire that burnt in his bright red cheeks, quietly smiling to himself as he recalled her enthusiasm, fully immersing herself into their increasingly hedonistic world. Even more aroused and animated than ever before.

Drowning in her own thoughts, Sarah privately sized up each family member, this was the first formal occasion where she had seen them all together since she and Ben had become an item, and it felt more than a little strange.

She felt the familiar warm glow as she briefly glanced sideways at Anna, her work colleague, her friend, her confidant, no further attention required in that department.

Facing forward again, her eyes fell upon Reg, sitting on the other side of the table opposite to her, his beer glass but a quarter filled, an empty one beside it, his chin resting on his hands, his grey beard wisping through his wrinkled fingers, his face a picture of misery.

Tilting her head, she gazed at him sympathetically, a broken man, his retirement plans shattered by the unwanted events of the past, his mind crowded with far too much uncertainty for a man who should be enjoying the golden years of his life.

Suddenly she recalled her conversation with Anna, no, he only had himself to blame, he had driven his poor neglected wife into the arms of another man, staving her of the attention she craved, the attention she deserved, turning her head, her eyes rested on Anna again, she was slim, she was pretty, she was sexy, how could he possibly have let her slip through his fingers.

Fixing her gaze onto her best friend, Sarah mentally re-enforced her assessment, she was quite unable to allow Anna to shoulder any of the blame for her little indiscretion, driven to her infidelity on the man she had married, the man for whom she had vowed to forsake all others, but who had been such a disappointment she had been left with little or no other option. Yes, the problems in their marriage started and ended with Reg, his shortcomings, his limitations, the fundamental flaws in the man would have made a happy marriage impossible right from the start, she was special, he barely adequate.

All of that cleared up to her satisfaction, taking a deep breath, she leaned forward and looked across at David, sitting at the head of the table, his body permanently turned towards Daniel, awkwardly facing away from his mother, unable to make eye contact with her.

Christ, she wouldn't want to be in his shoes. What on earth might be going on in his sorry little mind? Surely, he was the one who had lost the most in the past seven days. Completely ignored in Bill Williams' will, his parents' marriage now exposed as more than a bit of a sham, his brother, now not his brother, Jesus, how must he be feeling right now? surely, he must be slowly and painfully being driven into destruction.

Leaning further forward for a closer inspection, she looked into his tired but angry eyes, his glass almost empty, the first pint dispensed with rather too quickly, drowning his sorrows no doubt, she quietly ruminated to herself.

Her sympathies short-lived, she deliberated on how very uncomfortable David made her feel, he was ambitious, too ambitious, and not in a nice way either, he oozed confidence, but not in a way that made you feel safe around him, and he was always looking at her, eyeing her up and down, top to bottom, and not in a way that was attractive, in fact it made her squirm.

She had heard a rumour that he might be seeing that Tanya from the Cross Keys, well, at least that's what Ben thought. Good grief, anyone living within a ten-mile radius of the Cross Keys knew Tanya's reputation, she caught men with her long legs and see through blouses, imprisoned them with her sexual prowess, and then, once she was tired of them, discarded them like a piece of litter.

Mellowed by the red wine as it passed through her lips and into her mouth, Sarah leaned back in her chair, slowly turning her head into the opposite direction, and the relative security of her now boyfriend and lover.

Still feeling very pleased with herself, despite the cloud of tension hanging ominously over the table, Anna looked over her glass and across the table to Daniel.

"You're very brave, taking David in, Daniel."

"No problem Mrs J! A friend in need, and all of that." Daniel flashed an encouraging smile back.

"It's only for a time, Mother, just whilst I get myself sorted out."

David retorted, his attention immediately returning to his beer glass.

"Well, we're certainly not going to complain about having some extra space about the house."

Reg's contribution, a vein attempt to inject some humour into the conversation, whilst very much appreciated by his wife, did little of nothing to improve the situation, in fact, to describe the hour that followed, painfully filled, as it was, with awkward and truncated conversation, each member of the party treading on egg shells, each one not wanting to ruin the occasion, as almost impossible would have been perceived, quite fairly, as merely a generous act of charity.

His eyes resting on the empty glasses, Reg clumsily left his chair, his unsteady legs impeded by the excess of alcohol. Anna smiled, he was making an effort, doing his very best, there could be no criticism levelled in that direction, despite his excessive drinking. Frantically she motioned to Sarah to go and join him.

Their shoulders pressed hard against each other as they joined the throng of people standing at the bar, joining forces, each of them trying to attract the attention of the young man in the bright red jumper. He was young, not even in his twenties, with long brown curly hair and large tortoiseshell spectacles, his eyes scanned the crowd from behind the thin piece of polished wood no more than two feet in depth separating him from them.

Them being the rest of the endless flow of people on the other side, each and every one with a thirst to be quenched, each trying to make sufficient eye contact to secure themselves pole position ahead of the other, numerous, eager customers, leaning over the bar, ten, and twenty-pound notes in their hands, a declaration of the authenticity of their purpose.

Reg put his arms around Sarah's shoulder, protecting her as he skilfully negotiated his way to the front and rested his elbow on one of the damp beer towels, staking his claim at the head of the queue.

Balancing four pint glasses, two in each of his enormous paws, like a seasoned juggler, Reg returned to the table, with Sarah, his understudy, on a similar mission, but managing just one glass of wine in each of her own smaller, more delicate hands, hot on his tail.

Peaking over his father's shoulder as he stretched out his eager hand, carefully taking hold of the first pint glass of the quartet, as if guided by a sixth sense, David's eyes managed to pick out a couple sitting down at one of the small tables, ever so slightly obscured by an inconvenient pillar, deep in conversation, it was Craig and Tanya.

Instinctively, Tanya looked up, her eyes meeting with his, but not in the time-honoured way, her gaze making its way across the ubiquitous crowded room, forcing its way through the seating area, barging past any one inconveniently positioned in the intended line of travel, no, there was no such thing, there was no romantic notion with this particular connection, with Tanya immediately lowering her head, turning her chair away and back towards her more immediate companion.

For his part David returned his attention to his pint glass, his face was a white as a sheet.

Mixed emotion filled Anna's face. Having spied Tanya over five minutes ago and had hoped that, from where he was sitting, David would not catch sight of her himself, as that would certainly undo all of her plans for the afternoon. A smile flashed briefly across her face, was Tanya with her boyfriend? Perhaps the rumours hadn't been true after all and David had managed to escape the vile clutches of that evil, disgusting young lady.

Ben's elbow just managed to avoid a collision course with Sarah's left cheek, as he encompassed her with a loving arm, giving her a hug, he looked deep into her eyes, thanking his lucky stars that amidst all of the tension, all of the strain, and contrary to everyone else present in the room, he had somehow managed to find the secret to what felt like eternal happiness.

David's lips were contorted into an awkward smile, but his eyes were playing a different tune, unable to betray his true feelings, desperately trying to contribute to the sweet music, but unable to find the right key. As vigilant as he was in trying to concentrate his full attention on his family, there was an equal and opposite force dragging his attention away from them and back across to Tanya and Craig, pulling his reluctant eyes over into their direction.

He could feel himself stir as the outline of Tanya's shapely backside in her tight leather trousers flashed into his line of vision, a split second later both of the chairs were empty, instinctively his eyes followed the wall around and turned towards the two blue doors with brass handles leading to the toilets, the old wound still open and festering.

Suddenly a sharp tap on his leg made him jolt, Daniel sensing that his friend was distracted taking it onto himself to restore some essence of order.

"Come on mate, forget about those two, you're here with your mum and dad, remember, give them a break, for goodness sake."

Shrugging his tired shoulders, David looked at his friend.

"You're right, yes, of course you're right, sorry, mate."

Anna smiled to herself as she looked at her watch, it was half past three, she glanced around the table, metaphorically acknowledging each person in turn, discreetly patting herself on the back for a job well done.

The party, happily gathered around the table, Reg, David, Ben, her very own family, her best friend Sarah, and of course Daniel, God bless Daniel for taking David in tow. The whole of them, sufficiently fuelled with alcohol, the atmosphere laced with horseplay and ribaldry, in front of them their soiled, empty plates a testament to how much they had enjoyed the food, hungry appetites satisfied by the gastronomic delights set before them, yes, everyone was happy, yes, lunch at the one-time manor; Sutton Hall, had been an emphatic success.

A second, more discerning glance at her watch appeared to have an immediate effect on the people around her, suddenly, glasses were raised, emptied, and replaced onto the table, telephones carefully returned to coat pockets and handbags, the plates stacked up, each on top of the other, and carefully maneuvered towards the centre of the table, the knives and forks carefully balanced on top. Anna beamed at everyone, pride irradiating from her face.

"That was lovely, thank you all very much for coming."

Helping Sarah put her coat on. Ben grinned, affectionately, at his mother, a real tenderness in his smile.

"Our pleasure, Mum, we've have had a lovely time, makes a very pleasant change from the Narino."

"Yes, thanks a lot Anna, it was really nice to come here for a change, we haven't been here for a while, I'd quite forgotten how nice it was."

Sarah added, with equal enthusiasm.

Taking a brief and hurried look over his shoulder at his mother, the busy, efficient waitresses having already cleared the table in front of him, David had already tucked his chair safely away under the table, his coat draped over his arm.

"Thanks, Mum, thanks, Dad, see you all later."

A wooden chair crashed to the ground as he bumped into it, vacating the premises at breakneck speed. He didn't look back again, not for a second, not even to acknowledge Ben and Sarah, and he was totally oblivious of Daniel running after him, shrugging his shoulders apologetically at Reg and Anna.

In the meantime, Reg squeezed Anna's hand, leaned over, and gave her a peck on the cheek.

Chapter 17
Monday

The crumbs from the stale garage forecourt breakfast muffin fell onto his open laptop, nestling irritatingly between the keys, threatening to disappear from view completely as he sat gazing out of the window, his lukewarm latte, in its totally inadequate double walled paper cup, growing colder and more unpleasant by the second.

His office a rented space, just one room in a featureless building, on a lonely cul-de-sac in a faceless business park, was just ten minutes from Daniel's apartment. It was small and it was cold, positioned neatly on the slate grey carpet tiles were a cheap, boxy desk, a black swivel chair and a small light grey metal filing cabinet with three drawers.

Leaning back on the chair, David looked around the room, taking in the plain white walls, surveying the evidence of damp in the corner opposite to the door, discoloured patches on the otherwise unpigmented vertical surfaces, it was a grim, soulless place. The blank screen of his laptop offered very little in the way of respite, and the dark clouds of despair were soon descending, as if every time he paused, even just to catch his breath he was engulfed by a feeling of self-doubt, a rude reminder of just how miserable the previous week had been.

He blinked his eyes, his eyelids twitching involuntarily, and the unsettled sky immediately above started to clear, there was work to be done, and he was never going to make anything out of his life until he got on with it. Reluctantly he made a start, and, with the face of someone coming to the end of a ten-hour shift in one of the most monotonous jobs in the world rather than a man running his own business, he opened his emails, one by one, reading and digesting the content. Five and a half hours, and the first leg of a one-hundred-and-fifty-mile round trip completed, he was shaking the warm sweaty hand of his final client, gazing at his watch as they parted company.

Sitting in his car, he checked his watch once again, good, traffic allowing, he would be home by four o'clock, he smiled to himself, turning the key in the ignition and pointing the front of the car right and onto the main road, his nails vibrating as he quietly played a tune with his fingertips along the rim on the steering wheel as he drove patiently along the road.

Cruising along at fifty-five miles an hour, he reflected on the morning's work, a few more of those and he would very soon be buying himself a new car he teased himself, quite unable to hide the grin that covered his face. The further he drove, for every mile he clocked up, another hundred pounds miraculously found its way into his mental bank account, forty miles into the return journey he was adding revenue from the website, twenty-five miles after that he was moving out of Daniel's apartment and into his own.

The handbrake ratcheted into position, he gazed absent mindfully across at the other stationary cars, all compliantly lined up together with his own in front of the red traffic light. Suddenly, as if from nowhere, the familiar feeling of self-doubt crept up on him again, unwelcome and unwanted, like a grumpy old neighbour gate crashing a house party and turning the music down as everyone in the room had just started to dance, frowning to himself he contemplated the five thousand pounds he had invested in the website.

It was a huge amount of money, and there had been a niggle in the back of his mind ever since he had handed over that envelope filled with wads of cash to Craig, someone, incidentally, he barely knew, the torment continued silencing the jolly tune on the steering wheel, replacing by a vice like grip and a mournful melody in his stomach.

Speculate to accumulate, he mused to himself, desperate to lift his spirits, surely it was perfectly normal to be injecting that sort of money into a project, par for the course really, just good business. Try as he might, however much he struggled, he couldn't quite convince himself, still couldn't quite rid himself of that nagging doubt in the very back of his mind.

His leather messenger bag fell to the floor with a quiet thud, the old-style wall clock, its face protected by dark mahogany surround, was announcing the advent of the sixteenth hour of the day as he stuck his head around the door of Daniel's small, compact study.

"Drink and some food?"

Closing his diary, Daniel slowly looked up and acknowledged his friend's presence.

"What a splendid idea. I'll just grab a quick shower and we can be on our way."

By mutual agreement they had both made the decision to regale themselves with a decent session down the pub at least once a week, they had been firm friends for so many years now, and it would be a shame not to at least try and recapture those elysian days, time squandered drinking and eyeing up women. Ten minutes later they were standing in the hallway, Danial grabbing his coat and punching his code into the alarm panel.

"Let's go down to the Cross Keys, leave the car here, I fancy a pint or two of that Doom Bar. We might see that bird of yours as well, if we're lucky, very easy on the eye she is."

David laughed as he took a cigarette out, struck a match, and, cupping his hands lit it up.

"Leave it out, you're just jealous mate."

"Too right I am, and I bet I've got plenty to be jealous about, I bet she knows how to use that body of hers, mind you, has she anything else to offer, other than being bloody good in bed?"

Striding confidently long the broad pavement, David looked across at his friend. Tanya was attractive, in a sex sort of way, and was definitely bloody good in bed, as Daniel had so aptly put it, but was she anything much more than that? Was she really the type of girl he should be associating himself with right now? Was she the type of girl who would have the sort of friend that he should hand over five thousand pounds to?

Tension growing, adrenalin pumping through his body, David could sense his step quickening, the length of his gait leaving Daniel struggling to keep up. You've got to be prepared to take risks, live life on the edge, he told himself, no more pussy footing around, Christ he needed to make his mark on life. So, no, Tanya probably wasn't the type of girl any one in their right mind would want to settle down with, or even have anything to do with, but he had a certain level of control over her, a level of control that thrilled him, a level of control that intoxicated him.

The classic rock ballad, its chorus reverberating around the empty bar, failed miserably in generating anything that could be remotely construed as an atmosphere, and so, at six-thirty, the Cross Keys felt like a miserable place to be.

Without the distraction of the usual swarm of paying customers it looked a very different place too; a thick layer of dust appeared to have attached itself to a number of the picture frames, there were tears in the cheap imitation leather covers on more than just one or two of the seats, the dado rail, designed to protect the wall from the furniture, was itself in urgent need of attention, the white gloss paint chipped, and flaking away.

With Tanya conspicuous by her absence, disappointment written all over both of their faces, they got on with their allotted tasks, David leaning against the bar, ordering two pints, two steak and chips, and a plate of onion rings for the table, Daniel grabbing one of the small tables by the window. By seven o'clock they were halfway through their second pint, making short work of the food, served up on two generously sized white plates in front of them.

David cut into his steak, the serrated blade of the wooden handled knife effortlessly completing its allotted task, he fidgeted as he chewed the tender meat, his body made restless by his anxiety, agitated by his investment, five thousand pounds was an insane amount of money, he kept saying to himself, over and over, and to be investing in something you don't really know very much about, and, even worse, with somebody you don't really know very much about either. A piece of steak hanging precariously off the end of his fork, he stopped eating and looked up from his plate.

"If I told you that I had made a bit of an investment, what would you say?"

A couple of peas skidded off Daniel's plate as his fork fell from his hand.

"An investment? What sort of investment, how much have you invested, and with whom?"

David hesitated, he could hear the alarm in Daniel's voice. Scooping up the rogue former pod dwellers up from off of the floor, he looked earnestly into his best friend's face. This wasn't the first time that he had got himself involved in something not all together above board, and he knew that Daniel was well aware of that, but, having taken the plunge, and it was too late to stop now.

Three quarters of an hour and a pint and a half later, he had told Daniel everything. His relationship with Tanya, his savings account now lighter to the tune of the five thousand pounds he had invested into the new business, his partnership with Craig, someone he had only met once, a friend of someone with whom he was having a relationship that, at best, could only be described as casual.

Finally, he talked about the website, his gaze fixed to the table, unable to look his friend in the eye, his voice barely auditable, as he described the seedy, grubby details, of, perhaps, the most debased of his conceptions to date. Daniel looked at David, shaking his head in dis-belief, his face a ghostly white.

'For Christ's sakes David, you idiot, you stupid fucking idiot.'

His face red with embarrassment, his mouth uncomfortably dry, David looked up at Daniel, but there was no rage in his companion's eyes, no anger in his voice, just concern, the real, genuine concern, of a good friend.

Chapter 18
Monday

A beam of aureate light forced its way through the narrow gap in the bedroom curtains, its brightness temporarily blinding Ben. Stretching his arms as he swivelled his body out of bed, he glanced over his shoulder and across at Sarah lying next to him. The smile that filled his face was one of pure, unadulterated happiness, yes, he was in love, love and lust, lust and love, the best of both worlds. Suddenly he felt a warm touch on his knee, Sarah's bare arm, outstretched from under the covers, urging him back into bed.

"Don't get up just yet Ben, not just yet."

He gazed at her intently, she was leaning on her elbow, the covers thrown back, her nakedness enticing him to take another bite of the once forbidden fruit. A second invitation was not necessary, and twenty-five minutes later and they were both lying on their backs staring breathlessly at the white ceiling. Within an hour he was showered, dressed and once again standing in front of his girlfriend, totally captivated by the sight of her au naturel.

"Where are you going now?"

Tilting her head, she flashed a smile. Ben rolled his eyes, nodding his head.

"Now? Back home, I guess, to see how Mum and Dad are this morning. I could sense they were putting a bit of an act yesterday, covering up cracks, if you know what I mean?"

Sarah beamed at him, once just her friend, now her lover.

"Yes, I wonder how your parents are this morning? You're right, they were acting a bit strange yesterday, not their usual selves at all, it was almost as if they both desperately wanted everyone to be happy, you know, trying to keep the family together, I suppose. Do you think that they can save their marriage now, after all that's happened?"

Hopping about awkwardly on the polished wooden floorboards, his leg suspended in the air bent at the knee, desperately trying to line up his right shoe with his right foot, Ben replied.

"I don't know, Sarah. Dad loves Mum, I know he does, and she loves him, she must do."

"Oh, yes, she loves him, she definitely loves him."

Sitting at the end of the bed, Ben shook his head.

"I know, I know, but is love going to be enough? It all happened such a long time ago, that business with Bill Williams. Christ, I can't even bring myself to call him my father, but it still happened, Sarah, it still happened. I just wish we could do something to help, I couldn't imagine them not being together."

Fully dressed, Sarah sat down on the side of the bed next to Ben, shuffled up right next to him, and put her arms around him.

"Oh, come on, Ben, my love, they just need the time and the space, they'll sort it out."

Gazing into Sarah's eyes, Ben gently kissed her hand, her optimism, her lust for life, each was as infectious as the other.

"Well they've got the time, they've got all of the time in the world, just as long as they want to use it."

Her feet almost slipping from underneath her, Sarah jumped off the bed, her voice suddenly filled with excitement.

"Okay, they've got the time, so why don't you give them the space they need to? Of course, of course. David has moved out, so, why don't you?"

Ben smiled at Sarah, a wye smile filling his face.

"Move out! Where to?"

Her reply was instantaneous. "Well into here, stupid, move in here, with me!"

Ben smiled, both at Sarah and to himself. A short week ago, his life had felt so mundane, not to the point of unhappiness, but certainly complete indifference. All of a sudden, and taking him completely by surprise, it was moving at a hundred miles an hour, so fast he could barely keep up with it, out of nowhere he had the chance to move out of home, and move in with Sarah, it all felt too good to be true.

His own happiness making him feel guilty, his mind turned to his parents, especially his mother, would they really be able to sort things out if he wasn't there to remind them that it was all worth the effort? David had already flown the nest, but would it be just too much change in too short a period of time? That was their problem, he quickly concluded, he had his own life to lead now, and he certainly wasn't going to mess up any of his dreams of a life with Sarah just to save his own parents' marriage.

"Are you sure? I mean that would be brilliant, perfect. For me and you I mean, not for my parents, not just to help them sort out their problems, I mean."

Placing her index finger onto her lover's dry lips, Sarah retorted.

"I know exactly what you mean, and yes it would be perfect."

Having carefully and successfully negotiated the steep staircase, ten minutes later Sarah returned into the bedroom carrying a wooden rectangular tray with two large red mugs of steaming coffee and a plate with four slices of buttered toast. For the next hour, they sat on the side of the bed talking, like two teenagers, ten to the dozen, each anxious to have their say, each desperately trying to impress the other.

There was no need to wait, they concluded very quickly, they were old enough to know when they were in love, and yes, they loved each other, they loved each other very much indeed. Eventually they both stood up, Ben carried the tray downstairs, left it in the kitchen, and ushered Sarah towards the hallway.

"Now, I really must go Sarah."

"I know."

Sarah purred as Bens soft lips made contact with her left cheek, twenty minutes later he was standing in the hall of his parents' house.

"Good morning, good morning."

He shouted, closing the door behind him.

Stumbling about in the darkness, not wanting to switch on any of the lights, Ben stood in the hallway, smiling contently to himself, for whilst downstairs it was completely silent, upstairs was not so still, Sarah might be right, perhaps there was some hope for them all to cling on to after all.

Wearing an ironic smile, a dressing gown, and obviously nothing else, his mother came downstairs, her face positively glowing, squeezing his arm she shuffled past and into the kitchen, filled up the kettle with water and switched it on. A minute later steam was erupting from the kettle, the heat acting as a warning to anyone careless enough to come too close, Ben turned to his mother, two mugs in one hand, a couple of tea bags in the other.

"Do you want a cup of tea, Mum?"

Wrapping her white cotton dressing gown tightly around her naked body, desperate to maintain some level of decency, she shook his head.

"Actually, I thought we might go out for breakfast this morning?"

"What a good idea."

Reg shouted, bounding down the stairs two at a time, like an impetuous school child.

"I could do with a proper cup of coffee. Good morning Ben."

"Yes, definitely."

Anna spoke under her breath, the past eighteen hours had given her some hope, hope sufficient in quantity to allow for some confidence in what the future might bring for her family. For now, that was more than enough to keep her going.

Ten minutes later, the kettle standing cold and neglected in the kitchen, both had showered, dressed, and successfully managed to position themselves into their normal seats in the front of the car, with Ben un-ceremoniously shoe-horned into the back.

Reg smiled eagerly at the young lady standing behind the counter, one person's acquaintance often another's stranger, for she was aged about twenty years old, with short blond hair, wearing a short black leather skirt over her thick black tights and a white blouse decorated by the metal guitar badge pinned onto her chest. A student on a gap year earning the cash to finance a once in a lifetime trip to South East Asia, perhaps Thailand, Vietnam, Cambodia, exotic destinations ticked off her bucket list before embarking on a life in the workplace arena, Reg mused to himself, feeling every one of his fifty-eight years as he turned away from the counter, two lattes balanced in one hand, a skinny hot chocolate in the other.

"So, how are you this morning Ben?"

Anna asked, squeezing her son's hand, moving Reg's chair out for him, as he approached the table, the young lady following closely behind with a tray filled with two smoked bacon-in-soda bread rolls, and a croissant, flashing a familiar smile in Ben's direction. Brown sauce oozed out of the bacon roll as Ben took his first bite, the sweet taste of Applewood smoked bacon, a combination of both back and streaky rashers, it was his favourite and he chewed it slowly, enjoying the taste before replying.

"Very well thank you, brilliant in fact, and I bring some news."

"News?"

Reg responded immediately, wiping the crumbs away from the corner of his mouth. Ben smiled tapping his father's arm with his finger-tips.

"Nothing bad, Father, don't get yourself in a state. No, actually it's good news, very good news indeed. I'm going to be moving in with Sarah. I know it's quick, I know we should slow down, but…"

"That's wonderful news!"

Beside herself with excitement and unable to contain herself, Anna interrupted Ben mid-sentence. This was exactly what she wanted, what she had wanted for the past four or five years, one of her sons, one of her sons finally leaving home and settling down with a young lady, good God it's taken long enough, and with someone as adorable as Sarah as well, perfect.

"I agree, fantastic news, pleased as punch!"

Reg chipped in, slapping his youngest son fondly on the back.

Turning his head from side to side, Ben regarded his parents, first his mother, then his father, sitting together, grinning like a pair of Cheshire Cats. He looked up, suddenly, Sarah was standing over the table.

"How on earth did you get here?" Ben cried out.

Nodding at Anna, making a texting motion into the palm of her hand with her fingers, Sarah rolled her eyes, laughing. The drinks vibrated as Anna caught the edge of the table in her eagerness to embrace her closest friend, and, throwing her arms around her, almost squeezed the life out of her.

"It doesn't matter how she got here, she's here, and she has made me happy beyond my wildest dreams. Oh, come here, and let me give you a hug."

"I'll get you a hot chocolate, Sarah."

Reg gave Sarah's shoulder a squeeze as he walked past.

"Are you happy, Anna? I mean are you really, truly happy?"

"Yes, very much so."

Anna smiled, her arms seemingly locked around Sarah's shoulders.

Gazing at them both intently, Ben could not help but afford himself a smile, the two women in his life, he had grown much closer to his mother in the past week, the trauma of the events strengthening the bond between them, and at the same time, his relationship with Sarah had progressed so quickly, one minute they were friends, the next they're lovers sharing the same bed. Quite remarkable.

"So, what are your plans? The two of you?"

Reg asked, leaning over and placing Sarah's drink on the table, where she had sat herself down in between Anna and Ben. Ben looked at his father, his face suddenly serious, his voice considered.

"Well, I'm going to move in with Sarah and her mum, just for the moment. We're going to start looking for a place of our own fairly shortly to be honest with you, probably next week."

Resting her hand on to Ben's arm, Sarah concurred.

"Yes, we were thinking about having a look at those new apartments, do you know the ones I mean, on Waterslee Road?"

"Those new ones? The ones that were only finished last month? They're absolutely gorgeous! Oh, Reg, how nice is that."

Anna was in her element now.

"Yes, they're all finished now, and the show home is open. It's brilliant, you get to choose your own kitchen and bathroom. Do want to have a look with me Anna?"

Her face beaming, Anna turned to Sarah.

"Of course, I'd love to."

Anna and Sarah were soon engrossed in conversation, stoking up each other's fire, words coming out ten to the dozen, meanwhile Ben picked up his chair, repositioning himself next to his father. For his part, Reg had been married too long and knew better than to try to involve himself in the conversation with Anna and Sarah, the invitation was unlikely to be extended beyond the two them, and he had to content himself with that, and, looking towards the ceiling, he lifted his cup to his lips and took a long sip of his coffee.

Staring at his father rather too intensely, Ben mused, he was so conventional in so many ways, there must be tens of thousands of men out there just like him, in their late-fifties, retired, married with two grown-up children. Nothing too complicated about any of that, but life could never be completely void of complexity, and sometimes the entanglements can be too much, even for someone with that much life experience under his belt.

His map and chart life had been on an even keel for so many years, or at least so he had thought, then, suddenly, two pieces of news, one immediately following the other. A legacy, money suddenly in the family, well for one member anyway, more cash than they will ever use, or need, but along with that a feeling of greed and ambition, enveloping them all like a still mist over a stagnant pond. Next, a bombshell, so explosive that would rock the foundations of any family, shake it to the very core, an infidelity, a betrayal, marriage vows shattered, trust broken, perhaps beyond the point of repair. Embarrassment and shame will have surely followed very quickly on after that, leaving a tension, an uneasiness, that has brought the whole family close to breaking point.

His open hand outstretched, Ben smiled coyly at his father.

"A new beginning, a fresh start, something to look forward to, all of us, the whole family, what say you, Dad?"

Closing his tired eyes, Reg smiled, his favourite poem coming readily to mind.

"Be thankful you're living and trust to your luck, and march to your front like a soldier."

His eyes still firmly closed, he sighed heavily, yes, that was right, march to your front like a soldier, there was nothing else to be done.

"Yes, son, a fresh start, sometimes everyone needs that."

Clasping his son's hand, and, taking it into his own, he shook it firmly.

Chapter 19
Tuesday

Sitting down at the kitchen table, Anna frowned as she studied the two empty chairs tucked away gathering dust underneath the table, neither of them likely to see the light of day anytime in the foreseeable future. She had not slept well the previous night, tossing and turning, her head fit to burst with information, her mind whirling around at a hundred miles an hour, struggling to get to grips with the fact that in the space of just forty-eight hours both of her sons had, without giving any prior notice, left the family home. Now there was just her and Reg, alone again after all of these years, their marriage gone full circle.

Ben's circumstances she was more than happy with, he had fallen in love, head over heels in love in fact, with her best friend, a bright and beautiful young lady, they obviously had genuine feelings for each other, feelings that ran deep, feelings that felt like they might stand the test of time, financially they were well set up, Sarah having plenty of money of her own, so Ben's legacy was not going to be a significant factor, whether he decided to accept it or not. Good luck to them both, she smiled to herself, the satisfaction of good parenting written all over her face.

Suddenly a frown covered her face, like rain clouds spoiling a summer picnic, the early intermittent raindrops getting more persistent, the prospect of a positive thunderstorm on the horizon as she flipped the coin over, for there was David, and a lot less to be jovial about.

The charity shop had long been renowned as a gathering place of the elderly, somewhere they could meet for their morning repast of gossip and tattletale, and the rumourmongers were very vocal right now, talking endlessly to Anna about her eldest son and how he was dating, for want of a better word, a single mother of two children a full ten years older than himself, who served drinks behind the bar at the Cross Keys wearing tight leather trousers and leopard skin blouses that really didn't leave very much to the imagination. All of this she knew, but it still felt like a dagger to the heart every time she could sense those fingers pointing in her direction, those sympathetic glances at the cash register reminding her of the shortcomings of her family.

The time had well and truly come to awaken herself from the sense of denial surrounding her eldest son as on top of all of that, and even more perturbing if that were possible, one of the regular customers, someone she knew well and could be relied on, had seen David engrossed in conversation with someone who they did not know and did not like the look of, a male, in his mid-forties, who looked more than just a little shifty. The same man who had sat opposite Tanya at the London Road Inn on Sunday perhaps? She mused, her mind in overdrive. Of course, he had lots of clients he met through business, she knew that, but she also knew that he never carried out his business in local pubs or coffee shops, preferring to use his own rented office space.

In the way of a consolation prize she was grateful to be able to find some comfort in the fact that he was now living with Daniel. Good old reliable Daniel, she had known him for almost twenty-five years now, he was like a third son to Reg and herself, both of his parents having died when he was very young and him spending virtually his entire childhood living with his grand-mother, with Anna's role more that of a distant aunt than of a friend's mother. Yes, she knew Daniel very well, she knew where he lived and she knew that he could be relied on to talk to her, should David get himself into any kind of trouble.

Her face filled with resignation, her eyes switched from left to right, and right to left, transfixed onto the two empty chairs, no, the time had come and she had to let them both go. They were both old enough to make their own decisions, negotiate their own path along life's whirling merry go round, make their own mistakes, learn their own lessons, she had done her best for them, perhaps it was time to just let them get on with it.

The small table creaked under the weight of her elbows, yes, it all sounded so uncomplicated, so simple, her two sons all grown up and left home, very simple indeed, turn the page and get on with the next chapter. Recalling her own life, had that always been so uncomplicated and simple? Had she always learnt from her own mistakes?

Marrying Reg had certainly been one of her better decisions, she knew that, well she did now. But what about earlier on? Did it feel like such a good decision then? If that really was the case, why had she felt the need, the desire, to have somebody else? Why couldn't she have been content with just Reg? Why had she found it so difficult to be faithful to him? Granted, he was working away from home so much and that wouldn't have helped, but that was only during the week, only five days out of the seven, they had still had the weekends together, so why had it been so difficult for her? Had it been the company she craved, the attention, or just the sex? Or all three? Probably it was all three, she contented herself with that, it didn't sound quite so shallow.

The lonely table clear and tidy, its empty surface wiped spotlessly clean, the dirty plates and cups neatly lined up in an orderly fashion in the dishwasher, Anna put on her coat and gently closed the front door behind her. Reg was already in the driver's seat, sitting bolt upright as he always did, his eyes already fixed on the road, despite the car not having actually pulled out of the drive yet.

Taking her usual place in the passenger seat, she gazed at her husband, it would not be too long before he turned sixty years of age, she mused to herself with a gentle smile, noting that his beard was not especially well kempt, mentally adding the bottle of beard oil she had seen in Arnold's, with its promise of the magical properties of a combination of hemp, argan, and bergamot oils, guaranteed to rejuvenate even the most bedraggled set of whiskers, to her shopping list.

His clothes coming under closer scrutiny, she concluded that some additions to his inadequate wardrobe would certainly be advantageous, his being the sort of clothes that were generally left in cardboard boxes or black plastic bags in the doorway of the charity shop, generously donated by the wives of men a good ten years his senior.

She could feel her neck straining as she looked awkwardly down into her lap, her hands joined together, her fingers interlocked, he was all hers, and had been for more than three decades, for better or for worse, for richer or for poorer, she loved him, she always had and probably always would. So why had she had let him down so badly? He deserved so much better than her selfishness and faithlessness, he was a kind, loving man, who had shown her nothing but love and devotion throughout their marriage, he deserved much better, he did back then and he certainly did now. There was no turning back the clock now, what's done is done. Why it had happened was not important, not now anyway, one thing was for certain, it did happen, it was her cross to bear, she had to live with it.

The passing cars on the other side of the road were becoming more blurred as Reg accelerated along the by-pass, looking out of the passenger window, Anna's agitated cogitation continued.

Whatever had been missing from their relationship then was certainly not missing now, of that she was sure, they had built a good life for themselves, financially they were secure, they owned their own property, they had two sons, two fine lads, no grand-children as of yet, although that position may yet change given the relationship between Ben and Sarah, she checked herself quickly, reeling in those thoughts before she cast her line of fantasy out too far, no, she was happy, incredibly happy, and wouldn't change anything for the world.

Her elbow pressed hard against the interior of the car door, her head in her hand, she quietly cursed Bill under her breath. He had written to her on numerous occasions during the time immediately after Ben's birth, ardent epistles, handwritten leaves of paper burning with both passion and rage, begging, almost demanding that she took him back.

Flattered by the kind words of affection, she had kept the letters for months, squirreled away in a cardboard box, right at the very back of her wardrobe, carefully hidden under some old copies of the Sunday Times, reluctant to let the memories fade away like the words on the brown, dried up, newspaper, but even they were long gone now, put out with the rest of the rubbish, the inevitable refuse that litters every life.

She had thought, she had hoped, that she might get away with the indiscretions of her past, for this was a bed made up over twenty years ago, redundant for so much time, the sheets undisturbed, covering over the fabrication and falsehood. Well, she was certainly lying in it now, and every time she turned over she was smothered with more guilt, plagued by the prospect of more inquest and inquiry.

Seemingly oblivious to all of this angst and torment, Reg successfully turned off the by-pass and negotiated the small roundabout. He was never especially chatty when he was driving, preferring to remain in silence, giving all of his attention to the road and the other road users. This limitation, prevalent for much of their marriage, was not without a degree of selfishness, for it allowed him some time for deliberation, and for the past fifteen minutes, he had been deliberating about nothing else but Anna.

The seemingly impossible metamorphism from un-faithful wife to loving mother and head cornerstone of the family didn't just happen overnight, bringing up their two sons, the passing of years, a certain contentment with life that comes with age, all of these will have contributed. But how long had it taken? How many indiscretions had there been since Bill Williams? Equally important, how many had there been before that? And how much did all of that matter now anyway?

The perennial debate raged in his head once more, pestering and persecuting, battering his exhausted mind, On some occasions, he found that he could forgive and forget Anna's affair with Bill Williams, accept that it happened a long time ago, far too long ago to be of any relevance now, accept that, possibly, he just might have been partly to blame for what happened, perhaps he was away from home too much, perhaps he just hadn't given her the kind of attention she wanted, the attention she needed.

Pressing his foot gently on the brake pedal, he eased the car to a halt at a zebra crossing, the front bumper a good yard in front of the vertical black and white stripes, courteously he waved across a young family, a mother holding her two toddlers tightly by the hand, their lack of road traffic awareness pricking her maternal instincts, before making his way back up the gears and pulling away.

On other occasions, it was a different story completely, more anger, no, stronger than that, more fury and resentment, she had betrayed him, and by betraying him, she had betrayed their marriage, the whole basis of which was built on trust, and once that trust had been broken, could it ever be repaired, properly restored, or would it always just be patched up, mended, but weakened by concessions and compromise?

Was she so naive to think that his life had been totally free of opportunity, bereft of temptation? His eyes gazing over the prohibited garden fence of life and love, only to find someone looking back in his own direction? His hand tightened on the steering wheel as his mind drifted back almost a quarter of a century ago.

Inevitably, and as was often the case back then, his work had taken him away from home, almost six months working on a project right up in the north of the country. Karen was managing one of the main contractors, and they had spent much of the first week discussing timescales, reviewing resources and cost headings. By mid-way through the second week conversation had extended beyond the workplace, they were openly flirting with each other, having ascertained that they were staying in the same hotel.

As the project progressed so did the intensity of their entanglements, and very soon they were meeting up in the small intimate hotel restaurant, just six quiet tables and enough seating for no more than fourteen, enjoying a glass of wine with their evening meal together, both making excuses for having to go their own way by eight o'clock, each sensing in the other a reluctance to bring the night to an end.

Throughout the weeks that followed the flirting became less subtle, less discreet, a kiss on the cheek at the start and at the close of each day, dining together virtually every evening, touching each other at every opportunity, hugging each other shamelessly in the restaurant before going their separate way.

With the job drawing to a close, they met in the restaurant, as usual, for their evening meal. The food eaten, they gazed at each other across the table, as if two teenagers in love, only they were adults, not children, each of them old enough to know not to encourage the other.

"Shall we go into the bar?"

Reg had regretted making that invitation ever since, re-living the moment over and over, his stomach cramped by the dull ache of guilt of a man who dared to crave the forbidden fruit, and paid the price for it later.

"Why not."

It was almost mid-night when they finally found themselves alone in Karen's room, a bottle of wine between them, and a brandy each already under their belts, the hotel was fast asleep, the bar closed, the glasses washed up and racked away ready to do it all again tomorrow, the bar tender already safely home and tucked up in bed.

As they stood opposite to each other, his mouth suddenly bone dry, Reg could feel his stomach churning, the sexual tension, just a fantasy, just a game, a happy distraction in the restaurant, rapidly becoming very real now that they were alone in the bedroom. The buttons at the front of her white silk blouse were un-fastened, his eyes travelling involuntarily down from her face, past her slim neck, until they rested at her breasts.

Looking him straight in the eye, she took his hand and placed it onto her breast, squeezing his fingers and pressing them hard against her heaving chest, dropping his hand she stepped back, lifted the hem of her skirt and removed her knickers. Stepping out of them awkwardly in her high heeled shoes, she took his hand again and placed it in between her legs, he could feel the warmth and dampness of her naked crotch.

Suddenly he froze, blood draining from every part of his body, Karen, so sexy, so erotic just a second earlier, suddenly revolting and repulsive, her open blouse, her underwear lying in a heap on the floor, so seductive, so ravishing, now cheap and disgusting.

Frantically, he pulled his hand away from hers, mumbling an apology, pushing his way passed her and towards the door, he fled from the room.

Free parking and a café were probably the main draw for the small garden centre on the outskirts of town, Reg sat still, his arms stretched out in front of him, his hands on the steering wheel, the car stationary, the engine still running.

"You alright, love?"

Gazing across at her husband, Anna's voice was filled with concern.

"Fine, I'm fine."

Turning away, he recoiled, quite unable to look his wife in the eye, the unwelcome memories of how nauseous he had felt that next morning flooding back, packing his suitcase, taking one last look around his hotel room before finally closing the door for the last time.

In the small restaurant his own work colleagues, sitting around the large oval shaped table in the bay window, breakfasting together, debriefing each other, the job done, everyone ready to head back home. How happy they all were, smiling at each other, laughing and joking, content with their simple lives, no complications, nothing to agonise over, they could return to their husbands and wives, tell them how much they had missed them, tell them how much they loved them, enjoy something to eat together, everything back to normal.

How stupid had he been, all those weeks of playing an emotional, dangerous, game, creating an image of Karen in his mind, this image, this picture, where she was everything he had ever wanted, perfect in every way, flawless in every aspect of her shape.

He remembered reading in a book once that being married made a life of deception absolutely necessary, well, not for him it didn't, for he had spent the whole of the Monday back in the office riddled with guilt, peering around his computer screen looking for sly glances, heads discretely turning in his direction, the knowing nods of a secret revealed.

Turning the key and removing it from the ignition, he rested his forehead on the hub of the steering wheel, yes, he'd had his moments of weaknesses, and yes, he'd had opportunities, but he had never crossed the line, never allowed temptation to get the better of him, not once, not ever.

Maddened and infuriated by his own insecurities, perhaps it really was finally time to unburden himself of this debilitating anguish, this mental abuse, the psychological torture that had burdened his mind for over two decades.

Looking at Anna, his eyes tired, his face drawn, his shallow cheeks twitching, his haggard body sapped of all its strength, he ran his hand through his grey hair, and sighed, no, even after all of that, he simply hadn't got the energy.

"Shall we have a cup of tea love?"

He sighed, opening the car door.

Chapter 20
Wednesday

A quartet of regulars had already positioned themselves at the bar, each jealously guarding their own particular place along the wooden counter, hard-core punters, heavy drinkers, the condition of their respective livers a secondary consideration to their habits, according to the large round clock behind the bar it was barely midday and yet each was already well into his third pint.

Just past the hour Reg ambled in, joining the masses, nodding at each in turn, the easiness of familiarity. He ordered two pints of bitter, no Tanya this afternoon, Stephen will be disappointed he smiled to himself, as he picked up the two pints of beer and shoving the change into his jacket pocket, carried them over to one of the small tables by the window.

Looking up from his glass, Reg paused.

"How you doing Stephen?"

Suddenly overcome by a raging thirst, he hadn't waited for Stephen to arrive before taking his first sip.

"Very well mate, very well indeed," Stephen replied, catching up very quickly, drinking almost a quarter of his pint in one mouthful.

"I've ordered us both a steak and chips, is that okay mate?" Reg added, the question was rhetorical.

Stephen nodded his head in agreement. Fifteen minutes later, Stuart, the pub manager of twenty years, short, balding, fifty years old, the size of his stomach a testament to his dedication to the brewery industry, his slow pace and wide steps an effect of his obesity, arrived at their table skilfully carrying an outsized tray with two plates of piping hot food and two more pints of beer.

No Tanya today, Stephen sighed to himself as he nodded his approval at the rotund landlord.

Picking up a slippery chip that had fallen onto the table, dislodged by his enthusiasm in attacking the steak with his knife and fork, Reg looked earnestly at Stephen. By tradition, the Wednesday lunch time drink was an occasion reserved for ribaldry and ridicule, peppered with trips down memory lane and a running commentary of life in general.

However today he had something more serious to talk about, not that the two of them were alien to the occasional serious conversation, a problem shared and all of that, for the past twelve hours he had been deliberating, with some difficulty, as to how he was going to broach the subject.

With two empty plates sitting on the table in front of them, the both of them clutching their fourth pint, and, doing his best to keep his voice as nonchalant as he could manage, he finally took the plunge.

"Do you ever wander about your marriage Stephen?"

"What do you mean by that?"

It was more of a splutter than a reply, the question leaving Stephen both surprised and intrigued at the same time. Reg pressed on.

"Well, does anyone really know what is happening in their marriage? Can anyone be absolutely certain what their partner is up to? In fact, make that past and present tense. You know, if their partner wanted to keep a secret, or even lead a sort of double life, it wouldn't be that difficult, would it?"

Putting his pint glass onto the table, Stephen studied his closest friend's face intensely, taking in every detail, his eyes were slightly bloodshot, perhaps through lack of sleep, his mouth, thin lipped and unsmiling, an aggravated frown creased his forehead.

"I guess that would depend on what sort of secret are we talking about? Is it money? Trouble with the police? What sort of double life are we talking about? Infidelity? Job loss? A secret love child?"

Taking a slow deliberate sip of beer, Reg hesitated, he hadn't anticipated this level of enthusiasm, but fortified by his friend's level of attention, he continued.

"Oh, I don't know, what about money? Let's say that your wife had taken out a credit card without telling you, and had racked up a load of debt, say a debt north of say five thousand pounds, just from buying clothes, shoes, things that you probably wouldn't noticed she had bought?"

Chuckling under his breath, Stephen allowed himself a quiet smile, if Anna had gone out and spent a small fortune buying a wardrobe full of new outfits, then, no, Reg probably wouldn't have noticed, still he persevered with the conversation.

"I don't know, I think it would be difficult to hide that amount of clothing from your husband, even you Reg! Mind she could buy some expensive jewellery, you know, and keep it in a box on her dressing table? Anything bigger than that, say a new car, or something like that, well, you would notice that straight away, wouldn't you?"

Nodding his head in agreement Reg paused, he had certainly got his friend's full attention, it was time to start the conversation proper.

"Yes, yes, I see what you mean. Okay, how about something more serious, what if she had been seeing another man? Again, this could be in the past or the present, it doesn't matter, but could she hide that from her husband? If so, how?"

Leaning forward, more intrigued than ever, Stephen's eyes locked onto Reg's face, studying every detail, every line, every wrinkle, this wasn't the sort of topic of conversation he would normally have indulged in, not on a Wednesday lunchtime, not at any time for that matter.

"Difficult to say really, that's a different question entirely, spending money and having an affair are two completely different propositions."

Leaning forward over the table, their foreheads almost touching, his expression more intense than ever, Reg responded, "Well, of course they are. We've both heard of lots of people who have had affairs, so we know that it goes on, you read about it in the paper virtually every day of the week, and twice as much on a Sunday, but what about normal couples, not your celebrities or film stars, surely it would be much easier for the wife on the street to hide her indiscretions from her husband? I mean if she was really careful, he would probably never find out, would he? Answer me that question, and, while you're at it, answer this one as well, why would she bother in the first place?"

Finishing the last of his beer, and ceremoniously resting the empty glass carefully on to the table, Stephen placed both hands on his hips.

"Okay, let's break this down, let's take the man first and then the woman, shall we? Right then, what would make a man want to cheat on his wife or girlfriend? Surely this has got to be all about sex, hasn't it? If he isn't getting enough at home perhaps, or maybe his wife has let herself go a bit, you know, put weight on, that sort of thing. Or even he has just got bored with his sex life, maybe there's someone new started at his work, or working at the pub, like that Tanya for example, and he wants to try some of that action for himself?"

Stephen eyes fixed to the ceiling, mentally undressing Tanya, his sordid little mind working overtime.

"Yes, yes, I can see that, you're probably right with all of that, now let's move over to the wife or girlfriend, what would make them cheat?"

The words had been flowing freely and easily and Reg's abrupt interruption had not gone totally unnoticed, Stephen's response was slow and deliberate, his voice philosophical.

"I think that women would be in part very similar, but at the same time very different."

"What do you mean by that?" Reg probed.

"Well, for a woman sex is not just a physical thing, is it? No, women are much more complicated than that, aren't they? There's more going on in the mind. A woman wants her man to be attentive, wants her man to look after her, take care of her. It's almost like continuous foreplay, if you like, without it, you can forget about having any sex."

The last remnants of his pint almost completely disintegrated at the bottom, Reg played with his empty glass, turning it, first clockwise and then anti-clockwise with his finger-tips.

"You're probably right. Sure, you read about these girls and their sexual appetites in the papers, but that isn't real, is it? No, definitely, women are much more complicated than that, sex is not such a simple thing for them."

Stephen's eyes twinkled as he picked up the two empty glasses and stood up.

"That's right, they are. Mind you, if you take a look over there, yes, perfect timing."

Every part of Stephen's body appeared to be pointing over towards the bar.

"Now she, she might just be a different kettle of fish."

"We're not talking about her," Reg scolded.

His words fell on deaf ears, for Stephen was already half way across the room waving the two empty glasses in Tanya's direction, his eager gait powered with far too much enthusiasm. Flashing her most seductive smile, the one she saved for her most favourite customers, Tanya fluttered her eyes lashes as he ordered the drinks, his own gaze transfixed onto her slender neck.

Two fresh pint glasses in hand, Stephen placed his on the table, and, leaning over, he handed the other one to Reg, allowing himself one final leer, before finally sitting down.

"So, who exactly are we talking about?"

"No one, just a guy I used to work with."

Immediately cursing himself, Reg knew that was limp, it didn't sound remotely convincing, he muttered to himself, regretting that he had not put more thought into the conversation before-hand.

Captivated almost to the point of amusement, and enjoying his new role as the fountain of all knowledge, Stephen continued.

"Okay, so tell your friend this. If he isn't giving his wife the attention she wants, then she will find him less attractive in a sexual way, if you get what I mean. That will be made even worse if he isn't giving her the sex she wants either. At the same time, if she is getting that attention from another man, by that I mean that he is giving her the attention she wants, making her feel loved, making her feel special then, yes, she may well be tempted. Now, what would make that situation even worse would be if the man she is receiving all of this attention from was in need of attention himself. Let's say that he had some problems at home, something wasn't quite right in his life, well, this would make the woman feel that she was, well, wanted, needed, and this would make her even more attracted to the man, if you see what I mean. Of course, once the attraction starts, once she starts to fancy him, any shortfalls in her sex life will become an even bigger problem, and, eventually, she will start having sex with the other man as well."

"So, if you've got a woman who is being neglected at home, and she gets it together with a man who is happy to give her that attention, she may, will, be tempted? Tempted even to have sex with him as well."

Reg interrupted, seemingly seeking clarification at every juncture.

"Yes, that's about the size of it. Mind if you…"

"A half?"

Reg interrupted, again.

"Yes please, just for the road."

Whilst his voice was directed at Reg, Stephen's eyes were fixed on Tanya. God, there was a girl without much in the way of any form of complication, he mused, shuffling uncomfortably on his seat.

Her eyes sparkling, her mouth a permanent grin, Tanya was in her element, surrounded by her regular customers, the centre of attention, her electric blue silk blouse stretched to breaking point, the buttons barely able to hold the fabric together sufficiently to maintain even some order of common decency.

Standing deliberately away from the throng, Reg lent over the bar, the five-pound note felt smooth and greasy in his hand as he waited patiently for his turn, staring into space he sighed, a deep heavy sigh.

His work had taken him away from home for days, weeks, months at a time, so he couldn't possibly have given her the attention or the love that she needed to keep her sexually interested in him. Suddenly Bill Williams had entered into her life, he was there for her to talk to, to flirt with, and more than happy to give her the attention she wanted. That would have been how things started out, but it wouldn't have taken long before she had realised that she could make a real difference to his life too. He needed the love and attention that any man was entitled to, and yet he was lonely, living alone, going home to a cold, empty house every evening. Anna would have enjoyed the fact that she was making him happy, she would have enjoyed the fact that he needed her. He needed her, and she needed him, the sexual attraction, and the sex, would have soon followed. It couldn't really have been that simple, that easy, could it? Deep down he knew that, obviously, it had been.

"Two halves please."

Beer spilt over the top of the glasses and onto his hand as Tanya clumsily put the two halves in front of him. He handed over the five-pound note, motioned that she should keep the change, and trudged back to the table.

Chapter 21
Thursday

The seventy-mile drive back from a totally un-productive meeting with a new client had been littered with road works and speed restrictions, and by the time David arrived back at his office what little appetite he had for anything in the way of honest toil had all but completely disappeared.

The whole monotony of his work was starting to really grind him down now, the banal humdrum of meetings, emails, and his over familiarity of the country's painfully over-subscribed road network long since void of even the very elementary forms of enjoyment, let alone pleasure. Good God, the sooner he started earning money from of that website the better.

Sitting back in his chair, his arms stretched out over his head, he watched his MacBook Pro come to life as it dutifully accepted his password, leaning forward, he hovered the curser over the desktop, and selected the Safari icon. The cursor conveniently re-positioned itself into the browser, and carefully he entered the Uniform Resource Locator Craig had sent him via text message that morning. The desk shook, the cheap wood effect top vibrating as his clenched fist crashed down, a fourth attempt and none of the website keywords failing in proffering any results.

Perspiring profusely, he suddenly froze, his hands resting nervously on the keyboard, the magnitude of the situation becoming clear, panic starting to set in, all of the worst-case scenarios coming to mind at the same time, suddenly awake to the possibility that the website never existed in the first place, and the prospect that he had given up five thousand pounds of his hard-earned savings for nothing.

His heart beating faster, he could feel himself growing tense as that familiar red mist starting to descend once again, shrouding him in anger, cursing his misplaced judgement in handing over all of that money to a complete stranger.

Breathing in through his nose and out through his mouth he could feel himself calming down, and, his thinking more rationally now, concluded that the most constructive thing he could do was to find Craig and open his budget with him.

Pressing his fingers against his left temple, racking his brains, his own grey matter metamorphosing itself into a Global Positioning System, he set about pin pointing Craig's whereabouts. It was lunchtime now, and he knew that Craig hadn't got a job, well not a proper job anyway, just working cash in hand, running errands, and if what Tanya had carelessly let slip the other day was true, selling drugs.

Slamming the silver lid of his laptop down, the florescent lighting under the black keys immediately extinguished, he nodded his head slowly, recalling that Tanya had mentioned The Gladiator pub on a number of occasions in the past, his face suddenly a picture of self-contentment, a riddle posed and solved.

The Gladiator, positioned in the middle of a housing estate, was a throwback to the nineteen eighties, sharing a car park with a convenience store open seventeen hours a day in the name of serving its customers, and with a reputation for selling alcohol to fourteen year olds, a fish and chip shop with an extensive menu including pineapple fritters and two varieties of curry sauce, and a unit to let, formally a hair salon, now open to offers to the next entrepreneur brave enough to invest their money in that rather unsavoury neck of the woods.

Within twenty minutes he was pulling into the car park, his hands shaking as he removed the key from the ignition, he gazed mindlessly at the banners draped over the steel railings along the front, advertising live Premiership Football and two for the price of one Sunday Roast Dinner deals.

Wooden wedges held the first set of double doors open, and David wiped his feet on the heavy-duty matting that led to a second set and into the pub. The sound of the music was deafening, a stark contrast to the noise of the conversation, that had fallen dramatically as he entered the lounge, all eyes momentarily fixed in his direction as he negotiated his way through the tables and chairs randomly positioned in between himself and the bar.

The décor was simple, a dado rail with grey wooden panelling sitting on top of the black laminate floor below, above plain white walls, and a television set attached to a bracket on the wall, tilted and swivelled for the best viewing.

The atmosphere was already hostile, thankfully the pool table with its quality blue baize, fifteen balls, seven red, seven yellow and a black, neatly arranged in a plastic triangle, made for the only impediment separating the bar from the fire escape, should a sharp exit be required.

The four burly men sitting at the bar barely batted an eye-lid as David edged his way clumsily past them, their identical bar stools lined up, each one's backside hanging out of his identical grey fleece pants, their half-soaked eyes fixed onto the television screen above the bar, the highlights of last night's matches seemingly more interesting than an uninvited stranger entering the premises.

Opposite the bar a horse shoe shaped seating area, upholstered in a geometrically patterned fabric of grey and dark blue cubes, with the additional luxury of a carpeted floor, completed the arena.

A brief scan around the room and very quickly David picked up Craig, sitting by himself on a tall wooden stool at the end of the bar, a half empty pint of lager and a packet of spearmint chewing gum in front of him.

"I want a word with you, mate."

"Davey Boy, what can I do for you?"

David's body stiffened, his whole being erect, he eyes focused on his prey, every muscle in his body tense, poised for action.

"What can you do for me? What can you do for me? I'll tell you what you can do for me, you can tell me exactly what's happened to our website, remember our little website, our little joint business venture?"

His stool rocking abruptly from side to side, Craig slid awkwardly down onto the dirty, grimy floor, clutching his pint of lager precariously in one hand.

"Okay, okay, but first let me get you a drink."

"No, thank you, let's just get down to business, shall we? I went on line this afternoon, about fifteen minutes ago to be precise, and guess what? Our website doesn't seem to exist. Now, tell me, what do you know about that?"

"It didn't work out, mate."

Craig's pint glass dangled loosely by his side, his voice calm and nonchalant.

"What do you mean, it didn't fucking work out."

David's voice, more strident, more menacing, reverberated around the bar, loud enough to attract the attention of more than just the handful of the drinkers in the bar, their heads surfacing from their beer, their glasses now discarded, pushed away to allow space to prop their inquisitive heads onto their elbows, previously engrossed in the live pool on the television, four or five others got out of their seats, turning their heads towards the two antagonists.

"Well…"

"So that's that then."

David interrupted him, he was shouting now, his voice filling the whole of the bar area, his body shaking with rage. "I'm afraid so mate."

"What do you mean, I'm afraid so, mate."

Ears pricked up all around the bar area as David cruelly mimicked Craig's voice.

"Look, mate, we had an idea, we tried it out, it didn't work for us. Nothing ventured, nothing gained. Life goes on, you know what I mean?"

"No, I don't know what you mean. That idea, as you call it, the one that didn't work out, has cost me five grand, five, grand, you hear me?"

Betrayed by his own dark and shifty eyes, Craig tried to hide the smugness of the grin that was filling his cold face. David saw it, and erupted, "You bastard, you, fucking bastard."

His scream drowned out all of the other conversations that were taking place in the bar. The Gladiator was not immune to violence, and nor were the mortals who frequented it; a row over a football match, an unpaid debt, things routinely flaring up with little or nothing in the way of encouragement.

Sensing that this altercation was unlikely to end peacefully, drinks were returned to the tables and left there, neglected and unwanted, whispers and mutterings could be heard all around, hands in front of mouths, people murmuring and speculating, the tension and excitement growing by the second, suddenly there was a circle, a baying crowd surrounding David and Craig, as if present at an illegal dog fight demanding that each tore the other to shreds, a fight to the death.

Craig's back straightened, fortified by the familiar faces surrounding him, suddenly a voice was shrieking, piercing through his brain, reminding him that this was his local, his place of business, and that this unwanted guest had no right to be waltzing in, calling him out.

"Oh, piss off David, there's nothing I can do for you."

Suddenly there was silence, a pin drop would have been auditable, all of the noise sucked into a vortex of air as David swung his right arm back, the whites of his knuckles clearly visible under the taught skin of his clenched fist.

Then he punched him, he punched Craig right in the centre of his face, with a crack, a crack that could be heard all around the pub, its echo bouncing off the television screens, bouncing off the gambling machines, bouncing off every available surface. Craig's nose exploded, exploded like a volcano, blood running down his face like an unstoppable lava flow.

"What the…"

The words were still hanging in the air as Craig's lower lip split open, bright red blood running through his stubble, down his chin and onto the floor, a second later and David had followed up that punch with another, this one landing in his stomach, leaving Craig bent double and winded.

The relentless beating continued as David took a step back and kicked Craig, high and in the mouth, loosening one of his front teeth. Covering his head with his hands as collapsed to the floor, Craig curled up his body like a sleeping infant, praying for respite, but there was none, in a frenzied attack David carried on kicking him, in the body, in the head, he didn't care where, each time he made contact it was as if a pressure relief valve was being turned, regulating his fury, calming his temper, but it made no difference, his whole body was engulfed in a blind rage, a blind rage that had been gathering force, growing stronger over the last ten days, now so vehement that it knew no boundaries, the pain he was inflicting on Craig an irrelevance, the crowd gathered there watching invisible.

Craig's battered body lay motionless on the floor, the laminate flooring soaking up the drops of blood. The mob, baying for blood just five minutes ago like a pack of animals, was suddenly muted, struck dumb by the ferocity of what they had just witnessed.

Getting up from his seat, and walking across slowly towards David, one of the regulars, a man in his mid-fifties, wearing Adidas black tracksuit bottoms, a sweat shirt and grey training shoes, self-appointed as the official peacekeeper, grabbed him by the arm, and quietly whispered into his ear.

"Okay, mate, let's call it a day shall we, he's had enough, you've proved your point, whatever that was."

Standing over Craig's prostate body, David shivered, shaking his head, for a second unable to move, fixed to the spot, but gradually, as his composure returned, managing to step to one side. The blood was already drying up on his bruised face, a red crust covering his swollen cheek, as Craig staggered up to his knees, sucking his lip, he watched in horror as the front tooth fell from his battered and bloody mouth and onto the floor in front of him, showing little in the way of remorse, David looked down at him, his angry eyes pouring scorn over the pathetic form in front of them.

"I'll be back for the money you owe me as well, just make sure that you've fucking got it."

Sensing a seismic shift in the mood in the bar, David raised his eyes and shoved his way through the circle that had now taken shape around Craig, one of their own had just been beaten to a pulp, and he was the maker of all of that, people were getting restless, fingers pointing in his direction, it was time to leave.

Walking towards the door as nonchalantly as he possibly could, his hands thrust deep into his pockets, and keeping his eyes homed in on the green fire exit sign above the two wooden doors through which he could make do his escape, he passed through the wrathful crowd, and out into the car park, he didn't look back, he didn't dare look back, and, as he got into his car and turned the key in the ignition, he made the conscious decision never to darken those four walls again.

Chapter 22
Thursday

Pulling out of the pub car park at break neck speed, David gripped hold of the steering wheel tightly, his body frozen with fear, and by the time he had parked up next to the light blue Fiat 500 parked outside Tanya's house, his hands were almost completely numb, his finger-tips white through want of blood supply.

Standing on the doorstep, the irritating Big Ben chime of her door-bell making him frown, he braced himself to have it out with her. He didn't have to wait for long as ten short seconds later Tanya opened the door, skilfully turning the latch with her right hand whilst balancing a glass of wine and a cigarette in her left, her pink dressing gown loosely tied around the waist, her pale blue nightie arranged barely covering up her shoulders. Holding the door open, a big grin flashed across her face.

"Hi, my sweetheart, now there's a coincidence, I was just about to call you, the kids are away, and we've got the house to ourselves, fancy a drink?"

Suddenly she stopped dead in her tracks, her eyes and mouth competing with each other for which one could be open the widest.

"Christ, what's happened to you? Look at your hand, and your clothes, there's blood all over your shirt and trousers for God's sake."

His mouth twitching involuntarily, he studied her face as he quizzed himself at the doorstep. Did she know more than she was letting on? Surely, she knew what had happened at The Gladiator? Craig was a friend of hers, he must have been in touch with her by now? He was roughed up pretty badly, but he would have recovered fairly quickly, yes, she would know, she would know everything, Craig would have called her immediately, he would have known that he would come here straight after leaving The Gladiator, he would have warned her, he must have.

"What do you mean, what happened to me? You know exactly where I've been and exactly what happened there, you little bitch. Now stop pretending that you don't."

Tanya took David's hand, holding it gently in her own.

"Well, look at you. Your hand's all bruised, you're covered in blood and, obviously, well, obviously very angry about something."

Pulling his hand away from hers, David barged passed her, and moved into the hallway.

"What, are you trying to tell me that Craig has not been in touch with you? Trying to tell me that you know nothing about the website, nothing about the five thousand pounds that's disappeared into thin air? Nothing about what just happened at The Gladiator less than half an hour ago?"

His thunderous voice filled the tiny space.

"Look, I haven't seen Craig for ages."

Her protests fell on deaf ears.

"Yes, you have, you saw him on Sunday, at the London Road Pub. I saw you, and you must have seen me, so why lie, you fucking bitch."

His face was contorted with anger, his voice getting louder and louder, David continued.

"Yes, but that was four days ago."

Tanya's face still showed no signs of any emotion.

"Okay, okay, let me fill you in on a few details, get you up to date. I've just met Craig, and guess what?"

Feeling his breath against her cheek, his face right up against hers, Tanya's voice was still calm, almost a whisper.

"I don't know, really I don't."

"Your bastard friend has ripped me off, that's what."

'What do you mean, ripped you off. How has he ripped you off?'

Her face was still a picture of innocence.

"Five grand, that's how."

Suddenly Tanya's face changed, a slight change, barely noticeable, just a flicker of the eye, a flicker of recognition, a flicker of understanding, barely noticeable, but enough for David.

"You bitch, stop lying, stop lying right now. You set me up, you, you and your mate Craig, the pair of you have fucking stitched me right up."

His head pounding, David mentally groaned as he started to piece the events together. When exactly had Tanya and Craig first set up the scam?

After he and Tanya had started their relationship? Well it wasn't really a relationship, he had sex with her, whether she derived any pleasure from it was wholly irrelevant. Perhaps they had planned it all right from the start?

His mind was in overdrive now, news of Ben's legacy would have spread like wild fire, almost as if somebody was waiting outside Michael Hickman's office ready to fan the flames the minute Ben had left, closing the door behind him, clutching that brown envelope, saying his fond farewell to the receptionist, so prim and proper in her blue florescent spectacles and her perfectly symmetrical desk.

Tanya had humiliated him in the toilets on the Monday night, why had she done that? Why had she chosen that particular night to attach herself to him? Perhaps it was just luck? He went back to the Cross Keys on the Tuesday, to drown his sorrows again, and there she was again, this time joining him for a drink, all ears and sympathy, and he'd fallen for it, told her all about the money. Was that when it all begun, or could she have already laid down the foundation stones of the scam before then?

Scowling to himself, he continued with the mental destruction of his own self-esteem. Yes, she had taken him for a fool, she had known that he was jealous of his brother's money, she would have known that he was open to any opportunity in making some cash, and she had taken advantage of that. Christ, had she been using him in bed for the past week as well? She wouldn't dare, the bitch.

Thinking back to their nights together, David very quickly concluded that no, he was the person in charge, he was the one who always took the lead, she always submitted, no, the bedroom was the one place where he called all the shots, she was powerless to stop him. Well, he was going to show her who was in control, just one more time, just for good measure, then she could crawl back under that stone where he had found her, and die for all he cared.

"Yes, you bitch, you set me up, you little bitch, and now I'm going to sort you out once and for all."

One of the plastic buttons fell to the floor and bounced along the carpet before rolling under the living room door, ripped away from its jealous cotton thread fixing, as it succumbed to David's vicious tugging at the front of Tanya's cheap nightie. Suddenly he stopped, the sharp pain in his wrist making him feel sick and dizzy, his hand twisted backwards, his fingers breaking at his knuckles.

"What the hell do you think you're doing? You're hurting me, you bitch, you're hurting me." A shrill cry emitted from his twisted mouth.

The protests fell onto deaf ears, Tanya stood in front of him, her face a picture of arrogance and contempt, the pupils of her eyes jet black, still and dead, filled with hatred and loathing.

In an instant, he was lying flat on his back on the floor, her full body weight on top of him, restraining him, pinning him down with her left arm, as she made short work of removing his trousers with her right. The hallway was small, barely enough room to swing a cat, and yet, on the postage stamp of carpet she sat, knickerless, on top of him, her legs straddled either side of his body. Leaning forward, her face just a couple of inches away from his, her breath reeking with the stench of cigarettes and cheap white wine, she screamed at him, her mouth like a rabid dog, slavering as her words vibrated and soaked up the air particles filling the tiny space between their two mouths.

"You, stupid arse-hole, you really think that you're something special, don't you? With your suits, your flashy car, and your pathetic five thousand pounds. A real businessman, eh? That's a joke, a sad joke. Good God, talking about sad, let's not forget the sex, oh no, let's not forget that. Well, let me tell you all about the sex. Did you really think that I enjoyed it, you, you and your rough sex? Did you really believe that you dominated me, that you had my permission to use my body as your own little play thing?"

The combination of the taste of wine in her spittle and the smell the cigarettes on her breath were making David wrench, but he couldn't move, his body racked with fear, pegged down to the floor by her bulk, intimidated into arousal by her sense of authority he was powerless to stop her, as she closed her legs together, tightening her grip, squeezing him, degrading him both physically and mentally, ridding him of what little status claims he had left. Moving slowly backwards and forwards, she pressed herself against his pubic bone, completely in charge of her own pleasure, lying on his back, still, rigid, gasping for air, barely able to fill his lungs, he could feel her moving faster and faster, her body starting to tremble, her breathing slowing down, getting deeper.

"Stop it, stop it. You're hurting me, for Christ's sake, stop it Tanya."

He howled.

"Fuck you, David."

Her eyes were wild, her breathing, now shallow and more rapid, breaking up her words.

"Yes, actually, I think I will, that's if you don't mind, of course. The truth is, I've been fucking with you ever since that sad little episode in the toilets last week."

Suddenly her head snapped back on her neck, her hands pressing down on the top of his legs, her body suddenly tensed up, a rush of hormones and endorphins circulating through her body, her insatiable appetite finally satisfied,

David closed his eyes tightly, for whilst the waves of ecstasy radiated to every part of her body and brain, his own brain screamed at him, pleading and protesting at the torture, the humiliation, voices in his head, yelling at him, making his head ache, reminding him how useless and pathetic he was, the wretchedness of his pitiful life laid bare, the total degradation of his character, of his whole being, now complete.

Slowing down, and finally stopping, breathing heavily now, the taunting continued.

"You know, you'll never be able to prove that I had anything to do with Craig and your money, don't you?"

She panted, her hot forehead covered in beads of sweat.

"No way of proving it at all."

Suddenly her face was filled with contempt again, and, putting her hands on the floor she pushed herself up and glared at him.

"I'll tell you something else, David, you are a complete waste of time. You've been my play thing, yes, that's right, my play thing, for almost two weeks now, and now I'm bored of you, I've had enough of you, so get the fuck out of my house. Now!"

Her eyes were wild, wild and crazy, David could almost feel them, attaching themselves to him, burning through his flesh, wild, crazy, evil eyes.

"You bitch, you bitch."

Desperate to manage more, he couldn't, it was if he had a stuck record positioned in his mouth, with just those two words playing over and over, again and again.

"You bitch, you bitch."

"Oh, shut up David, and fuck off out of my house."

Tanya glared at him, her eyes filled with hate.

Shaking like a gibbering wreck, holding the door open with one hand, David turned and looked at her, standing at the front door, his voice as quiet as a mouse, he attempted one last parting shot.

"So, the rumours are all true, you are an animal, using men for your own pleasure, getting what you want and then dumping them like a piece of trash."

"Yeah, that's right, just like your fucking mother. You men, you deserve it. You think that you can take what you want off us women, don't you? Use our bodies to satisfy your own perverted needs, not giving a damn about what we might want. Well, not this one mate, this one has got her own needs, her own wants and desires, and, thank you, you've just satisfied them all. Now, close the door behind you, and piss off."

Chapter 23
Thursday

His headlights on full beam, David crawled into a dark layby at the side of the road, the engine as still and silent as the air that surrounded it. Closing his eyes, he broke down, shattered by the events of the past ten days, he felt exhausted, a spent force, it was as if his body were wearing a coat, a great thick woollen coat, soaked through from being caught out in a thunderstorm, dripping wet, dragging him down, pressing against his body, suffocating him, paralysing his limbs, shutting down his brain.

Nor was it an enervation borne solely through lack of sleep, although there was precious little of that, his paranoid mind keeping him awake, seeing and hearing things that were not there, hearing voices, voices calling him, telling him to do things, urging him to take actions against his wishes, convincing him not to trust anyone.

It was a tiredness coming in both forms, physical and mental, his body starved of exercise during the day, his mind working incessantly through the night, life had become one catastrophe after another, slowly losing the basic social and occupational functionality required to even exist in a world full of stimulus and incitement, he had lost all control, his had become a nervous existence, in constant fear of a constant danger.

His heart beating faster and faster he sat there, all by himself in his car, the engine fast asleep, the outside temperature falling, his eyes tightly closed, the outside world at arms' reach, desperately trying to shut out reality, erase the past twenty-four hours.

Try as he might he could not remove the image of Tanya from his mind, straddled on top of him, crushing him, destroying him, her pleasure, his downfall, Good God. Closing his eyes more tightly, all light now excluded, there was still no respite, for in front of him, clear as day, was Craig, lying on the floor, beaten to within an inch of his life, Jesus Christ. Suddenly his mind was in overdrive, his skin turning cold, what if he decided to press charges? There were plenty of witnesses there, witnesses who would surely jump at the opportunity of putting the matter right, a prison sentence for grievous bodily harm, Good God, Jesus Christ.

Almost enjoying the sharp pain under his eye lids as he closed his eyes even more tightly, desperately trying to shut it all out, but it was too late, all attempts were futile, he was past cure, his world pitch black now, suicidal thoughts starting to creep in, barging their way through, making an unwelcome visitor to an already hostile space.

Stretching out his arm he grabbed his phone from the passenger seat. Staring at the white numbers on the black background, he sighed, he must have fallen asleep, another hour of his life had disappeared, another sixty minutes totally un-accounted for.

Pulling a cigarette from the packet he lit it up and inhaled deeply. Absorbed straight into the bloodstream, within two seconds the nicotine was having the desired effect on his brain, the rush of adrenaline, his heart rate increasing, suddenly his whole body entombed in the pleasure and calm that every smoker craves.

Sufficiently recovered, a second cigarette already burnt beyond the half way point, his confidence growing with every eager draw, he managed to manoeuvre his troubled mind into the direction of the future, desperately seeking to get some order back into his life, some sense, some normality.

Top of the list, he decided, was to distance himself from that Tanya, tipping the ash outside through the open car window his thoughts ventured further, and perhaps it was time to find another pub to drink in as well, he was getting tired of the Cross Keys anyway, so it was definitely time for a change. In fact, he concluded, they served a much better pint at The Flag, and it was only a couple of minutes further away, yes, he would start drinking in there from now on.

The tobacco tip glowed bright red as the flame of his lighter took hold of his third cigarette, he could feel the tension slowly lifting, the outlook improving at a rate of knots, he had found himself a new watering hole, now he just needed a new girlfriend, rid himself of Tanya once and for all. His arm dangled loosely out of the window, engulfed in a cloud of smoke, he inhaled and exhaled incessantly, as if convinced that the answer lay somewhere in the relentless hits of nicotine. His eyes lit up, a vision of Sarah's face suddenly filling the space immediately in front of his face.

His heart was racing again, adrenalin pumping around his body, he had always quite fancied her, she was sexy, very sexy in an innocent sort of way, she had class, and plenty of it, perhaps that was part of the attraction, a bit of a challenge.

Suddenly he stopped in his tracks. She was with Ben, wasn't she? They were all lovey-dovey at the London Road Inn on Sunday, but that didn't mean anything did it?

His mind travelled back eight years in time when he had gate crashed a house party with some friends, only to find Ben there with his girlfriend. An hour and copious amounts of alcohol later he was lying on top of the bed with her, Ben frantically searching the house for the pair of them.

His head buzzing, he took one final, long draw on his cigarette, yes, he would make a move on her, he had taken his brother's girl from him before, he would do it again, for God's sake, he had all of that money, what else could he possibly need?

The smouldering cigarette end hit the tarmac as David retracted his arm and closed the car window, pulling out of the layby, he re-joined the main road.

*****

A faint mist of furniture polish hovered over the mahogany coffee table, the smell of beeswax, that combination of honey and wood, such a pleasure to the nasal cavity, filling the air. Sarah shook her hand vigorously, her arm was aching now, an hour of non-stop polishing starting to take its toll, and there was a real chance that her tennis elbow might rear its ugly head again unless she put an end to it soon.

Elsewhere in the house it was quiet, her mother was working away and Ben had been out since eight o'clock that morning, rising early to attend an appointment with some people about a new nature reserve that was going to be opening three miles out of town. Finally letting the yellow duster drop onto the shiny surface, she smiled fondly as she thought about Ben, he was practically perfect, always doing good, always getting involved in things that actually meant something to people, always doing his best to make a difference where it really mattered.

Five minutes later, a cup of steaming coffee positioned on the perfectly polished table, she was back in the living room, sitting on the settee, her hand stuffed down the side of the cushion blindly searching for the television remote control.

Rolling her eyes, she tutted as she heard the doorbell ring, reluctantly she putting down her precious cup of coffee, and, leaving the shy channel hopper still safely secure in its hideout, walked the short distance into the hall and opened the front door, stopping abruptly, one hand on the door handle the other gripping onto the door frame.

"Oh hello, David."

Standing in the doorway her voice was barely a whisper as she shuffled uneasily from one leg to the other. She found David to be both intimidating and intrusive, for some inexplicable reason he always managed to make her feel uncomfortable, the way he looked at her, almost as if his eyes were peeling off her clothes, his mind conjuring up an image of what might lie underneath, it made her skin crawl.

Staring at her reflection in the long mirror hanging unobtrusively in its clean frame in the hallway, she quietly cursed herself for having not bothered getting dressed, her navy-blue microfleece pyjamas with their grandad button collar and red checked trousers totally inappropriate for the time of day.

With seemingly impossible difficulty she tried to force a smile as she greeted her unexpected and unwanted guest, but, in reality there was no hiding the frown that covered her face.

"Hi Sarah, pleased that you're in, I thought that I might pop round for a chat, is that's okay?"

His tone was friendly, almost polite.

"I suppose so, you'd better come in then."

Her voice was hoarse, barely a whisper her hand shaking uncontrollably, she motioned David to take the seat opposite to her own, sitting down herself, her coffee cup carefully positioned on her lap, she quietly congratulated herself for allowing at least an essence of security with some sort of barrier between them.

The conversation spluttered along cumbersomely, inch by inch David gradually steered his chair towards her own, getting closer and closer, he was now virtually within touching distance. Sarah froze, breathing in through her nose and out through her mouth, desperate to calm the panic, the inexplicable fear that held her in a vice like grip. Why hadn't she got dressed? What must he be thinking, her pyjama top was far too tight, far too revealing, she panicked, her hand trembling as she raised up the inadequate coffee cup again, pressing it against her chest.

Her heart pounding in her ears, the heat from her cup against her chest offering little in the way of comfort, she sank back in her chair, her nerves shattered. What was he doing here? What on earth did he want? She didn't have to wait long to find out, for David suddenly lent over, his face just inches away from hers.

"Sarah, let me take you out, you know, for a drink."

The small talk was clearly well and truly over; the question could not have been more direct. Luke warm coffee soaking the buttons as it trickled down the front of her top, she steadied the cup with both hands.

Racking her brains, she shrank back into her chair, had she ever given him any indication that she might have had any feelings for him in the past? Had she ever given him any signs to that affect? No, she hadn't, in fact, they had never really indulged in any form of real conversation in the past, indeed, never been in the same room alone before today. In fact, she had always found that she shared much more in the way of common ground with Anna and Ben, those were the two she found herself leaning towards, never David, or his father for that matter. Oh! Why hadn't she got dressed?

She looked across at David, discreetly moving her chair further away from him, lifting it up an inch from the ground so as not to make a sound, leaning backwards, her back pressed hard against the cushion, desperately trying to reclaim some distance between them.

"David, you know that I am in a relationship with Ben, don't you? In fact, to be honest with you, he will be moving in here very soon."

David's body twitched involuntarily with that unwelcome piece of news. Of course, he had got an incline at the London Road Pub on Sunday that his younger brother and Sarah had been up to something, but moving in together? Typical of his luck, Ben does sweet Fanny Adams for most of his life and, all of a sudden, he's absolutely loaded and he's got a gorgeous bird under his arm.

"I know that you two have been getting close, but I am asking you out for a drink, nothing more than that, just so we can get to know each other better."

Despite his best efforts there was no hiding the un-welcome menace in David's voice.

"I'm afraid that really won't be possible David. I'm going out with Ben, and that's that, there is nothing more to say."

She felt like a swan, gliding serenely across a lake, above the surface she appeared composed, her voice as calm and assertive, yet underneath her heart was pounding, her breaths short and rapid, she felt light headed, her body shrouded in a blanket of terror, her mind galloping away in a state of blind panic.

"Look, Ben will be home soon. He goes swimming on a Thursday afternoon after work and likes to take a shower before we have our tea, it's late already, so he won't be long. We're off out this evening for a drink together, so I know that he'll want to look clean and fresh. He stayed here last night, you can check if you like, his clothes are hanging in my wardrobe, he'll be back any minute now, yes, definitely any minute now."

She was rambling, her face was filled with fear, she was clutching at straws, and David wasn't fooled by it, he was now out of his seat and standing over her.

"Oh, come on Sarah, I've fancied you for ages, you know that I have. You little fucking tease, sitting down at our house in your short skirts and dark tights, you've got a nice pair of legs and you know it, you've caught me staring at you loads of times, and yet still you kept coming round didn't you? You little tart! Give me a chance, I can show you a good time, I'll give you everything you ever wanted, that's a promise."

"The answer is no David, I am seeing Ben, and that's that."

She did not quite know how, but, somehow, she managed to stand her ground.

David finally cracked, what little self-control he exhibited completely gone for a Burton.

"It's because of the money, isn't it? You women want everything don't you? You can never be happy with just something, you have to have more. Just like my mother, not content with just one man to sleep with, she had to look elsewhere, had to have somebody else, a bit on the side, had to have more than she already had, greedy little bitch."

"No David, it's not like that. I love Ben and have done for weeks now, nothing to do with the stupid money, in fact I've got plenty of my own thank you very much."

Sarah screamed as David grabbed her by the sleeve, she screamed again as the buttons at the front came open, her naked flesh exposed, she screamed a third time, as she reclaimed her arm and adjusted her top. Looking down at her chest, she could see the outline of her nipples, Christ, what did she think she looked like? Oh my God, she looked just like, just like Tanya. Oh, why hadn't she got dressed? She could at least have put on some underwear. God, now he could claim that she had led him on, encouraged him with her unrestrained breasts, the complete absence of any visible panty line, fuelling the fire of his lust, leading him on, inviting his attention, his engrossment.

She had read all about sexual assaults in the newspaper, seen it on the television. Was this what it was like? Was this how it started? A seemingly innocent conversation spiralling into something physical and revolting? Christ, he wasn't even a stranger, and she was in her own house, where could a girl feel completely safe? Her head was spinning, she felt dizzy, she felt stupid, everything leading back to the same question, why the hell hadn't she just put some clothes on?

"Leave me alone, David, you're hurting me."

She screamed, her shrill voice pleading, begging him to stop.

"Shut up you little tease, come on, you want me as much as I want you."

Holding him at arms' length, Sarah stared at David's contorted face, his voice was that of a mad man, a man who had lost all sense of reality, all sense of dignity, completely out of control.

Suddenly the front door opened, Sarah looked up, her face pleading for salvation, as she listened to the sound of Ben's swimming bag flying through the air and landing at the foot of the stairs with a dull thud.

Standing in the doorway Ben was frozen to the spot, his mouth wide open, his eyes digesting the unanticipated and appalling scene that was taking place right in front of his very eyes.

His mind in overdrive. What the hell was his brother doing there? What the hell did he think he was doing in Sarah's house? Good God wasn't it bad enough that he was jealous of his money without him wanting his girlfriend as well.

David winced, his face contorted with pain, as his younger brother grabbed hold of his arm with his left hand and twisted his fingers with his right, forcing him to release his grip on Sarah. For her part, she took full advantage of the brief window of opportunity and ran into the relative sanctuary of the kitchen, looking over her shoulder just to confirm that David had not followed her in pursuit.

His hands on his hips, his body erect and alert, Ben shook his head as he contemplated his brother, it was as if a complete stranger was standing in front of him, someone he couldn't recognise, someone he simply didn't know.

Instantaneously he was transported back to the house party eight years ago, standing outside of that bedroom, his ear against the cheap paper-thin plywood door, listening to his brother fucking his then girlfriend, she was only sixteen for goodness sake, no doubt flattered by the attention of an older man, a man in his early twenties.

Silently opening the door ajar, he had peeped inside, there they were, lying awkwardly underneath a pile of coats on the single bed, he could see the back of his brother's head, his body obscured by the heap of hap-hazard garments, he could see her naked legs, one either side of David's arched body, her skirt and knickers discarded, thrown onto the floor in her raging teenage desire, an uncontrollable yearning to feel the older brother inside her.

Suddenly, he snapped completely, the sense of déjà vu simply too much to bare, and with his hand balled into a fist he set about his older brother in a most vicious and violent manner, pounding him with punches, four, five, six of them, in a ferocious and brutal attack. The fierce assault finally coming to an end only when Sarah, her courage sufficiently returned, intervened, holding his clenched fist in her tiny hand, wrapping her delicate finger around it, pleading for him to stop.

Blood pouring from his nose, his lower lip cut and swollen, David swayed from side to side, staggering backwards and forwards, before eventually falling, heavily, to the ground, his head banging into the arm of the chair as he fell.

Sitting up, overcome by dizziness, he struggled back up onto his feet, his body still rocking unsteadily, his face covered in blood, his shamed eyes fixed to the floor, humiliated and crestfallen. He recoiled as Ben grabbed his right arm and pulled it up behind his back, almost suspending him up into the air, before frog-marching him out of the living room, into the hall, through the front door and throwing him outside.

"Now, get out, get out you, you, sick bastard."

Leaving his brother's motionless body sprawled out on the pavement Ben slammed the door behind him, and, holding out his hands he pulled Sarah towards him, wrapping his longs arms around her, drawing her closer to him, caressing her tenderly, his lips making just the slightest of contact on the top of her hair. She buried her head into his chest, and sobbed uncontrollably.

Chapter 24
Thursday

Holding a tissue to his nose, his thumb and fore finger squeezing it tight against his nostrils in a futile attempt to stem the flow of blood, David managed to stagger and stumble the short distance down the road towards his car.

Standing uneasily by the door, his hands shaking as they fumbled around in his coat pocket, exploring every nook and cranny, desperately trying to locate his keys, eventually they fell out, straight onto the pavement, and lodged under the front wheel.

The sole of his shoe left a small brown mark, spoiling the paintwork of his car door as it made contact, not satisfied, he kicked it again and, once inside, he sat, rocking backwards and forwards in the driving seat banging his head on the steering wheel, the magnitude of his own stupidity becoming patently clear.

Of course, he had known that Sarah and Ben were an item, that had been pretty obvious on Sunday at the London Road Inn, the pair of them already settled down, perusing the menu together by the time he had arrived, their knowing smiles, the casual brushing together of their bodies, all pointing towards a night spent together, sharing the same bed.

What on earth did he think he was playing at, imposing himself on her. She had never given him any encouragement, in fact she had never shown the slightest bit of interest in him in the past. The truth is, this morning had probably been the first proper conversation the two of them had ever had together. Stupid, stupid, stupid.

Unable to move, he sat there, screaming to himself, his head throbbing, banging his fists against the dashboard, until he was totally overcome with exhaustion, too tired to even raise his hands from his lap.

His exhausted, aching body screaming back at him, the torture almost unbearable and seemingly without end, his body physically numb, cut off from his brain, a brain wracked with pain, completely over whelmed by negative thoughts; revenge, guilt, shame, totally isolated, trapped, hopeless.

Lifting himself up in his seat by his bloodstained hands, he summoned all of his strength, put the key into the ignition, looked over his shoulder, started the engine, and pulled away.

If only Ben had not taken that money, then everything would be fine, he muttered to himself, trying to restore some remnants of order back into his life. Suddenly, almost involuntarily, his right foot hit the pedal, slamming on the breaks, the car screeching to an abrupt halt.

Was the money really to blame for the state of his life? Was it really the money that sparked off the chain of events that have left his life in tatters? No, it wasn't, Bill Williams wasn't to blame either, he was just some old geezer who had passed away bequeathing everything he owned to his only son, nothing wrong in that, in fact all perfectly normal. No, none of this had anything to do with him, or that letter that had arrived so unexpectedly a week last Monday, innocently folded up in its perfect brown manila envelope.

In that second everything became very clear in his mind, crystal clear, there were only two people to blame, and they were his parents, his pathetic parents, his whore of a mother and the sad little figure that was his father, well, today they were going to get a piece of his mind. They might have been happy to destroy their own lives, content to put up with each other's shortcomings, but now the depravity of his mother and the weakness of his father had ruined his life, and he didn't deserve that, he didn't deserve that at all.

Ten minutes later, and still cursing his parents under his breath, he pulled up into the empty driveway. how typical that they should both be conspicuous by their absence at the most inappropriate time he muttered under his breath, as he rang the doorbell, his face filled with resignation as the hall light illuminated his mother's distorted form silhouetted through the glass door. Wearing a pair of tight-fitting jeans, complimenting her slim legs, and a bright yellow blouse, her face beaming with delight, Anna pulled the door open.

"Well, what a lovely surprise. How lovely to see you, David, Good God, what's happened to you? Come in quickly."

Ushering her eldest son through the door and towards the kitchen, she put a comforting arm around his shoulder.

"Leave me alone, Mother, just leave me alone will you."

David protested, waving his arms about ferociously in the air. Being fussed over had always irritated him, and, to be fussed over by someone he had nothing but contempt for, just made it worse.

"What's happened? What on earth has happened? You poor thing."

Her voice shaking with emotion, her maternal arm still wrapped around her eldest son's shoulder despite his best attempts to remove it. Finally, David managed to pull himself away from her, physically removing her arm from his shoulder, he screamed.

"What's happened? What's happened? I'll tell you what's happened. You, you have completely ruined my life, that's what's happened."

Anna froze, barely capable of supporting herself with her own two legs, she sat down, stunned by his outrage, intoxicated by his voice, filled with so much venom.

"What do you mean, I've ruined your life. How could I have possibly ruined your life? And stop shouting please."

His face filled with mockery and derision, David stared at his mother, as she sat in her chair, his back perfectly straight, his arms folded tightly in front of him.

"What do I mean? Well, let me tell you what I mean. More than twenty-four years ago, when you were supposed to be head over heels in love with my father, you got friendly with a bloke called Bill Williams, and guess what? You couldn't control yourself, could you? Couldn't keep your hands to yourself, couldn't keep your knickers on."

Anna's face turned red, and then white, she remained sitting down, her head buried in her hands.

"Oh, David, that was a long time ago, a long, long, time ago."

Her voice was barely auditable.

"Yes, it was, as you say, a long, long, time ago."

David pressed on, his voice a metaphoric dagger aiming right for her heart.

"But it has come back to haunt you, hasn't it? Only, actually, the problem is that it's come back to haunt all of us, the whole family, all of us caught up in your mess. You didn't think of that at the time, did you?' No, of course you didn't, lying on your back with your legs wide open, all you cared about was yourself and your own pleasure, your own enjoyment."

Her eyes shining with tears, Anna held her head in her hands, he had always been an angry person, his had always been a world teeming with demons, both as a child and even more so when he was a teenager, but had her son finally been pushed over the edge?

"David."

She tried to interject.

"No, let me finish. We were, well at least I thought we were, a happy family, but no, that's all gone out of the window now, I mean for God's sake, my brother and I don't even have the same father. Can you imagine how that feels? My mother and father haven't been capable of having a normal marriage, you know, the sort with a bit of trust and decency about it?"

Tears rolling down her cheeks she stared down at the floor, quite unable to look her eldest son in the face. He had every right to be angry, he had every right to hate her, but now it was time for him to hear her side of the story, learn some more of the truth of her marriage, and, as she got up slowly and deliberately from her seat, the tears suddenly stopped flowing, her eyes suddenly dry and crystal clear.

"Okay, David, let's talk, yes, let's talk, but, adult to adult."

Shocked by the change in her voice, David's exhausted legs suddenly giving way as she spoke, her voice hissing like a snake disturbed from its nest, its head retracted, its neck coiled into a curved stance, positioned to strike, he sank nervously into his chair.

"Right then, your father, your father and I, well, things were not easy at the start. We didn't have much money, actually, we had no money at all, in fact, we were badly in debt, things were almost impossible. He was offered a promotion, much better pay, and it meant working away, working away for weeks, months on end, but at least the extra cash gave us something to look forward to, a light at the end of a very dark tunnel."

For a split-second David managed to look up at his mother, and immediately turned away, too frightened to meet her eye.

"Whist your father was away, yes, I had a relationship with a man called Bill Williams, and I enjoyed it, I enjoyed it very much indeed, especially the sex. I've always had a craving for sex, good sex, and yes, Bill was better than your father, much better."

She paced around his chair, circling around him like a vulture, waiting its turn to feast on the prey.

"It filled a gap, a void in my life that was torturing me, it made me feel wanted, made me feel desired. That might shock you David, but I really don't care anymore, you wanted to know the truth, well here it is. Bill was single, Bill was lonely, his mother had just died of cancer, so, yes, I guess it made me feel kind of useful as well, as if I was doing some good. Do I regret it? No I don't, never have done, and probably never will do. I've never forgotten Bill, you know, I just put him right to the very back of my mind, and get on with my life. Do I think of him when I look at Ben? Sometimes. More now, of course, obviously, because of what's happened."

David stared at his mother, his mouth wide open, speechless. Anna continued unabated, her face more intense than ever, the sentences short and sharp.

"Look, I'm not making excuses, and I am not going to try and make any excuses. I'm just being honest with you, Christ, give me some credit for that at least. Mind, I probably don't care that much if you don't, you're old enough now to have your own opinion. What happened, happened, we can't change it now, so you just need to deal with it the best way that you can."

Her voice trailed off, David remained seated, his gaze fixed to the floor. Of course, he had been suspicious of Bill Williams, that seemingly special friendship with his mother, too close, too intense, and from that, even way back then, he had learnt that his mother was not to be trusted, seeds of doubt planted early in his life, germinating throughout his teenage years, his very being now a strong stem from which hung leaves of wariness, and suspicion.

Tanya's face suddenly flashed before him, her smug little smile, her fiery eyes filled with lust and hatred in equal quantities, reeling him in with her pathetic submissiveness, before unleashing the full force of her twisted and perverted mind.

His mother had done exactly the same to his father, getting married, and then promptly breaking their marriage vows, meaningless, shallow, words spoken out loud for all of the congregation to hear, meaningless, shallow promises that she must have known that she would be unable to keep.

His father had fallen for her, hook, line, and sinker, taken in by her long slim legs and sexual appetite, but, sadly blinded by his pathetic nature, for he would surely have had some sort of inkling as to what she was up to, he would have lacked the strength, the courage, to take the necessary steps and take her to task over her wrong-doings.

Glaring across at his mother, how he hated her, how he despised her, her depraved habits, her perverted mind. She kept an old photograph album under her bed, he'd seen it, its synthetic leather cover creased at the bottom corner, the photos protected by the aging, now brittle, plastic interleaves, photos of her when she was younger, more attractive, she had obviously used that and her sex to get what she wanted.

She had needs, needs and desires, sadly none of which his father could satisfy. His father, his sad, pathetic father, who had married a beautiful, young, women, captured her in the prime of her life, full of energy, ambition, filled with a zest for life, only to leave her by herself, neglected and uncared for, all he had to do was to satisfy her, satisfy her mentally, satisfy her physically, give her what she wanted, the attention she craved. Bill Williams obviously had something that she wanted, and so they had both fed from the trough, that disgusting trough of faithlessness and betrayal.

Anger and hatred are never a good combination, only bad things can happen when those two meet up, and, sitting back in his chair, his head pounding, his stomach churning, David was thick with both. He had come to the house to confront his parents, he had heard his mother's account, now he wanted to hear his father's, and would not settle until he had. His voice so soft it was almost noiseless, he gritted his teeth and turned his head slowly and deliberately towards his mother.

"You make me sick, do you know that? Now where is my father?"

The sound of a key turning smoothly in the lock interrupted Anna before her mouth had finished forming the first word of her response, the glass front door opening and with it a draft appeared to enter the house, a cold breeze chilling the very bones of those present, seconds later Reg walked cheerfully, and un-wittingly, into the room.

Chapter 25
Thursday

His car keys bounced off the heavy carriage clock on the mantelpiece, as a bag of shopping landed on the floor with a thud.

"Hello, David, how good to see you, and what brings you here?" Reg asked his voice chirpy, bordering on the flippant.

"I think you'd better sit down, dear, I'll make you a cup of tea."

Anna spoke to her husband, her voice nervy and uneasy, before quickly moving into the kitchen, safely hidden behind the noise of the china cups clanking together as she removed them from the cupboard and the kettle came to boil.

For a second David remained in his seat, his arms folded in front of him, scowling at his father, whilst not actually acknowledging his presence. Reg sat down, totally oblivious to the situation, unaware of any tension that might or might not be hanging in the air.

"You'll need something a lot stronger than that by the time I've finished."

David taunted his father, ridiculing him, mocking him. Anna, still in the kitchen, poured the tea carefully into the cups, tears welling up in her tired red eyes.

"What do you mean, something stronger?"

His voice filled with surprise and naivety, caught completely off guard, his eyes blinking furiously, opening and shutting quickly as he started to piece things together in his mind.

His head was filled with questions. What was David doing there? Why was he so angry? God, he had never seen him so angry. What has happened? He could see dried blood on his hands, his knuckles were grazed too. Oh my God, what on earth has happened? He could feel himself starting to panic, a feeling of dread in the pit of his stomach.

A cup of tea in each hand, Anna came back into the room. Shaking his head, David smirked to himself, a cup of tea, classic, that'll make everything better, won't it? Of course it will, a couple of sips of that great British solver of all problems, curer of all ills, yes that should do the trick.

As if reading David's mind, but carrying on regardless, Anna handed out the two cups of scolding tea, an olive branch, a plea for peace, her unsteady outstretched hands laying bare her desperation.

"Now, why don't you tell me what you know, Father?"

David's cold eyes, the whites of which had turned pure black, drilled into his father, his face right up against his, less than two inches separating them, goading him, prodding him.

"Tell you what I know about what?"

His voice was calm and non-committal, for whilst Reg had slowly moved his face away from that of his impetuous son, his cards were still very much firmly pressed up against his chest, the expression on his face illegible.

Almost two weeks had passed since Ben had spent that eventful three-quarters of an hour in the company of Michael Hickman, almost two weeks since that brown envelope had been passed around the family, finally landing in rightful hands of his youngest son, changing his life forever, leaving David firmly out in the cold.

This confrontation had not been un-expected, in fact he was surprised it had taken David quite so long to put two and two together, piece together the damning evidence. In any event he needed to ascertain exactly what his eldest son knew, keep testing the water, but for now, keep his powder dry. He did not have to wait long.

"Your wife, my mother, the mother of my brother. You, my father, but I'm guessing not the father of my brother."

Resignation written all over his face, Reg, gazed at David. The question could not have been any more direct, he sat up and lent forward towards his son.

"If you're referring to Bill Williams, and your mother's affair, then, yes, I know all about that, and yes, I have always known all about that."

Suddenly, almost a quarter of a century later, he felt like a ton weight had been lifted off from his shoulders.

The table legs lifted clear off the floor, its top covered in a lake of spilt tea, as David's fists came crashing down.

"What? And you're happy about that, are you? Happy just to get on with your life?"

"It happened a long time ago, son, it was a difficult time for both of us, and yes, I have forgiven your mother."

It was getting more difficult to stay calm, but Reg knew that he had to, for David's sake as well as his own.

"It happened a long time ago? Oh, that's alright then, let's sweep it all under the carpet, out of sight, out of mind, pretend that it never happened, shall we? Only it did, it did happen, didn't it, Father?"

David would not be placated, not by his father, not by anyone, his desire for a fight too strong.

"You neglected our mother, you virtually pushed her into the arms of another man, no wonder she had an affair, no wonder she went somewhere else, to get what you were obviously incapable of giving her. Now, twenty-four years later, here we are, a family ripped apart, rotten to the core, but, never mind all of that, you've forgiven her, and everything's all rosy in the garden. God, you're pathetic."

"Enough, that's enough, David, and, please, stop shouting, stop everything. Stop it now."

Standing at the kitchen doorway, a quivering wreck, her head buried in her hands, her face red, two soaking wet tissues on the floor at her feet, Anna had heard enough now, enough of her son's verbal assault on her husband, enough of his insults. Positioning herself in between them both.

"I think that David may have got himself into a bit of trouble dear."

She added, moving next to Reg, placing her hand onto her husband's, standing shoulder to shoulder beside him, a grand gesture of solidarity, the espirit de corps that comes with a long relationship. Reg turned his head to David, raising his eye brows.

"Yes, I am in a bit of trouble, as you, so eloquently, put it Mother, and why? Well, I'll tell you why, because in the past two weeks my life has been completely turned upside down. It was never brilliant, I will concede that, but it was certainly a damn sight better than it is now."

His facial expression a combination of depression, frustration, and resignation. Deep down David knew that he was a victim of his own stupidity, his actions over the past week, a series of adrenalin rushes, one kick after another, coming back to haunt him, the steel frame of the roller coaster with its steep climbs and sharp descents for so long making him giddy and lightheaded, now leaving him feeling sick as he disembarked.

He had persisted in having a relationship with Tanya despite her having given him a very clear insight into the depths of her depravity in the toilets on that Monday evening, laying bare her warped, perverted mind, pinning him against the wall, stripping him of all his dignity. To add insult to injury he had allowed her to coerce him into investing five thousand pounds into a business venture with someone he scarcely knew, and, after today's exploits, and to compound matters, he could now add assault, both physical and sexual, onto the grubby, disgusting crime sheet, inevitably the time to pay the piper could not be far away.

Despite all of that, and his full submission to the facts before him, the compulsion to fight back was over-powering. He simply had to find someone or something to blame, someone to hold to account, and that someone or something was his parents.

"The first few years of your marriage were not exactly a bed of roses, were they Father? Don't worry, I already knew about Bill Williams, I remember him from when I was younger, and now I know all the rest of the disgusting details. I know all about my mother, and why she felt the need to seek attention elsewhere, why she had no choice but to turn away from you and into the arms of another man. What I don't understand is why you put up with it? You must have known what she was up to? If you have had the courage to get shot of her all those years ago, then things might have turned out differently. If only you'd had the balls to tell our mother that no, you weren't prepared to be cheated on, you weren't prepared to be shafted, then perhaps, just perhaps, we would all be able to look forward to the rest of our lives, you know, normal lives, a happy retirement for you and the prospect of perhaps happy marriages with children for me and Ben."

David paused, his face contorted with anger, his cheeks bright red, a brief pause, catching his breath before lashing out again.

"But no, no you couldn't manage that, could you? You were happy to pretend that it never happened. Years of playing happy families, years of living a lie. Well, a letter, one poxy letter from a poxy small town solicitors has certainly put paid to all of that. Only now it's too late. Oh yes, the horse has well and truly bolted. How can we possibly hope to move on from this? What do you suggest we do, Father? Pretend it all never happened? Carry on living out our little lie? Well, it's a bit late for that now, isn't it?"

189

Reg sat motionless, his hands gripping the arms of the chair, studying David's face intently. Respect for his father had been sadly lacking since David was a teenager, up until now the whys and wherefores had been a mystery, well not anymore! Was he really as weak as David thought? Was that really the image he portrayed to his eldest son? It was very apparent that David thought so. Closing his eyes, pain wracking his whole body he brought the past to mind.

Of course, he had had his suspicions all those years ago, deep down he had known that something wasn't right. He had been working away for such a long time and suddenly this Bill Williams' name kept popping up. On the face of it, he was just the man from the wine merchants, on the face of it, he was just the person who sold Anna her bottle of wine on a Friday evening. But, he should have asked more questions, he should have been more inquisitive. He should have started asking questions then, right at the start.

Why had she suddenly taken such an interest in wine all of a sudden? She was never that bothered before, in fact, she had always gone for what was on special offer at five pound a bottle in the local supermarket, price much more of a consideration than the name of brand or the variety of grape. The signs were there, virtually right from the start, they were there, some were obvious, clear as day, others much subtler.

During the early trips away from home, Anna had been very attentive on the Monday morning, fussing over him, checking that his suitcase was all packed up properly, nothing was missing, sufficient quantities of clean underwear and pressed shirts. She had looked up where he was going to stay on the internet, looking at the reviews on line, taking a real interest in the facilities, making sure that he was going to be comfortable, well looked after.

That was at the start, the first three or four trips, but it didn't last for long, and, as he looked back at those times, over twenty years ago Reg recalled that, after what seemed like a very short space of time, Anna showed a good deal less interest in his arrangements, much less dutiful in her work, more concerned with going about her own business than the contents of his suitcase, eventually reaching the point whereby and could barely seem to find the time to stand at the front door of the house and wave him off on a Monday morning.

Looking back the signs had all been there, words unspoken, actions unnoticed, he should have nipped it in the bud there and then, for as Ben grew up any doubts that might possibly have existed were completely extinguished, the truth confirmed by his physical attributes. He had known the truth then, as he knew the truth now, but he had chosen to ignore it, with a small child already in the family he had no choice. He loved Anna, he loved her un-conditionally, he still did, and he knew that he would never, could never have found another like her. He had buried his head in the sand, he had convinced himself that Anna would never cheat on him, never betray him, not ever. It had been so much easier that way, living a lie, turning the other cheek, focus on work, focus on the family.

On top of all of that they had David, that rendered the chance of any confrontation impossible, and so, somehow, he managed to put everything to the back of his mind, and that's where it all stayed, surfacing from time to time, only to be shoved back into place.

"What's it all got to do with you David?"

His head finally rising from its sweaty ten-digit haven, his voice louder, his eyes wide open, his eye-brows wrinkled. Instantly he knew that was a mistake.

"What's it got to do with me? For Christ's sake, what about the shame, the embarrassment, and that's just for starters."

Sighing heavily, Reg knew that the time had come to make his point, time for David to listen, and understand.

"Surely only your mother and I should be feeling any shame and embarrassment, as you put it. You've done nothing wrong, you've got nothing to be ashamed of. Yes, of course I know that I am not Ben's father, well not his biological father anyway, I've known that virtually all of his life, I had doubts even before he was born. I had to make a decision back then, and I have stuck by that decision ever since, I decided not to confront her over it. Was that the right thing to do? Well sometimes I don't actually know, but what I do know is that I had other things to think about, more important things. Yes, my pride had been damaged, but I already had a son, you, and she had another child on the way. I had responsibilities, I had a family that needed me. How could I possibly turn my back on two innocent children? Could you have done it? Well, could you? What would you have done in my position? Run away from it all? No, you would have done exactly what I did, stay with the family, care for the children, try to re-build the marriage, fight tooth and nail for everything you had worked for."

David glared at his father, his face filled with disgust, his mouth twisted into a sneer.

"Did you now," he growled in a low tone.

"Yes, David, yes, I did, I decided to put all of the doubt to the back of my mind, yes bury my head in the sand if you like, but I had to fight for what I had, win your mother back, I wanted her all to myself, every single bit of her. I took a pay cut and stopped working away from home, and not so I could keep an eye on her. No, to give her the sort of marriage that she wanted, the attention that she wanted, everything she wanted."

Her cheeks glowing a bright shade of crimson, and looking incredibly embarrassed, Anna gazed at her husband, completely overwhelmed by the feeling of love she felt for the man sitting next of her. They had never really discussed her relationship with Bill Williams before now, there had always been an element of doubt, a niggle in the back of her mind, had she got away with it?

That indiscretion, that crime of passion? Now she knew the truth, no, she hadn't, and, yes, she had. No, in that Reg's life had been one of compromise, doubt and suspicion in abundance, and yes, in that he had put the family first, put the security of the children ahead of his own feelings, his own pride. She squeezed his hand gently, she certainly didn't deserve him then, she probably didn't deserve him now.

Gazing into his father's tired bloodshot eyes, David stood up from his chair, his anger thawing, the numbness driven by the pure hatred of his father slowly disappearing, replaced by an overwhelming feeling of admiration. His mother's affair had hurt him, the fear of any future betrayals as waring as the pain of the reality, but rather than making his father weaker, rather than breaking him, it had made him even more resilient, more determined to have what he wanted.

Through him their marriage had become stronger, he had made it into what it was today, he had made them into what they were today. His father had been the cornerstone, the stone rejected by his wife, and yet, almost as if chosen by God to be the foundation stone of the family, he had persevered, soldiering on against all adversity, through thick and thin, for better and for worse.

Blinking away the tears welling uncontrollably in his eyes, the lump in his throat so huge he could barely swallow, David stared at his father, sitting in front of him was the head of the family, the same person but, suddenly, bigger in stature, more demanding of his respect, the head of his family, someone to admire, someone he could be, and, indeed, should be, proud of.

Turning to his mother, sitting so close to his father, their chairs touching, she was almost on top of him, her tiny hand cradled in his, he scowled, a dark, fierce scowl, filled with hatred and revulsion.

Oh, how she had fooled him, led him right up the garden path. She was the one that he had placed on a pedestal, elevated her above all others, especially his father, she had always been the one, the one he had turned to, whenever he needed help, whenever he needed advice, the one he had respected more than anyone else in the world. How wrong he had been. She was nothing but a cheat and a liar, cunning and devious, taking what she wanted and leaving others to pick up the pieces from the trail of emotional destruction left behind her.

She was no better than Tanya, sick, disgusting Tanya, both of them taking whatever they wanted, from where ever they wanted, the pair of them self-indulgent to the point where they had little or no concern for the feelings of others, totally wrapped up in themselves, having their fill, and spitting out what little there was left at the end.

Staring at his mother, all other feelings shut down, what microscopic feelings of love that remained well and truly extinguished, his mind sick with hatred, and with his only obsession to inflict as much pain as was humanly possible, David ran the dagger home.

"You make me sick, you stupid fucking whore, don't ever come anywhere near me again."

Chapter 26
Thursday

His seatbelt un-fastened, the rear-view mirror un-checked, David reversed sharply out of parents' driveway.

"Christ, look at the state of you, what the hell has happened?"

Daniel's eyes travelled slowly up and down his best friend's body, as he watched him stagger into the hallway, the dried blood on his raw knuckles, his shirt sleeve ripped and hanging loose from his arm, the purple bruising surrounding his split lip, Jesus Christ!

"Coffee?"

Daniel motioned towards the living room.

"Or perhaps something stronger?"

His tired, aching, legs stretched out in front of him, David collapsed onto one of the brown leather armchairs, the cushion sinking, submitting to the dead weight of his exhausted, shattered frame.

A friend in need is a friend indeed, and edging his way carefully around David's chair, his hands filled with two heavy glass whiskey tumblers and a bottle of twelve-year old single malt, Daniel sat down opposite his emotionally penurious friend, and poured out two generous shots of whiskey, pushing one of the glasses across the dark wooden coffee table.

"Well, what have you been up to then?"

David eagerly held his glass in his fragile hands, wrapping his blood-stained fingers lovingly around its smooth surface, and took a gulp, it did the trick, the misery of his life seemingly fading away as the pale, pungent liquid coated the back of his dry mouth.

Daniel sat in silence, nodding his head up and down, as he spent the next two hours listening to David recount his sad and sordid saga. The altercation with Craig in the bar at The Gladiator, the money would not be so problematic, lesson learnt and all of that, but in front of all of those witnesses, that would surely spell trouble? He quizzed himself silently, as he made a mental note to watch out for his friend trying to borrow money any time soon in the future.

There was more than a pang of jealousy as he listened to the erotica laden facets of the indecent, almost prurient nature of the relationship between David and Tanya, and an equal amount of horror as he learnt of the incident at Sarah's house and his un-gamely ejection at the hands of his younger brother.

The decorative hands on the broken arch walnut mantel clock flashing a lop-sided smile at the pair of them as they sat together in a welcome silence, it was five past nine, the twelve-year old malt had all but disappeared, the ashtray full to the brim with cigarette ends buried in a pile of ash.

Suddenly the sanctuary of calmness was abruptly broken, the chime of the doorbell echoing from the hallway. Tutting under his breath, Daniel jumped out of his seat, leaving David sitting by himself, stewing in his own introspection, his empty glass on the table, his discarded cigarette end balanced perilously on the corner of the ashtray.

Thirty seconds later, Daniel was back in the room, standing awkwardly in the doorway. Two men stood behind him, both jostling for the same space inside the narrow door frame, the taller one was in his forties, wearing a tatty blue suit and brown shoes, his grey hair brushed tidily across his round head in a side parting, the shorter was younger, podgier, more casually attired in jeans and a jumper, his frizzy ginger hair and beard seemingly untameable and completely out of control.

His face as white as a sheet, drained of any colour, his voice scarcely audible, Daniel formally announced the un-expected guests.

"David, these gentlemen are plain clothes policemen, they want to ask you a few questions."

Chapter 27
Thursday

Sitting in silence, on the two leather chairs that had been a much welcome wedding present from Anna's mother, each of the four looking as tired and worn out as the other, Reg and Anna had been staring into space for almost two hours, only the copious consumption of French red wine separating the pair of them from the eternal hope of a better world and total oblivion.

The bamboo alert tone of her phone brought Anna back down to earth with a start.

"Oh my God, Reg, it's a text from Ben, David's been arrested. He's spoken to Daniel and has all of the details and we are to give him a call. Christ Reg, what's going to happen? What are they going to do to our son?"

The words leaving her mouth at a hundred miles an hour, Reg rubbed his eyes, trying to keep up with her.

"Now, hold on, hold on, let's call Ben first and find out exactly what's going on."

Five minutes later, he put the overworked mobile device back down onto the table, his face a picture of apprehension.

"It doesn't sound good love. If what Ben has told us is correct, and my guess is that it will probably be worse, as David won't have told Daniel everything that's for sure, David could be in big trouble. The police have arrested him, and they wouldn't have done that if that Craig bloke hadn't decided to press charges for the beating David gave him. Now, given the number of people in the bar at the time, all of whom I would imagine would gladly step forward and give evidence, then David could be looking being charged, and found guilty of grievous bodily harm, and that could mean a prison sentence. Christ Almighty. The five thousand pounds we can replace from our own savings, it'll mean less for us, but, we'll survive. We always have, but we can't help David if he ends up in court, no lawyer is going to be able to save him, given the evidence that is stacked up against him."

Anna frowned as she considered her husband, he had always been very matter of fact about things, always so good in a crisis, but this time he was so different, looking tired and drawn, as if he had aged ten years in less than a couple of hours.

"Perhaps Ben will help him out with the money?" she offered.

"Perhaps he will." His voice now barely recognisable.

Anna took a deep breath, fortified by almost half a bottle of wine, and with Reg more than just a little vulnerable, she knew that there would never be a better time to talk, to talk about Bill Williams and Ben. Earlier she had learnt things from Reg that she was totally unaware of before today, if they were to give David the support he would certainly need they would have to stand together, in unison with each other, side by side, with no distractions of their own. Tears rolling down her cheeks, Anna looked at her Reg, her eyes pleading with him.

"Reg, Reg, look, I'm so very sorry about what happened, you know, with Bill, with Bill Williams, so very sorry indeed. That must have hurt you very much, very much indeed."

She held her hand out to her husband, a gesture, a futile gesture of hope, but, just as their fingers tips met, he pushed it violently away.

"I thought that I had dealt with all of that, well, the best I could, but Ben's money has bought it all flooding back, worse than ever. Yes, I had my suspicions at the time, I was convinced that you were up to something, but as I said, I couldn't face causing any trouble between us, I wanted to be with you so badly, I wanted us to be a family, and I didn't want to force you to choose between him or me, I was so scared you might choose him over me. But why, why did you do it Anna?"

Sinking further into her chair, Anna closed her eyes, this was the question she had been dreading for the past twenty-four years, and she had not been idle, for during that time she had prepared hundreds of answers, carefully crafting an explanation, a justification, but she had never been satisfied, never quite able to square the circle, with any of them. Hesitating uncomfortably, her mouth dry, her lips withered and cracked, her voice little more than a stammer.

"Oh, oh I don't know love. You were working away so much, I think that was the main problem, and we never seemed to have any money, we were broke

197

all of the time. I was lonely, I was bored, I felt unloved, neglected. I know this sounds like a load of rubbish and just excuses, but it really was just that."

Pausing, she caught her breath.

"And, of course, there was Bill."

Those final words coming at him like a steam train, Reg visibly recoiled, hit for six, his tired eyes suddenly filling with rage, his white face suddenly flushed red.

"But, why Bill? What had he got that I hadn't? Why Bill?"

The wine glasses fell off the table as it vibrated, rocking violently from side to side, scattering splinters of glass all over the floor, as his clenched fist slammed on the table, the words and actions in perfect unison with each other.

Startled, frightened, and staring into the empty table, her face seemingly void of any emotion, Anna continued.

"Well, Bill, oh, I don't know. It was all so different then. It felt like you were never around most of the time, and Bill, and Bill. Well Bill had lost his mother almost a year before we first met, she died of cancer, very quickly, he was still in a state of shock, still grieving, he needed someone to talk to, someone he could rely on, and he made it quite clear that someone was me, he needed me, and yes, I found that attractive, very attractive. We first met each other at the opening night at The Premier Cru Bottlehouse, right from the start I knew he was keen. I would make an excuse to go there, and then the Friday evening routine started. I kept telling myself that I was buying a nice bottle of wine to celebrate your coming home for the weekend, but deep down I knew what was happening, I knew exactly what I was doing. Every time I went in to see him, and it was him I was going to see, we would talk for twenty minutes, half an hour, even an hour sometimes, just chatting, nothing too heavy, nothing too serious, he would do anything to keep me there with him, it was very flattering, and I was very flattered by it. Going to the wine merchants on a Friday evening soon became the highlight of my week, the only time when I really felt wanted."

Shaking his head, Reg winced uncomfortably as his mind gave a reluctant audience to his wife's viva voce, the words having a familiar trait to them, but where and when?

"Go on," he whispered, his head in his hands.

"Well, then we started meeting during the week, not just on a Friday. We were careful, of course we were, always meeting away from the town. Then we started having sex. I missed sex Reg, I missed it so much. You were always too tired when you came back on Friday, and I understood that, but fifteen minutes after we had put David to bed and had a couple of glasses of wine was just not enough, I needed more. Any way we started by having sex in his car, and soon we were booking a room at the Royal Oak."

"The Royal Oak?"

Like a wild animal, its prey at its mercy, Reg sprang from his seat.

"Yes, the Royal Oak. We never stayed overnight."

Immediately Anna knew that her attempt to soften the blow was a mistake.

"Oh, that's alright then."

Reg screamed, his angry voice shattering the still air.

"No, it wasn't alright Reg, it was wrong, it was all wrong, I know that now, but I needed it back then. You weren't giving me what I wanted, what I needed, so I went elsewhere, and that elsewhere was Bill."

Returning to his seat, Reg rested his arms on his seat, a fruitless attempt to catch his breath, but it was simply too little too late, completely overwhelmed by his nausea he rushed out of the room and into the hall, frantically pulling the door of the downstairs toilet open, he sank to his knees, and, leaning over the pan, groaned as the contents of his stomach splattered against the porcelain bowl.

Staring at his vomit at the bottom of the pan, a revolting broth, a disgusting combination of both his lunch and breakfast, he froze, the repugnant smell filling his nostrils, his head throbbing, his hands shaking as he lifted himself away from the pan, as freezing as it was, the water from the cold tap felt warm against his skin, his fingers blue with numbness fully enclosed in the hand towel, suddenly everything was clear, crystal clear.

Back sitting opposite his wife, he stared into her eyes, cutting through her defences, hacking his way through the wild grasses of deceit, her lies and falsehoods.

"Was there anybody else, apart from Bill?"

"What do you mean?"

"I said, was there anybody else, apart from that fucking Bill?"

"No, no, of course not."

Faltering for just a split second, Anna hesitated before answering, a blink of an eye, not even a heartbeat, but Reg picked up on it straight away, leaning forward, his face so close it nearly connected with that of his wife, the revolting cocktail of red wine, coffee, and vomit on his breath making her feel queasy, he grabbed her tiny forearm in his massive hands, squeezing it, pinching her skin.

"Okay. I'm going to ask you one more time, just once more, you little bitch, was there anybody else apart from Bill, and don't lie to me, I want the truth."

All fortifications breached, any resistance now pointless, her tear-stained eyes fixed to the ground, Anna wept hysterically.

"Yes, yes there was."

"Who and when?"

His teeth gritted together, his whole face twisted and contorted into an ugly frown, Reg continued with the relentless barrage. Suddenly a smile filled his face, not a happy smile, but a sardonic smile, the smile of a man betrayed from all quarters. "The lady doth protest too much methinks."

He quietly recited to himself, only this time it wasn't a lady remonstrating, it was a man, and not just any man, it was a man who he knew very well, a man in whom he trusted, a man who, right up until this moment, he had considered his closest friend.

Anna looked at him, tears were rolling down her face, her cheeks red raw.

"It was Stephen."

She stammered, her voice spluttering through her tears.

"It was Stephen, I'm so sorry, I am so very, very sorry."

This revelation was not news for Reg, the conversation with Stephen in the Cross Keys just a few days previously still ringing in his ears, it didn't quite match Anna's explanation word for word, but the similarities were there, words running parallel with each other, it didn't require a sleuth's brains to work it all out, but when, when did it happen?

His head in his hands, Anna's words turning over and over in his exhausted mind, her craving for attention, she attracted to that attention. Taking a deep breath, he thought about Stephen, and closing his eyes, he could picture him, leaning at the bar, cradling his dimpled pint glass jug in the way he always did, his thumb hooked onto the handle, smiling in the way he always did, seemingly without a care in the world.

But had it always been like that? Racking his brains, his eyes still shut tight, he rummaged through the past, cursing and swearing under his breath. Then, all of a sudden it came to him, as if in a flash, a thunderbolt from the very bowels of his memory, suddenly he remembered, yes, he remembered everything, and it all started with Stephen's wife, Cath.

Her horrific injuries confining her to a wheel chair for almost a year, a road traffic accident in which a car had unwittingly collided into her own as she was exiting a roundabout, her useless legs finally, and mercifully, bought back to life by an intensive course of physiotherapy. The accident hadn't been her fault, but fate does not always take that into account, and whilst Cath was battling her own demons, both physical and mental, Stephen had installed himself as an almost permanent resident in Reg and Anna's front room, spending hours with the both of them, a lost soul seeking redemption in a world that had turned against him.

Exhausted and at the end of his tether, Reg's mind wandered back to the holiday they had shared together the summer before the crash, renting a four bed-roomed villa in the Algarve, an almost idyllic setting, with its clean white walls and sun-bleached terracotta roof, the sun loungers positioned around the sun-drenched rectangular pool, practically perfect.

Married for barely eighteen months, Reg had been a reluctant traveller, but Stephen had been adamant that the four of them would make the perfect quartet, enjoying each other's company as much as they enjoyed their own. Fast forward six months, his wife's accident leaving his own life in tatters, the landscape could not have been more different.

Slowly the tiles of the jigsaw were all falling into place, the oddly shaped pieces interlocking together creating a clear picture, revealing the truth. Looking up, he scowled at his wife, a death stare, a stare filled with pure hatred, for he had become hatred itself, and he wished her dead.

"Let's work this out, shall we? We had been married for about two years when poor Cath was involved in that car crash, married just two years when you started fucking Stephen."

Rocking backwards and forwards in her chair like a demented child, Anna ran her tear-soaked hands up and down her cherry red face.

"Reg no, no."

Reg leant forward, his hand squeezing Anna's skinny leg just above the knee in his massive hands, his vice-like grip making her wince with pain.

"Reg, no, no, stop."

Reg didn't stop, he couldn't stop, it was too late, all of the events now chronologized, everything laid out in order, the car crash being two years after they had got married and one year before the birth of their eldest son.

There could be no going back now, his fury channelled through from his raging mind to the hand on her leg, squeezing it tighter, halting the blood flow, that current, that river of life that flows effortlessly through the body, quietly and efficiently going about its work nourishing and cleansing, suddenly stemmed, and with it her very existence and the existence of their shattered marriage.

Her face covered in red blotches, she pleaded with her husband, "Reg, please, oh Reg, I'm so sorry, please Reg, please."

Her words fell deaf ears, his was now a silent world, his shattered mind completely shut down, oblivious to everything going on around him, the straw had finally broken the camel's back.

"You cheap tart, you cheap fucking whore. Not David as well, for God's sake."

Chapter 28
Thursday

The car was freezing, his fingers fumbling with rage and numbness from the cold, Reg pulled his coat tightly around his chest, and took his phone out of his coat pocket, five seconds later he could hear Stephen's voice at the other end of the line, and, composing himself, he talked into the handset.

"Hi mate, you busy right now, fancy a couple of jars at the Cross Keys? I'll drive you home."

"Short notice, but yes, please mate, always up for a night out, yeah, that sounds great."

Reg smiled to himself and, taking his foot off the accelerator, slowed the car down, indicated and crawled into the roadside, stationary, he un-fastened his seatbelt, the sound of the engine drowned out by the blast of the heater. Ten minutes later he pulled into the Cross Keys car park, slowly and deliberately he got out of the car, and closed the door, he had used the time wisely and was now sufficiently calm, ready to face Stephen.

The bar was relatively quiet, just the inevitable handful of regulars huddled together, shoulder to shoulder, a solid mass of hunched backs and stamping feet, pints of beer lined up randomly on the bar in front of them. Through the corner of his eye, Reg spotted Stephen sitting at their normal table, bolt upright, his hands on his hips, staring up at the ceiling, two pints of beer in front of him.

Striding confidently towards him, Reg made a mental note his friend's promptness in arrival, contemplating whether or not there had been time for Anna to have spoken to him, forewarned is forearmed and all of that, he smiled to himself.

"I've got you a pint in mate, you said that you were driving, but you can have one, can't you?"

Stephen smiled, getting up, his outstretched hand pointing in Reg's direction.

Not wanting to arouse any suspicion, Reg shook his best friend's hand warmly, at the same time looking into his face, searching for any hint of any contact with his treacherous wife.

"I'm driving, but yes, I'll have a pint please," he replied sitting down, lifting up the glass and taking a sip.

Forty-five minutes passed quickly, the conversation flowing effortlessly as it often did, Reg held the base of the glass in his hand and rotating the last of the contents into a whirlpool of froth and liquid before depositing it all into his mouth. That was his second, Stephen had managed four in the same time, it was Thursday night after all, he had said, practically the start of the weekend. Putting the empty glass on the table, Reg suddenly stood up.

"Tell you what, mate, I'm tired, need to head for home, can I give you a lift?"

Stephen's face dropped, he was just settling down for the evening, just getting a taste for the beer, each pint slipping down more readily than the previous one, plus Tanya was working behind the bar, and she definitely wasn't wearing a bra.

"Okay, mate, if you're tired. We can always finish off the session another night."

Edging their way passed the bar, Stephen flashed a smile at Tanya, predictably she was surrounded by eager punters, all competing for her attention, each wanting more of her than the other, she was lapping it up, enjoying every moment of it, suddenly he caught a glimpse of her nipples underneath her thin blouse, she caught him looking, and smiled back, her white teeth gleaming against her heavily made-up face.

Patting his coat pockets clumsily with his gloved hands, Reg searched for the keys, Stephen stood patiently at the passenger door, stamping his feet, the ache in his groin reminding him that a visit to the toilet on the way out might have been preferable to being distracted by Tanya. Turning right onto the main road, they drove for about a mile and then took a left onto the bypass. Stephen frowned, his house was towards the east, and they were travelling northbound.

"What's this Reg, The Magical Mystery Tour?"

Surprised by the pitch of his own voice, which was significantly higher than normal, Stephen could feel himself feeling more than a little uncomfortable, shuffling from side to side in the passenger seat. Reg never normally had a drink when he was driving, he cogitated to himself, and yet tonight he had dispensed with two pints in a very short period of time, and there had definitely been the putrid smell of wine on his breath when he had arrived. Christ, was he actually safe to drive? What the hell was going on? He felt cold, a cold shiver running down his spine, he rubbed his hands slowly between his legs.

"How's Cath, Stephen, how's the wife?"

Reg's question came bolt out of the nowhere, his eyes focused on the road, making no effort to turn and look at Stephen.

Stephen shot a nervous glance at Reg through the corner of his eye, unable to control the sense of uneasiness taking over his entire body, an unsolicited wariness taking over his mind. Reg hadn't enquired after Cath for months, they didn't really talk about their wives or family, far too engrossed in their own tiny little world, they had a heritage that preceded all of that, their topics of conversation always more self-centred, more juvenile.

"Cath's fine thanks, Reg, not as young as she used to be, but then again, the none of us are."

His eyes firmly fixed on the road, Reg continued, "That's nice, that's very nice, yes, pleased to hear that. In fact, Anna and I were talking about Cath just the other day, so we were. Yes, talking about that terrible accident she had all those years ago, must be, what, over thirty years ago now?"

Almost afraid to turn and look at him in the face, Stephen continued to study Reg through the corner of his eye. Looking downwards, he caught a glimpse of the speedometer, the matt red pointer moving smoothly around its perimeter, was already at fifty miles an hour.

A sheen of sweat forming on his brow, Stephen wiped the salty droplets away from his eyes, as he tried to make some sense of what was going on.

Firstly, and out of principle, Reg never had a drink when he was driving, his father's life having been brought to an abrupt end by a teenager, his full driving licence barely six months old, drunk and behind the wheel driving himself home after a Friday night stag night.

Secondly, Reg never broke the speed limit either, frustratingly he was one of the most cautious drivers in the whole world, and yet tonight, for some unfathomable reason, he seemed determined to kill them both. A keen fan of Formula One, Stephen's blood ran cold, as that horrific picture of Ayrton Senna's mangled car, almost entirely engulfed in a cloud of dust at the San Marino Grand Prix, flashing before his eyes as he watched the speedometer dial moving up to sixty-five miles an hour.

Even more concerning than all of that was his sudden interest in Cath. They hadn't talked about Cath's accident for a very long time, it was a good thirty years now since it had happened. His body shuddered as he recalled how difficult that time was for the both of them, she being confined to a wheel chair for a good twelve months, her sheer determination to come through it, she still walked with a limp, but that was barely noticeable, time heals, and they had managed to put the whole horrendous experience behind them now, the whole episode forgotten about. Or at least he thought that it was.

"Christ, that was a long time ago now Reg. What on earth got you and Anna onto that subject?"

His desperate attempts to keep some degree of calm in his voice thwarted by an involuntary and unwanted stammer, desperate to avoid any meaningful eye contact Stephen kept his eyes transfixed onto the road.

Both of his arms rigid and locked out straight at the elbows, his hands gripping the steering wheel tightly, Reg replied.

"Can't remember exactly how we got onto the subject, but we were just saying what a difficult time it was for you. How low you were, down in the dumps, in fact for about a year really, when you think back to it."

Staring up into the car roof, Stephen spotted a tear in the fabric that he had not seen before, a brief distraction but not one that lasted for long, his mind very quickly back to work. There was a point to all of this, he knew that. with Reg, there was always a point to everything, and all that the tone of Reg's voice told him was that the point of all of this was going to be very unpleasant, and was unlikely to have a happy ending.

"Yes, it was a difficult time, a very difficult time, you and Anna were brilliant to me, you couldn't have done for me."

Reg turned and looked at Stephen, staring at him, an intense hatred etched all over his face, and for the first time since they had got into the car their eyes finally met.

"Especially Anna?"

Stephen could feel the blood draining from his face, there was a real menace in Reg's voice now. something wasn't quite right, that was obvious, but what? Why was he talking about what happened all those years ago? Why was he so concerned about Cath? Is this to do with that money, had he and Anna been discussing Ben's legacy, had that raised questions about Ben's paternity? Had those questions lead to others? Suddenly, he started to think about Anna. Was this about his affair with Anna? Had Reg finally found out about that? No, not a chance! There was no way that Anna would have told him anything about it, no chance in this world. So, what was he getting at? Stephen could feel the car going faster, he looked at the speedometer, it read seventy-five miles an hour.

"Yes, if you like, especially Anna."

The words stumbled quietly from his mouth.

Reg turned and looked at Stephen. The bastard. Oh yes, Anna had looked after him all right. She knew that he couldn't get it off his own wife, that side of their relationship had been left in tatters following the accident, so she had decided that he could get it off her instead. Stephen was depressed, feeling un-loved, Anna would have enjoyed that, him lapping up all of her attention, she more than happy to oblige.

On her part, her husband working away during the week from time to time, she would have been lonely, felt neglected, her life bereft of tenderness, of passion. Yes, Stephen had always found her attractive, he had told Reg that on numerous occasions, this would have given him the opportunity he had been waiting for.

All of that happened so many years ago, but now the disgusting truth had finally made its way up through the sewers and come to the surface, Reg froze, his body over-whelmed by a deep, irreversible, hatred for his once best friend, his wife, and for his own depressing, pathetic life.

He glowered at the man, the man sitting beside him in the passenger seat, a man he no longer recognised, a man perhaps he had never really known. Stoking the fire further, he continued with the mental torment. Poor Cath, how long after her accident, how long was she in that wheelchair, that damn wheelchair, relying on the good nature, the charity of friends and family to push her around having never quite had the strength in her own arms to work those impossible grooved hand rims attached to the outsized rear wheels, how long was it before her husband started sleeping with one of her best friends?

Where did they do it? His mind was working overtime now, his head spinning out of control, and when? He was often working away, so that would have made it easy for Anna to get away, make herself available for those secret tristes, but what about Stephen? Of course, Cath was at the physiotherapist every other day, he would have dropped her off, and she would have relied on him to pick her back up again to take her home, perfect.

Crippled with emotion, his paralysed body unable to move, his head fixed into one position, his arms like the branches of a tree, dark horizontal immoveable boughs, his foot, a dead weight, pressed harder down on the accelerator pedal.

As much as Reg was leaning forward, Stephen was pressing himself harder and harder against the back of passenger seat, as if sitting on an aeroplane bracing himself for take-off, moving faster and faster along the runway, the scenery outside fuzzy, the grey of the runway tarmac merging with the green of the grass forming its borders, pulling a boiled sweet out of the packet just at the right moment waiting for your ears to pop, only after the ten to fifteen seconds it would normally take to get up into the air, the wheels were still firmly on the ground spinning round faster and faster.

His stomach churning, his eyes closed, he took a deep breath, yes, Reg must know all about the affair with Anna, there could be no other explanation. Suddenly, and very un-expectantly, through the nausea he managed to smile, his spirited brain reminding him of the first time with Anna.

Three months after the accident, and completely out of the blue, she had invited him round to her house, of course, he had expected Reg to be there, but he wasn't, he was working away, and, quite innocently, Anna had suggested that they opened a bottle of wine, it was the afternoon and very quickly the two of them were feeling that warm glow of too much alcohol too early on in the day.

Sitting on the small settee in the living room, they were chatting away, their empty wine glasses on the coffee table, when he had accidently put his hand on her knee, he tried to pull it away, but Anna had taken it into her own, and moved it up under her skirt and onto her smooth naked leg. The smile changed into a smirk, yes, he remembered their first time, he remembered it very well indeed, her appetite had been insatiable, an unquenchable thirst of desire.

"You haven't got any children have you, Stephen?"

His face deformed and ugly, his whole body shaking, his eyes locked onto Stephen's, and with little or no consideration for the road ahead, Reg continued the verbal battery.

"That must have been a real disappointment to you and Cath? You know, the family incomplete."

"Okay, stop the car, I don't know what you're getting at Reg, but stop the car. I said stop the car Reg!"

Stephen's voice filled the car, his screams reverberating all around their heads, he was scared, scared for his life. He could see that Reg had completely taken leave of his senses, totally lost control.

This was a man whose whole life had been turned upside down, it really couldn't get any worse. He had bought up two sons, two fine young men, whom he had loved, cherished, and protected, yet in the past two weeks he had learnt that he was the biological father of neither, he had been bringing up the offspring of two, not one, but two other men.

He had met the girl of his dreams, enjoyed a brief and intense relationship before celebrating their nuptials, he had thought they were happy, he had thought that he made her happy, and now he knew differently. He looked into his friend's face, contorted with hatred, loathing, the friendship terminated, any hopes of a happy ending well and truly extinguished.

Suddenly, Stephen was silent, his hands clenching the seat so tightly his knuckles turning white, his finger nails tearing at the fabric, his mouth open, his voice barely auditable, he couldn't shout any more, he simply hadn't got the strength.

"Come on, Reg, stop the car mate, let's talk this through."

Would he be able to reason with Reg? Would Reg be capable of listening to reason? That question was soon answered.

"Talk about what, mate. Talk about the fact that you were screwing my wife thirty years ago, fathered a child with her, the child that I thought was my son, and then carried on like nothing had happened. Shall we talk about that?"

With every syllable of every word, Reg's foot pressed just a little bit harder on the accelerator, eighty, eighty-five, ninety miles an hour.

"Yes, let's talk about that, shall we? Or shall we talk about the fact that my other son is also some other man's fucking child too. Two children, two fathers, neither of which are me, for fuck's sake."

Unable to look his friend in the face, and in desperate need of some respite, Stephen averted Reg's glare and focused on the other side of the road where, a hundred yards away an articulated lorry, a full fifty-four feet long, its bright orange cab illuminated by the street lights, was travelling in the opposite direction.

Its tyres slip-sliding over the short grass, the car mounted the central reservation as Reg abruptly spun the steering wheel around, forcing the unchecked vehicle onto the other side, his foot pressing harder and harder on the accelerator, the very fibres in his muscles almost tearing with the exertion, his foot seemingly attached to the pedal, the speedometer now reading close to a hundred miles an hour, ninety-seven, ninety-eight, the car travelling faster and faster, the top of Reg's head almost touching the windscreen, his eyes fixed on the dashboard, his chin stuck fast against the rim of the steering wheel.

His brain anaesthetised, his eyes now wide open, Stephen looked through the windscreen, the two vehicles were less than a fifty-yards apart now, he could hear the deep, hollow, sound of the lorry's horn, its lights flashing furiously, blinding him, the speedometer now pushing a hundred miles an hour.

Desperate for yet another perspective, he stared out of the passenger window, everything was a blur, images flashing before him but nothing was visible, everything travelling too fast for his eyes to focus.

Facing the front again, his clammy hands getting in the way, and not knowing where to put them, the hairs on the nape of his neck bristling, he could see the lorry's flashing lights, illuminating the whole road, the noise of the horn now deafening, the smell of burning rubber, the wheels of the trailer locked, the trailer itself swaying from side to side, the rear end crossing into the opposite lane, thick black smoke engulfing the outsized front wheels, his eyes open wider now, as if waiting for the fatal blow to be delivered. Delivered by the poor innocent lorry driver, a man in his mid-fifties just going about his normal business five minutes ago, now desperately applying all of the breaking systems in a futile attempt to avoid the collision that was now inevitable.

Stephen screamed, he knew that it was too late, and closing his eyes, he counted down from five.

Chapter 29
Thursday

The rain beating against the window panes almost drowned out the passing strike of the gilded bronze carriage clock, a gift to Reg, in recognition of his twenty-five years of loyal service, as it struck eleven o'clock. Picking up a tissue from the box seemingly permanently positioned next to her, Anna patted her red, tear-stained cheeks.

Slumped in her armchair, the lights out and the last of her wine long since drained from the bottle, she sat thinking about her marriage, of which the honeymoon period of the first twelve months had been perfect, filled with limitless joy and endless devotion to her new husband.

A year in and she had started to feel trapped, tied down by the vows she had made at the alter on their wedding day, like a nun, observing the spiritual practice of monastic silence, with only prayers and fetters of the Roman Catholic faith to look forward to, she couldn't bear it, she wanted more, she needed more. Oh, why had she been so stupid? Why couldn't she have just been satisfied with what she had.

The room was pitch black, as black as it was cold. There she sat, wallowing in her own self-pity, shivering, rocking backwards and forwards in her chair, biting her knuckle, the skin all but broken, tears rolling down her cheeks.

It was well past eleven o'clock, and there was still no sign of Reg. An hour ago she had still been reasonably content, only mildly concerned, at that time she could still find some reason, some rationale for his absence, but not now, that time had long since passed. Irrational thoughts filled her anxious mind, perhaps he wasn't going to come back at all? If he didn't she couldn't really blame him, not after what she had done.

Her first sexual experience had been painful and uncomfortable, she was just fifteen at the time, but very soon she found she had an insatiable appetite for it, and at seventeen years of age, she had already slept with a majority of the boys in her class at school.

She had the looks that made her very attractive and a perfectly proportioned body, all of which made her very fanciable, she knew which buttons to press, the right noises to make, and that made her very desirable, her addiction to intimacy fuelled by the fact that, after the thrill of the chase, the excitement and the newness of each conquest very quickly wore off, leaving her almost immediately craving something new, someone different.

Five years later, and mourning the death of her own father, everything changed, her interest in sex all but completely disappeared, her desires suppressed by an intense grieving for the man she respected and loved most in the world, leaving her cold and emotionally drained.

For almost two years she remained celibate, her mind telling her body that it did not need that type of pleasure, that sort of gratification.

Time heals all wounds and gradually her body began to re-ignite itself, and then, all alone one evening in the house she shared with her mother, surrounded by scented candles and tea-lights, a half-empty bottle of red wine standing on the carpet next to her empty glass, she lay on the settee, aroused by Elgar's *Salut d'Amour*, the soft metallic shrill of the violin combining effortlessly with the mellow feathery tinkle of the piano, the mood as intense as it was melodious.

Whilst one hand gently smothered her right breast, a familiar tingle suddenly running down her spine, her breaths getting longer and deeper, the other, its fingers outstretched, wandered slowly down over her stomach and towards the top button of her jeans and the waistband of her knickers.

Four months, and a whirlwind romance later, she was married to Reg, and twelve perfect, almost blissful, months ensued, but into the second year, she could feel those old urges, those un-welcome yearnings, returning. Sitting in the pitch black, she mentally recited her marriage vows, for sickness and in health, for better and for worse, all said with the very best of intentions, but forsaking all others? How in Heaven's name did she ever think that she could commit to that? With enough lovers to fill the roll call at a school assembly, there was real inevitability about her inability to remain faithful to one single man.

Just over a year into the marriage, those old yearnings having returned with a vengeance, leaving her openly flirting with her customers at Arnold's where, working in the underwear department, she found that it wasn't difficult to tempt even the most loyal of husbands from the comfort of even the most loving of relationships when the main topic of conversation was whether they should be buying French cut panties or bikini briefs.

In her element, enjoying the thrill of the chase, the anticipation of what might follow, every empty minute of her day filled with whimsical fantasy, she spent three months merely wetting her appetite, teasing and denying herself, whilst flirting, philandering, tormenting the eager, hungry men that queued at her counter craving her attention.

The relationship with Stephen hadn't been planned, no one would possibly hope for those circumstances, but from the very first kiss it had been passionate, intense, trysting when every opportunity presented itself. Rocked to the very core when she fell pregnant with David, on the day of his birth she pledged to live a monogamous life until the end of her days.

For almost five years she managed to suppress her feelings, all inappropriate urges ignored, right up until the fateful occasion when she had stepped innocently into that wine shop on opening day, when she had met Bill, suddenly her desires uncontrollable, her urges overwhelming, stronger, fiercer, than she had ever experienced before.

Her arms crossed tightly in front of her chest, she shivered irrepressibly as she remembered the feelings of both excitement and panic when she had learnt that she was pregnant with Ben. With another young child no more than five years old, and both of them in need of a stable home there was no question of her leaving Reg, however much she might have been in love with Bill, with two children she simply had to make it work with her husband, and that's exactly what she had done, learning to be happy with what she had, initially making the most of it, but in fact, happily, there had been little in the way of compromise for ten years now.

As unpleasant as it was, sitting alone in the cold dark room allowed time for introspection, and the more she ruminated, the more ludicrous it was that she had imagined that she might escape both episodes completely unscathed.

She had played her part well, portraying the image of the doting wife, with the attentive husband, and two respectable grown-up sons, the house, a regular three-up, two-down at the head of a cul-de-sac, their gleaming car, parked in the driveway, washed and polished every Sunday by her devoted spouse.

Subconsciously she had taken the charade further, working in the charity shop, giving something back to society, contributing the most precious of all things, her time. Well, she could give as much back as she wanted in the future, but that wouldn't change the past, not one little bit.

She had lied and cheated her way through those early years. Giving two good men a child each and then snatching it away from each of them, depriving them of any chance of being a proper father. On top of all of that she had let an honest man live his life believing that he had two sons and a loyal, devoted wife, totally oblivious to the sordid truth hidden behind their sham marriage.

Yes, she had behaved atrociously throughout her life, an appalling wife and a flawed mother. She deserved all that was coming to her, and nothing less. She wouldn't blame Reg if he left her, he wouldn't blame her two sons if they disowned her. She would lose her best friend, Sarah, as well, of course she would, and she deserved that too.

A cold chill ran through her body, less than a fortnight, not even two weeks, that's all it had taken for her whole life to implode, her world to completely cave in, just a dozen days, and she had lost everything she had built up over the past thirty years, every single little bit of it.

Pressing the palms of her hands down against the arms of the chair, she tried to lift herself up, exhausted she slumped back down again, a second attempt and she could feel there was more energy running through her shattered frame, no, she would not lose it all, she would fight tooth and nail to hold on to them, hold on to the family that she loved so dearly. Sitting bolt up now scolding herself, she harshly reminded herself of her responsibilities.

She needed to be there for David, shoulder to shoulder, regardless to how much she repulsed him, she was his mother and she would stand at his side, supporting him in any way she could, after all, they had been so close before all of this started, surely, he would welcome her rallying around.

There was a very good chance that her youngest son was going to be marrying her best friend, and she desperately wanted to be part of their special happiness, she couldn't possibly miss out on that.

Most of all, yes, more than all of that, she wanted to grow old with Reg, be the wife that he always wanted her to be, the wife he deserved. That loving man who had lived his entire life, selflessly, for the sake of his precious family, never a thought or consideration for himself, making sacrifice after sacrifice so they would never go without. Working away for weeks on end, nights spent in soulless, faceless hotel rooms, endless miles sitting in the car driving up and down the congested motorways, tirelessly providing for his family, those whom he loved and cherished unreservedly.

Looking into the darkness, desperately seeking some light, some hope, in the dimness of her surroundings, tears flooding from her eyes, flowing down her cheeks like a raging river, every muscle in her face trembling, her body racked with pain and guilt, the wail of her sobs reverberating around the pitiful surroundings of her self-made pitiful life.

No, she was not prepared to lose him, not prepared to give him up. she would fight, fight to save their marriage, battle to keep the man who had stood by her, despite all of the doubts and uncertainties. Leaning forward, her hands clasped tightly together she wailed.

"God. Please God, just give me a second chance, just one more chance."

Her words trailed off, the new silence interrupted by the sound of the doorbell. Her head spinning violently, faster and faster, out of control, making her feel physically sick, she struggled to get up onto her feet, the doorbell still resonating in the background. The outside light, so thoughtfully and cleverly fitted by Reg the first winter after they had moved in, automatically switched itself on, illuminating the hallway, a dull beam of light forcing through into the blackness of the living room.

Convinced that Reg had returned home, her heart was beating uncontrollably in her chest. Yes, safely home and on the other side of the door, come back to forgive her, make a start on re-building their marriage, the thought of growing old without her simply too much to bare.

Wiping away her tears, straightening herself up, making herself as presentable as possible, she eagerly made her way in to the hall, automatically reaching out to turn the front door handle.

Suddenly she froze, stopping short of the front door, her eyes slowly adjusting to the light, and through the mottled glass door, she could see the distorted image of a flashing blue light, and beneath that the outline of the police car parked in the driveway.

Immediately her heart sank, instinctively she put both hands onto her chest, as a sharp pain radiated around her fragile torso. The front door open just six inches, she bravely, tentatively, peered through the gap.

Balanced on the edge of the doorstep, their faces filled with emotion, a hint of tears in their eyes, the two police officers, both female, braced themselves, preparing themselves to carry out the hardest and most heart-breaking work a police officer faces.

The shorter of the two, the seniority of her rank displayed through the two diamonds on the epaulettes of her uniform, the windswept blond hair of her fringe sticking out untidily from under her helmet, stepped forward, her voice as soft and as gentle as was humanly possible.

"Anna, Anna Johnson? Can we come in please?"

The front door felt like a dead weight, but Anna, her hand shaking uncontrollably, somehow managed to pull it open sufficiently to allow them to enter the house, motioning them both to go into the living room, before closing the door slowly behind them.

Letting them pass, and standing with her back to the door, her full body weight pressed against it, the palms of her hands desperately trying to gain some purchase on the mottled glass, she could feel the colour completely draining from her face as she rubbed her bloodshot eyes. Her mind swirling round and round, she felt dizzy, totally disorientated, her lung capacity shrinking with every breath she took, the whole world turning black, her beaten and abused body finally calling it a day, finally giving up the ghost, and, powerless to prevent her legs from buckling from beneath her, she sank into a motionless heap onto the floor.

More Than Two Years Later

David had not slept well last night, in fact he had not had a decent night's sleep for more than two years, his back ached, his left arm was stiff as a board. His brain having awoken from its fitful slumber, almost immediately his nose started to twitch, for despite his time served he still couldn't get fully accustomed to the smell of prison, that repugnant stench of sweat, tobacco, stale food and the foulness of being contained in such a small space was something he would not be missing in the future.

Taken down to serve a four-year prison sentence for grievous bodily harm, he had been totally complicit whilst residing under Her Majesty's pleasure, completing his time quietly and without fuss, diligently repaying his debt to society. Sitting on the edge of his bed, rubbing the sleep out of his eyes as he took one last look around the cell, furnished with a toilet, a sink, a small bookcase and a bedside table, that had been his home for most of that time.

Conspicuous by his absence at his father's funeral, he had made it quite clear that he didn't want any contact with any members of his family whilst he was incarcerated, and, to his relief, everyone had respected that wish, and, barring for the two letters which Ben had sent him, he had managed to keep himself in perfect isolation throughout his sentence.

However, he had been very glad to receive those two epistles, mercifully they had allowed him some familiarity and comfort to an otherwise alien and hostile world. Many a cold, miserable night, alone in his cell, had he spent reading and re-reading them, retracing every word time and time again, keeping both of them safely stored away, one on top of the other, in the corner of the drawer in the small bedside table.

Holding them carefully in his hand now, both worn at the creases and dog eared at the corners, but still legible, he recalled the first time he had opened them, the first six months into his sentence, and the second a year later, the anger that his wishes not been respected quickly replaced by the fortitude he felt when he had finally completed reading each of the neatly typed documents and reached Ben's carefully handwritten stamp at the end of them both.

In the first letter, after a paragraph of sympathy for his brother's predicament, Ben had provided a comprehensive resume of all matters family, paying special attention on his mother and how she was coping with life as a widow with a son in prison. Evidently, she had returned to working behind the lingerie counter at Arnold's, her life turning full circle, slowly re-constructing her life, one building block at a time. The letter closed with a bombshell, Ben was planning to give him one hundred and fifty thousand pounds, an appeal that at least something positive might come out of the whole episode followed, with an offer of more money if he should need it.

In the second letter were further updates on his mother and her steady progress, but also a warning, a warning that she had aged, and to brace himself for a shock when their paths should next cross. The letter closed with a second, and more explosive bombshell, Sarah had given birth to their first child, a baby boy, he was an uncle. Time and tide waited for no man.

The front of the prison was a grim and intimidating place, no frills, no effort made to encourage either its customers or their visitors, just a mild steel fence, topped with barbed wire, with a single large gate for vehicles and a smaller one for pedestrians.

A white prison van, with four rectangular port holes for windows, its back door filthy with dirt, was pulling through the large gate as David was escorted through the smaller one by a prison officer, an overweight burley man in his sixties, with an expressionless face.

Keeping his attention on his prisoner, the officer looked keenly across at the white van as it crossed the threshold, completing the mental arithmetic of plus one and minus one in his head, the status quo maintained to his satisfaction. There would always be gameful employment to be found there, he afforded himself a wry smile as he closed the gate behind David, he himself remaining on the inside, a prisoner in his own place of work.

Shivering as the cold crept underneath the out-sized civilian clothes, hanging awkwardly from his body wasted away through his lack of appetite for prison food, David breathed heavily, sucking up the clean air, forcing it into his eager lungs, as he gingerly stepped across the threshold and into the outside world. His head drenched by the incessant drizzle, he shrugged his shoulders and carried on walking.

Positioned just a few yards from the gate, but significantly on the right side of liberty, stood a small crowd, five or six people forming an orderly and typically British queue as if waiting for a bus, huddled together in their hats, scarves and raincoats, sharing umbrellas, patiently waiting to visit their loved ones.

Twenty yards beyond that another group had assembled, three in number, one of them slowly nudging a pram slowly backwards and forwards. David recognised his brother first.

The two siblings stood facing each other in silence, after more than two years apart, just the same number of paces separated them, both void of any prior knowledge of prison gate etiquette, neither quite knowing where to look.

Suddenly, Ben held out his hand, it was cold and it was wet, but David took it, and they shook hands vigorously. Opening his arms, Ben pulled David towards him, and they wrapped their soaking wet arms around each other, the embrace a grand gesture of the love they shared for each other, words being an unnecessary distraction. Eventually, simultaneously, they dropped their arms, and stood back and looked at each other. Ben was the first to speak.

"Welcome back, David."

David's eyes immediately filled with tears, his whole body completely overcome with emotion.

"Thanks, Ben, thanks mate, it's good to be back."

The rain water running uncontrollably off her fingers and onto the handle as she held onto the pram, Sarah was just as he had remembered her, the birth of her first child having made little or no difference to her appearance.

Looking into her eyes his stomach starting to ache, he remembered the last time they had been together, Ben pulling him away from her, his eyes ablaze with anger, raining punches down around his face and his head before throwing him out of the house by the scruff of his neck.

Would she still remember how he had behaved, of course she would, how could she possibly forget that little incident? But would she be able to forgive him? His brother had, but of course blood was always thicker than water. He looked into her eyes, desperately searching for an answer.

Just the pram separating them, and so ashamed, so humiliated, David shrank back as Sarah approached him. She moved away from the pram, lent towards him, and smiled, a magical smile that filled her face, radiating with love and warmth.

"Give us a kiss, David."

Nervously obliging, David kissed her tenderly on her wet cheek, immediately she put her arms around him, embracing him, surrounding him with her love and affection, neither of which he deserved, tears streaming down his face.

"Thank you, Sarah."

Forewarned is forearmed, and David mentally thanked Ben for taking the time out to write to him, warning him of the changes in their mother's appearance, and she was changed, quite changed, for standing just ten feet away from him, David could see her quite clearly now.

She had stopped dying her hair, and whilst still hanging just onto her shoulders, it was now grey, almost white, her face looked older, thinner, more wrinkled, her oversized coat almost entirely hiding her figure, she was still slim, perhaps too slim, her lower legs like sticks, and, looking at her hand, her small, pale, wrinkled, soaking wet hand, he noted that she was still wearing her thin, gold wedding band.

Shoving his hands into his pockets, he gazed into her eyes, and took a deep breath. Standing in front of him was the person he had hated the most in the world, the woman who was to blame for all that had happened, the tragic death of his father, his own imprisonment, the total destruction of their family, the person he had loved unconditionally for so many years, and yet in less than two weeks over two years ago, had come to despise. He could feel his mother's eyes as they locked on to his own, for a second neither of them wanting to make the first move.

Suddenly he looked across at Sarah, she had forgiven him for how he had abused her, his disgusting repulsive behaviour in her house on that dreadful Thursday morning, his own life at its very lowest point, surely he could find it in his own heart to forgive his mother as well, put the past behind them, look to the future?

That was exactly what he intended to do, his mind made up eighteen months ago sitting all alone in his prison cell grasping hold of the wooden crucifix, given to him during the first desperate six weeks by the friendly Prison Chaplin, the tiny wooden cross a constant companion, squirreled away shamefully on the top shelf of the bookcase.

Alone in his cell, rehearsing the words, those two precious words, time and time again, over and over, as he kissed the tiny feet of Jesus, He who had died on the cross to save the all of us. Yes, he knew what he wanted to say, and the time had come to say it. He walked towards his mother, his arms wide open.

"Hello, Mum."

Two simple words, two syllables and then one, but two words that Anna had heard a thousand times before, their own personal greeting, the one they had used when he was a teenager, growing into adulthood, finding his feet, making his own way into the world, and they meant the everything to her. Her face contorted with emotion, her cheeks red with tears, her voice barely a croak.

"Hello, Son."

They stood locked in each other's arms, neither wanting to be the first to break away, each breathing new life into the other.

Ben stepped forward and touched David's arm.

"Don't forget your new nephew, David."

Anna squeezed David's hand and let it drop, releasing him to complete his next task.

"Yes, David, go and meet your nephew."

Turning slowly away, David shuffled nervously towards the bright red pram, the rubber rims of its silver wheels soiled with mud, the brakes locking them into position. Inside, and completely oblivious to everything going on around it, the baby was lying fast asleep inside, safe and dry under the rain cover, its head protected by a white knitted wool hat.

Reginald David Johnson, his face young and innocent, as yet un-tarnished by the toils of life, un-spoilt by the passing of years. David looked into the pram and smiled, a baby boy, a new life, the first born of the next generation, and surely nobody could possibly be taken to task for willing it to make a better job of it than those of the previous two.